Buckley, Christopher

The White House
mess

Buckley, Christopher

The White House
mess

DATE	ISSUED TO
AUG 3 '88	78-843
AUG 19 '88	84-575
SEP 5 '88	77-178
SEP 12 '88	82-350
SEP 22 '88	

ALSO BY CHRISTOPHER BUCKLEY
Steaming to Bamboola: The World of a Tramp Freighter
My Harvard, My Yale (contributor)

THE
WHITE HOUSE
MESS

THE
WHITE HOUSE
MESS

Christopher Buckley

Alfred A. Knopf   New York   1986

THIS IS A BORZOI BOOK
PUBLISHED BY ALFRED A. KNOPF, INC.
Copyright © 1986 by Christopher Taylor Buckley
All rights reserved under International and Pan-American
Copyright Conventions.
Published in the United States by Alfred A. Knopf, Inc., New York, and
simultaneously in Canada by Random House of Canada Limited, Toronto.
Distributed by Random House, Inc., New York.

Library of Congress Cataloging-in-Publication Data
Buckley, Christopher
The White House Mess.
I. Title.
PS3552.U339W5   1986   813'.54   85-45586
ISBN 0-394-54940-6

Manufactured in the United States of America
FIRST EDITION

FOR MY WIFE, WITH LOVE

CONTENTS

Contents

THE
WHITE HOUSE
MESS

PROLOGUE

At 11:48 a.m. on Friday, January 20, 1989, the heavy iron gates of the White House grounds swung open and moments later the President-elect's motorcade drew to a halt beneath the North Portico. In accordance with custom, the President-elect and Mrs. Tucker were escorted inside, where they would escort President Reagan and the First Lady to the motorcade for the trip to Capitol Hill.

It was a clear and cold Washington winter day, a fine day for an inaugural ceremony. There was an air of excitement and history in the air. For the Tucker team, this was not the end of a twenty-two-month-long road, but the beginning of a dream.

Mike Feeley, the President-elect's press secretary, and I waited in our own limousine several Secret Service cars behind the President-elect's. Feeley filled the inside with so much cigarette smoke that I began to worry I might have a bronchospasm.

Ten minutes passed. Feeley began to fidget. Then I became concerned. Presidential movements are scheduled down to the minute. A delay like this, with the entire nation waiting, was unusual.

An advanceman in the front seat of the limousine pressed his earpiece to his ear, then said into the microphone clipped inside his shirtsleeve, "Echo One Tango. Say again, Headmaster?" He listened intently to the repeated message and turned to face me.

"Mr. Wadlough, Firebird wants you immediately in the Roosevelt Room." Firebird was President-elect Tucker's Secret Service code name.

"Christ," said Feeley, looking at his watch. "This is an outrage."

"Relax, Feels," I said merrily, for I was feeling very gay that morning. "It's probably just a photo op."

I was escorted through the West Lobby directly to the Roosevelt Room. The President-elect, Mrs. Tucker, and several Reagan officials and cabinet members who were to accompany the President up to Capitol Hill were clustered at the far end of the room. The looks on their faces were grave. The President-elect waved me over. As I approached, I was conscious of entering a scene charged with drama, though that may just have been the inset spot lighting.

"Herb," said the President-elect barely above a whisper, "we seem to have a situation here." He drew a deep breath. "The President won't leave."

I did not at first understand.

"I beg your pardon, sir?"

"His doctor's in with him now. They're talking about maybe giving him a shot of adrenaline."

During the transition President Reagan's inner circle had privately and delicately confided to me that their chief had been showing increasing signs of his advanced years. (He was at this point only weeks short of his seventy-eighth birthday.) The Defense Department had recently drawn up a contingency plan to provide, in their gruesome idiom, "command-chain continuity."

My immediate concern was less for the integrity of our nuclear response than for the 120,000-odd spectators, VIPs, media, security agents, air-traffic controllers (I had even arranged for landings and takeoffs from National Airport to be suspended during the President's inaugural speech), and others who were waiting for the start of an inaugural that was now threatening to be a logistical nightmare.

"Have you spoken to him?" I asked.

"Yes, I have," said the President-elect. "He told me his back was bothering him, that he was feeling tired, that it's cold outside, and that he just didn't feel like moving out today."

"Oh," I said, for I could think of nothing else to say.

"He was very nice about it. Hoped it wouldn't inconvenience me."

"I see. Did he say *when* he might feel like moving?"

"Yes. Spring."

"Spring."

I had spent weeks drawing up contingency plans for everything, including the disposal of 1,800 pounds of horse manure that would be "processed" during the parade. I had not anticipated this.

Mrs. Reagan and Jim Knott, President Reagan's deputy chief of staff, were in the Oval Office trying to persuade him to get dressed. Apparently he had not changed out of his pajamas that morning.

President-elect Tucker turned to the cluster of officials and said softly, "Gentlemen, perhaps we should discuss this in private. Why don't we convene in the Situation Room?"

As we all walked down to the ground floor of the West Wing, Defense Secretary R. Hannibal Bowditch grumbled quite audibly, "Acting like he's already President."

A fine sentiment, I thought. The transition had been a difficult one.

Eight of us, a mix of Reagan and Tucker officials, took our places around the burled-white-ash conference table in the Situation Room. The room has the feel of the inside of a bank vault. A hissing sound emanates from the floor that makes the room impenetrable to electronic eavesdropping. Every time the door opens, a red sign lights up red and flashes: ROOM STATUS: NOT SECURE FOR SENSITIVE DISCUSSION. There were seven phones in front of us, six white and one red.

Steady, Wadlough, I said to myself. I confess that red phones make me nervous.

Apart from the President-elect and myself, the others were all Reagan inner circle: Bowditch; Knott; Mortimer "Skip" Billington of the National Security Council; Virgil "The Butcher" Hooper, Office of Management and Budget; Attorney General Atticus Simpson; Commander William Crimmins, the President's physician. Vice President Bush had injured himself playing racquetball the day before and was still in the hospital. I rather missed Bush. He would have brought the average age of those assembled down considerably.

It was now 12:06 p.m.

"Gentlemen," began the President-elect, "I know this is awkward, but I think we'd better try to find a solution quickly. There are a lot of people waiting for us up there. You know the President much better than I do. Do you have any suggestions?"

Bowditch volunteered his. "Go to DefCon Three."

Def(ense)Con(dition) Two is the designation for a high-level nuclear alert. The lowest is DefCon Five; the highest is DefCon One. DefCon Two puts U.S. forces worldwide on a virtual war footing. The Secretary's suggestion was thus, well, surprising.

The President-elect said in what I thought was a very reasonable tone of voice, "I see. The reason being—?"

"Mr. President-elect," said Bowditch heavily, "we have here a situation of extreme"—he lingered on the word—"criticality. Never during my four years at Defense have I moved higher than [DefCon] Four."

"For which we are all extremely grateful, sir," interjected the President-elect.

Bowditch furrowed his brows. "This speaks to the President's and my temperance, *despite* the more"—he cleared his throat noisily—"intemperate charges made during the campaign."

Here it comes, I thought.

"Your friends in Moscow—"

"My what?" said Tucker. It was an interesting contrast, the forty-eight-year-old President-elect and the hoary Bowditch.

Bowditch let the question pass. He then launched into a harangue the point of which—as I understood it—was that the Soviet Union was at this moment undoubtedly about to take advantage of our present dilemma. When the President-elect asked him why he thought this was the case, Bowditch merely harrumphed that it was "instinct" and then rambled for some minutes about his lengthy career of public service. It was necessary to interrupt this flow of words, which seemed greatly to annoy him.

Faced with this rather awkward and deteriorating situation, President-elect Tucker turned to Mr. Billington, the seventy-nine-year-old director of the National Security Council, and asked him for his assessment. Unfortunately, Billington had not been following the discussion, owing to his hearing problem.

The President-elect rubbed his forehead with the tips of his fingers. "That's all right, sir," he said wearily.

He turned to the President's physician. "Commander," he said, "is there something *you* can do?"

The Commander said that the President might respond to two cc's of adrenaline, but that at his age it might provoke an "undesirable reaction." When the President-elect asked what sort of undesirable reaction, the commander replied, "Death."

A tabloid headline played before my eyes:

REAGAN KILLED BY INJECTION
GIVEN ON TUCKER'S ORDERS

I am not usually forceful at meetings, but I spoke up and offered my frank opinion that this was not a viable option.

Virgil Hooper of OMB began speaking of actuarial tables and the savings on Secret Service protection and pension in the event of President Reagan's demise. I was beginning to understand how he got his nickname, though I do fully understand the need for a tough helmsman at OMB.

One of the white phones rang, interrupting Mr. Hooper's gloomy discourse. Jim Knott took it.

"Trouble," he said. "The networks are reporting a White House news 'blackout.' It's affecting the stock market."

"Mr. Tucker," said Bowditch, clearing his throat, "I think it's time I made that call."

"In a minute," said Tucker with a trace of annoyance. "In a minute."

Atticus Simpson, the Attorney General and at eighty-one the second oldest member of Reagan's cabinet, rasped that he thought Tucker should invoke section four of Amendment 25, the constitutional provision whereby a President is declared unable to serve out his term of office.

The President-elect was silent a few moments. Then he said, "I don't want him to go out that way."

Bowditch snorted. "Didn't think you cared *how* he went."

For a moment I thought the President-elect was going to speak sharply to this rhinoceros, but he displayed admirable reserve.

I looked at my watch. 12:25. We were now alarmingly late. I asked an aide to switch on one of the television monitors. The camera panned the front row of the west front of the Capitol, where justices of the Supreme Court were conspicuously looking at their watches. I had a fleeting glimpse of my wife, Joan, sitting to one side of a pillar. She looked very presentable in her new overcoat with the beaver trim. There was much hubbubing, everyone looking at their watches and shaking their heads.

Think, Wadlough, I said to myself. But no solutions presented themselves. It was most vexing.

A phone rang—the red phone, to my great dismay. Both the President-elect and Bowditch reached for it. Bowditch practically snatched it out of his hand. Most unseemly.

Bowditch listened, grunted, and cradled the receiver on his collarbone.

"Mr. President-elect," he said with great solemnity, "we've just received word a squadron of Blackjack [long-range bombers] has just passed out of Soviet airspace."

The words sent a *frisson*—French for "a tingling sensation"—up my spine. For a moment all that could be heard was the hissing noise.

The President-elect was obviously taken aback. "I see," he said. "Are there hostile indications?"

Bowditch treated the question with impatience. "Do you consider forty megatons hostile?"

The President-elect considered this. "If they're dropped on my head, I do," he said.

He reached over and took the phone from Bowditch. He asked if the flight pattern appeared other than routine. His face creased into a smile. "Thank you," he said. "Thank you very much. You'll keep us informed, then? Thank you." He hung up and shot Bowditch a hot glance. Bowditch's lower lip protruded unpleasantly.

"Where were we, gentlemen?" said Tucker.

One of the white phones rang. Knott took the call.

"That was the First Lady," he said after hanging up. "It's no use. He won't change out of his pajamas. And I'm afraid he's just ordered lunch."

There was murmuring around the table. I leaned over and said to the President-elect in a hushed voice, "We have to leave for the Capitol in five minutes. With or without him. We can't wait any longer."

We huddled. "Let's look at this rationally," he whispered. "We've got a doctor who may kill him, an Attorney General who wants to declare him bananas, and a Defense Secretary who wants me to start World War III."

I agreed. The options were not encouraging. First, we ruled out starting World War III. We were down to killing the President or having him carted off by the men in white when the phone rang. An aide handed it to me.

"What the *fuck* is going on in there?" It was Feeley. In a hushed voice I quickly explained the situation.

"For Chrissake," he said. "The nets [networks] are going out of their heads. Tell him the Soviets are attacking and he's gotta get the hell out of there."

I whispered Feeley's idea in the President-elect's ear. He nodded. I also made a mental note to speak to Feeley about his language.

"Gentlemen," he announced, "I believe we have a solution. Mr. Bowditch, please inform the President we are under attack by the Soviet Union and that he is to assume direct command of operations."

With the expression of a bulldog that has just been given sixteen ounces of fresh red meat, Bowditch picked up the phone. The red one.

"This is Caesar," he said. "DefCon Two, stand by." Cupping his hand over the receiver, he said to Tucker, "Intelligent decision, sir. My compliments."

It took a few moments for the President-elect to realize what had just happened. "Mr. Secretary," he said, "what have you just done?"

"I'll call the President. He'll need to be briefed."

"Wait a minute. Do I understand you have just ordered a nuclear alert?"

"As you directed, sir," said Bowditch.

"Cancel that order, Bowditch. Immediately."

Bowditch scowled. "If this is to appear convincing—"

"Cancel the order, Bowditch."

Beneath the oceans, submarine commanders were requesting verification. From Guam to South Dakota, bomber crews were scrambling.

"It seems to me, Mr. President-elect—"

"It seems to me, Mr. Secretary, that you have taken leave of your senses. *Cancel that order.*"

With a histrionic clearing of phlegm, Secretary Bowditch reluctantly gave the command and rescinded the nuclear alert he had moments previously issued. Around the world, U.S. forces stood down. The President-elect loosened his tie.

The President-elect left the Situation Room for the Oval Office. There he told President Reagan that NORAD had confirmed over two dozen incoming SS-28 missiles which would strike their targets on the eastern seaboard within twenty-one minutes. He told the President that it was essential to the national security, under the provisions of established White House Emergency Procedures, that he leave at once for Andrews Air Force Base aboard his helicopter, Marine One. At Andrews he would board NEACP (the National Emergency Airborne Command Post, a converted 747 nicknamed "Kneecap"), from which he could conduct World War III. Apparently the President was quite animated by this last prospect, and began immediately to change out of his pajamas.

Arrangements were conducted swiftly. Five minutes later Marine One was on its way to the South Lawn of the White House. Once the President's helicopter reached Andrews, he would be transferred not to NEACP, but to Air Force One.

There was, however, a problem. What if he began issuing retaliatory atomic orders? He *was* still President. It was decided that if he started giving orders to annihilate Soviet cities, his military aide would go through the motions of following his orders. Indeed, the President could have himself a grand old time on the way back to the ranch.

At 12:41 President-elect and Mrs. Tucker finally embarked in their limousine. He instructed me to work with Feeley on a speech insert explaining the delay. We had seven minutes to come up with it.

I suggested putting out the story that a gun barrel had been sighted along the motorcade route and that Secret Service had delayed departure until the area had been "sanitized," as they say.

Feeley said the *Washington Post* would find out it was phony and we'd be accused of lying to the American people on our first day in office. "Listen," he said, "I think we should just tell everyone the man went crazy, pissing on the drapes, the whole works, and tried to start a war. It's not *our* fault we're late, goddammit."

"No," I said. "I don't think that's the approach he wants to take."

Muttering, Feeley began scribbling on a legal pad. He finished just as the motorcade pulled up at the Capitol.

The press was swarming, but at a safe distance. The Secret Service kept them well back. We could hear the shouts, however: "Where's the President!? What's wrong!?"

The President-elect merely waved at them, despite his well-known propensity for marching over to the roped-in area and taking any question put to him—an unfortunate tendency, in my opinion, and one which had led to some of the more spontaneous, troublesome moments of the campaign.

Feeley and I rushed to join the President-elect as he was hustled through the marble corridors of the Capitol. Feeley handed him a sheet of legal paper.

He read it quickly and frowned.

" 'Emotionally disturbed'? Feeley, this is terrible. What were you thinking?" He crumbled the page into a ball. "Now I'll have to wing it."

It all seemed to happen very quickly after that. I remember coming through a doorway into cold January air, the bright blue sky, television lights, and Marine band striking up the theme music from *The Magnificent Seven*, our campaign anthem.

"Where on earth have you been?" hissed Joan. "People are *furious.*"

"Averting disaster," I said enigmatically.

To judge from the looks on the platform, Joan was right. They did not look pleased. Some looked downright incensed. The twenty-five-degree cold had not helped. Justice Marshall had turned cerulean, and was apparently experiencing cardiac trouble. My stomach muscles tightened into a Gordian knot. I reached into my pockets for milk-of-magnesia tablets, but they had crumbled. All that remained was a linty powder.

The President-elect moved to the podium. A murmur rippled

through the crowd as it took stock of this unprecedented breach of protocol: the President-elect was about to speak before taking the oath of office.

"Mr. Chief Justice, Senator Hastings, distinguished members of Congress, friends and fellow Americans," he began. "I guess I have some explaining to do."

Alas, those words would become a *leitmotif* of the Tucker Presidency.

"The President is not with us on this occasion. He . . . could not be with us. He is about to leave the house and city he has lived in for the past eight years. He told me he hopes you would understand and that you will forgive him. He could not trust his emotions at such a time as this. And so he asked me to say goodbye to you for him."

The audience was hushed.

"And so we do, knowing that as he takes his leave of us, our prayers and our thanks go with him."

The sound of rotor blades was heard in the distance down the Mall, at first faint, then louder. The President-elect paused. Tens of thousands of heads turned. Few Americans are unfamiliar with the dramatic television footage, the poignancy of the moment, as Marine One banked its rotor blades in what everyone took to be a gesture of farewell before disappearing over the edge of the Capitol. I heard sniffling around me as the noise of the blades receded in the southeast and the stunned, almost reverential silence set in. I remember thinking, *How moving*. But possibly it was the beginnings of the flu that so many people got on that historic day.

BOOK ONE
HONEYMOON

1
IN THE OVAL

The President appears not to understand the gravity of the
situation. Are we destined to spend the crucial moments of the
Presidency huddled in lavatories? I worry.

—JOURNAL, FEB. 12, 1989

I do not propose, as so many White House memoirists do, to give
the last four hundred years of my genealogy. But since I am frequently asked why I speak the way I do, I shall explain.

I was born in England during World War II. My father had been
wounded by a malfunctioning crane while serving with the Corps
of Engineers. He recuperated at an English Army hospital, where
he met my mother, a nurse. Eventually they married, and I was
born. At war's end Father moved back to Boise, Idaho, where he
resumed work as assistant manager of a paper mill. Though she liked
Idaho well enough, Mother missed England and inculcated in me a
fondness for my maternal country. I was sent to school there, and
it was there I fell in love with chartered accounting. But, being an
only son, I returned to Boise to be with Father and Mother in their
autumnal years.

It was while working at Dewey, Skruem and Howe, Certified
Public Accountants, that I first met Thomas Nelson Tucker. He
was then a figure in Boise society, scion of Thomas Oglethorpe
Tucker, the lumber and tinned-trout impresario. My wife, Joan,
and I did not participate in the glitter and glamour of *le tout Boise*,
as the French say, so I knew him only from the gossip columns,
which I read infrequently. Mr. Tucker, as I called him until
the day of his inauguration, had been put in a spot of trouble
with the Internal Revenue Service because of some sloppy tax

preparation. Old man Tucker's returns were done by DS&H, and so I was called in to clear them up. I was only too glad to help.

Thus began a friendship that—aside from religion and my own family—has been my most enriching life experience. I knew right from the first moment that this was a young man destined to go places. I was not disappointed. I served as finance chairman of his successful gubernatorial races. I also became a sort of counselor without portfolio, managing the personal arrangements, such as travel and accommodation, making sure the household ran smoothly. If I had a coat of arms, it would read: SEMPER IBI. Always there.

And I *was* there, from the beginning—unlike so many others, such as Chief of Staff Bamford Lleland IV and National Security Council director Marvin Edelstein. During Governor Tucker's celebrated courtship of Jessica Heath, it was I who snuck her into the Governor's mansion in the back of my Ford station wagon. And during their engagement it was I who prevailed on her to take his name in marriage. When their son, Thomas, was born, I stood by him at the baptismal font as godfather.

I had my finger in the policy pie, as well. I well remember the night the Governor told me he was going to announce his controversial demand that the federal government remove all Muscleman missile silos from Idaho and that the state be declared a nuclear-free zone. While I might have recommended a more cautious approach, I said to myself, *Courage, Wadlough. This is just the story of bold initiative that will land Thomas Tucker in the White House someday.* I was not wrong.

When the great moment arrived on election night and Ohio put us over the top, I began almost immediately to worry about moving to Washington. How would it affect Joan, who had never been further east than Denver; and our children, Herb, Jr., and Joan? I resolved that the transition should be a smooth one. Instead of renting a house in fashionable Georgetown or Maclean, I found a pleasant and modest house in Arlington, with a small garden and within walking distance of church.

·   ·   ·

I had visited the White House a number of times during the transition, but I was not prepared for the sense of awe and history that I felt as my car pulled up in front of the Southwest Gate at 6:48 a.m., to a smart salute from the uniformed guard. As I made my way to my spacious office on the first floor of the West Wing, I was greeted with a crisp chorus of "Good morning, Mr. Wadlough." *Yes,* I thought, *this will do quite nicely.*

As I walked in, my secretary, Barbara, a loyal, clean, and efficient public servant, handed me a slip of paper. It was one of those pink WHILE YOU WERE OUT slips. She had put a check next to the PLEASE CALL box. Under REMARKS she had written only two words: "The President."

The President. I would be dishonest if I said that the words did not send a *frisson* up my spine. I pocketed the slip of paper. Perhaps a grandson of mine would someday be asked to bring it to school and show it to his classmates.

The past twenty-two months flashed through my mind like film run at high speed, and suddenly I felt rather tired. Democracy can be a bit of an ordeal, you know. I had put on weight. My hairline had ascended another inch or so. My glasses had developed the tendency to fog after I climbed a flight of stairs, and my knees throbbed in overcast weather. I was approaching fifty and felt it. Was I fit, I asked myself, to advise the President of the United States?

But had I come this far, I wondered, only to clutch on the threshold of power?

"Mr. Wadlough?"

Barbara's voice brought me out of my reverie.

"Are you feeling all right?" she asked.

"Yes, Barbara," I fibbed. "Fit as a fiddle."

She knew me better.

"Shall I bring your hot water?"

I do not drink coffee or tea; in the mornings I find a nice, hearty cup of hot water soothing and stimulative of the digestive functions.

I sat down for the first time in my new office. I had asked August Hardesty, the White House curator, to do it over in the style of the administration of Rutherford Hayes, one of my favorite Presidents.*

Hardesty and I had exchanged sharp words over the matter. He was a persnickety old fussbudget and, in my opinion, probably Republican. He looked on our occupancy of the White House with the undisguised distaste of a retainer who has been sold along with the estate and left to assist with its desecration. He had stiffly informed me that he was not "a decorator."

He had indeed redone my office in the style of the 1870s. An enormous brass spittoon squatted beside my desk, which had probably last been varnished while Hayes was alive. The desk was split in eight places. The oak veneer top was so warped it resembled the surface of the sea in a moderate chop. The crowning impertinence was the phone. It was one of those antique stand-ups with the earpiece. To compound the travesty, the old goat had installed another, similar phone painted a garish shade of red and labeled SECURE.

When I attempted to swivel in my chair, I nearly caused scoliosis. On closer examination of my chair, I found I was sitting on a mahogany commode.

"Barbara!" I simmered. "Get me Hardesty!"

Just then the blasted antique phone rang. *Brrrring brrring.*

It was the President. It sounded as though he was speaking to me through a long pipe.

"Herb? I can barely hear you. Where the hell are you?"

Mortified, I told him it was a technical dysfunction. Hardesty would pay dearly for this.

He was sitting behind his desk—the one that had once belonged to FDR—in his shirtsleeves, tie loosened, feet propped up, enveloped in cigarette smoke. I wasn't surprised to see him in such a casual posture, but I was stunned by the cigarette smoke. His smoking had been one of the most closely guarded secrets of the campaign.

No presidential candidate since Nixon had smoked, and certainly never in public. Though we tried to see to it that he was never

---

* Some found my admiration of a Republican inconsistent with service in a Democratic administration. But Hayes was a man of rectitude who enforced a sound money policy.

photographed with a cigarette in his mouth, one or two photos of him smoking had made it into the press.

But when that wretched eleven-year-old elementary-school girl in Ames, Iowa, asked him in front of all the cameras if he'd please give it up "for me," we were in a spot of bother.

Afterward, he'd sat there that night in front of the TV chain-smoking and becoming gloomier with each testimonial to what a great thing he'd done.

"What are we going to do, Herb?" he said with a stricken look.

I told him that "we" had best live up to "our" promise.

"Don't ask me to do that. Not in the middle of a campaign."

I reminded him that I hadn't asked him to do anything. Little Mary McInnis had.

I brought in cigarette-quitting specialists; I brought in a hypnotist. They only managed to put the candidate into a foul temper. At one point he went eighteen hours without one.

But since the consequences of going back on a promise to an eleven-year-old girl were unthinkable, he agreed only to smoke in bathrooms. In return for our consent, he swore he would give it up the day after he won the election.

We made it through the campaign without being found out, no small miracle. I always carried a bottle of Listerine with me. Before interviews he would have a furtive glug from the bottle.

On election night he told me "come hell or high water" he would give it up the day after the inauguration. Now here we were, first full day in office, enveloped in smoke.

"Mr. President, may I speak frankly?" I said as I stood there on the Oval Office carpet for the first time.

"No," he said.

"This just won't do." It was not easy to speak this way to the President of the United States. But it was my duty. "Shall I have Feeley come in and paint headlines for you? 'TUCKER BREAKS PROMISE TO LITTLE GIRL, NATION . . .' "

"Feeley smokes two packs a day."

"Feeley is not President. And anyway he spends the early morning spitting out little pieces of his lung," I said. "A disgusting spectacle."

"FDR smoked. He was a great President. Suppose I got a holder?" I said I did not think a holder would solve the problem. But it was useless. All I could do was get him to agree to the campaign conditions. Later that day I made arrangements with General Services Administration to install special NASA-designed air-purifiers in the Oval Office. They were told it was for the President's hay fever.

Major Arnold, the President's Air Force physician, was very distressed by the President's smoking. I was present one day shortly thereafter when he launched into one of his sermons. These exhortations had obviously begun to grate on the President. When Arnold was through, the President lit another one and asked him if he had ever been to Greenland. When the Major expressed puzzlement at the question, the President reminded him of our Air Force missile-tracking installations there and said he would be more than happy to arrange for his transfer to one of them. "*Northern* Greenland, Arnold," he said.

The Major did not again bring up the subject. It was he, in fact, who arranged for the special flesh-tone dye that the President applied to the nicotine stain on his middle and index fingers.

Later that first day in office Feeley and I were in the Oval and I noticed a number of books piled up on the desk. It occurred to me that in all the photographs I've seen of desks in the Oval Office, I've never once seen *books* in any of them. Feeley noticed them too and told the President he wanted one of the White House photographers to shoot a roll of him behind the desk, reading.

"It'll appeal to the pinheads," said Feeley. Feels wasn't high on intellectuals; he was a meat-and-potatoes politico. That explained in part his dislike of Marvin Edelstein, head of the NSC. Having grown up in a Pennsylvania steel town, he was suspicious of our chief of staff.

"Catching up on your reading?" asked Feeley.

"No," said the President. "Trying to figure out how to keep the reading from catching up with me."

The books were all White House memoirs. Hamilton Jordan's *Crisis*, John Ehrlichman's *Witness to Power*, Emmet Hughes's

The Ordeal of Power, A Thousand Days, With Kennedy, Blind Ambition, Breaking Cover. There must have been about fifteen of them.

"Remember what Oscar Wilde said?" asked the President.

"Who?" said Feeley.

"Christ, Feeley. Oscar Wilde."

"Fuck if I know."

The Oval is hardly the place for such expressions, but Feeley and the President had a good relationship. He was casual with the President, and the President liked that, since there is no dearth of bowers and scrapers in the corridors of power. Next to me, the President was closest to Feels.

"Surprise me someday, Feeley. Read a book. Oscar Wilde said every great man has his disciples and it's always Judas who writes the biography."

"Uh-huh. You hear about the guy goes for his physical—"

"Feeley, you're missing my point."

"Well, what is your point anyway?"

"These memoirs, Feeley. They make me unhappy. It makes me unhappy to think that you and Herb and Edelstein and Bam Lleland and all the rest of you are going to write books."

"So don't think about it." Feels usually had an answer.

"Even the valets. Did you read that book by Ford's?"*

"Yeah," said Feeley. "That stuff about the cold cream. Jesus."

As we talked about Donald Nixon's shady business deals and Lyndon Johnson's fondness for conducting business astride the toilet, I could see the President was deeply perturbed that all his private moments would someday be available on the paperback racks at airports. Something else was worrying him.

"I told a joke this afternoon," said the President. "There were about eight people here. They all laughed."

"So?" said Feeley.

"It wasn't funny. That's why I told it. To see if they'd laugh. They all did."

---

* *One Hundred Years of Solicitude*, by Manolo Rivas.

As the late-afternoon sunlight played on the bare branches of the oak trees outside, the President was philosophical.

"Who knows?" he said as his eyes scanned the curve of the Oval. I sensed it was a historical moment, a man reflecting on the immensity of power and on the implacable forces that would come to bear on him in the years ahead. "This place could turn us all into assholes."

The phone rang. The President picked it up. "Oh." He turned to us. "It's Jimmy Carter."

Feeley said: "What does *he* want?"

"I have a feeling he wants to give me advice."

"Oh, Christ," said Feeley. "Tell him you're out."

"On my first day in office?"

2

THE STAFF

Wrote heated letter to Safire of *New York Times* in response to calling me President's "bootblack" in column. Joan *very* upset.
—JOURNAL, JUNE 4, 1989

I confess that Bamford Lleland IV and I did not hit it off from the start. Sig Beller, our campaign manager, brought him in after the New Hampshire primary when we realized that the Governor now stood a chance to be elected President. His arrival did much to change the flavor of the campaign. He fired fifteen people the first two days. When I found out that he had tried to sack me, I confronted him and gave him a rather large piece of my mind. He was apologetic, but I had no doubt it was because he realized by then that I was "untouchable" owing to my long, personal relationship with the First Family.

Bam Lleland was an adenoidal Bostonian of considerable (inherited) wealth and breeding, with perhaps a little overmuch of the latter. He was a congeries of Eastern affectations: hair pomaded straight back, suspenders, lizardskin briefcase, bow tie, Porcellian Club cufflinks, clear-rimmed glasses, and a show-offy knowledge of French menus. He had increased his wealth by marrying into more, with the result he was able to afford such trifles as his 130-foot motor yacht, the *Compassion*. This unfortunate manifestation of conspicuous consumption he kept in Norfolk, Virginia, the waters in nearby Chesapeake Bay not being deep enough to accommodate it. It was a most maladroit political symbol, given President Tucker's egalitarian philosophy. Lleland always referred to it as "my wife's boat." More than once Feeley and I tried to persuade the President to get Lleland to get rid of the wretched thing.

Marvin Edelstein was another Ivy Leaguer, a Yale professor of political science whose book, *Toward a Grain of SALT*, had made a deep impression on the Governor. Marvin was only thirty-nine, very young to be given such an important post as director of the National Security Council. He was brilliant, with a tendency to arrogance; perhaps that explained why he got along so well with Lleland. They seemed to speak the same language. Despite this, I was fond of Marvin. In a way I felt a bit sorry for him. He was a transparent young man. He wanted to be respected; more than that, I think, he wanted to be liked.

Marvin was very taken with the mystique that went with his job. He carried his penchant for secrecy to great lengths. Whenever we spoke over a non-SECURE telephone line, he would resort to a code incomprehensible to anyone but himself or a skilled cryptanalyst. Before he left on one of his secret missions, he would give us one-page keys to whatever code he had chosen for that particular mission. Invariably, no one paid attention to them.

The first time he tried it on me, the system did not work well. One day my secretary told me there was a call for me from a "Maximum Effect." I assumed it was one of the deranged people who every now and then penetrate the White House switchboard. I simply told her to hang up. She did, but within minutes this Maximum Effect fellow was back on the line. "He says it's urgent," said Barbara. I told her I couldn't be bothered and to inform whoever it was

that there were severe consequences to tying up important government lines. A minute or so later Barbara buzzed me again.

"What *is* it, Barbara?" This was most annoying.

"It's Mr. Edelstein calling from Cincinnati," she said.

I got on. Marvin was nearly hysterical. "What's going on?" he
demanded. "What's wrong with your secretary? It's me!"

"Oh, yes," I said. "How is everything, Marvin?"

"*Don't* call me that!" He cringed. "The code. You forgot the code."

"I'm sorry," I said. "I've been very busy."

He was on his way to Havana to meet with Fidel Castro. For
reasons of secrecy he had insisted on flying there via Cincinnati,
though that seemed out of the way to me.

"Well, how's it going?" I asked.

"I met with Cucumber," he said. "The dressing was delicious."

I rummaged through my drawer for his key. But I could not find
the key.

"Good," I demurred. "It was a good lunch?"

There was a pause. "You don't know what I'm talking about. Do
you?"

"I seem to have misplaced the key, Marvin. It must be here
somewhere. Hold on, I'll find it."

"Never mind," he said. "Never mind. I'll be in touch via Crown.
Over and out."

"Roger," I said, thinking it would help.

I don't mean to make light of Marvin's undercover diplomacy or
of the need for secrecy. The latter is a real and vital part of the
former. But Marvin's system did produce some confusion.

Next to me, Mike Feeley had been with the President the longest,
having joined the campaign well ahead of all the johnny-come-
latelies. Feels, as we called him, had come up through the hawsepipe,
and had served briefly—four days—as Geraldine Ferraro's press
secretary. (He had the most unpleasant memories of that experience,
apparently.) He was a pugnacious fellow of Irish descent, with a
florid complexion and unruly hair. (I often had to ask him to brush
it before a press conference.) Feels was not a man of delicate sen-
sibilities. I suppose press secretaries can't afford them. His trademark

was his propensity to resign. His cries of "This is a fucking outrage!" were a familiar sound of the *Spirit of Greatness*, our converted Boeing 707. One day he resigned twice. His foibles amused the Governor, and he was very good with the collection of jackals and unscrupulous swine that make up the White House press corps; ladies excluded, of course.

Any White House staff is divided into two classes: those who have access to the President and those who don't. Access is the coinage of the realm. Those who have it do not take it lightly. Hal Jasper, Assistant to the President for Communications, was so worried about being "cut out of the loop," as they say, that he kept coming to work throughout a severe bout of the chicken pox. He applied a cosmetic to hide the unsightly skin eruption. Poor Hal was convinced that if the President could manage without his "input" for even a week, he might begin to consider him dispensable. Unfortunately, he managed to infect the President. Though extremely generous by temperament, the President was not pleased, and that was the end of Hal's access.

The various offices, or "shops," within the White House are not unlike medieval dukedoms or baronies. They seem to spend as much time conniving and plotting against each other as they do in running the country. This is sad, but a fact of White House life. I did my best to keep the tensions among the domestic, press, foreign-policy, and other shops to a minimum. In some ways that was a thankless task. I was surprised at the lengths—or depths—to which some would go.

One morning, for instance, my phone rang at 4:30 a.m. The voice identified itself as that of the duty officer in the Situation Room, and said the President had instructed senior staff to assemble immediately in the Situation Room at the White House. Alarmed, and thinking that my President needed me, I dashed to get there, driving at foolhardy speed. When I arrived at the Situation Room, I found only the duty officer, who yawningly informed me that the President was asleep and all was well.

My sense of humor is as good as the next person's, but this kind of childish prank has no place at the White House. I asked the

Attorney General to have the FBI investigate the incident and issued
a very sharply worded memo to the junior staff warning that such
pranks would in the future be grounds for dismissal.

In time I began to think of myself as a shock absorber. I would
get home to Joan and she would say, "Dear, you look like a shock
absorber." "Yes, Joan," I would say, "I feel like one." Of course, I
was speaking metaphorically.

On one occasion the people in Lleland's shop had my security
clearance reclassified so that I suddenly found myself being denied
access to documents of which I had urgent need. When I confronted
him, Lleland suavely denied any culpability on the part of his staff
and chucked it off to some bureaucratic gremlin. I was not amused.

They say that revenge is a dish best served cold, and as it happened I was perfectly situated to provide such a meal, since the
White House mess, run by the Navy, was under my direct control.
Every time Lleland's myrmidons visited some fresh humiliation upon
me, they found themselves getting very slow service, overcooked
food, and watery Coca-Cola.

Perquisites are a key part of the White House, and staff members
measure their importance by them. Access, limousines, tennis-court
privileges, mess privileges—these are the talismans of power. Frankly,
I wish there had been less attention paid to who made the Air Force
One manifest than to running an efficient operation.

My decision to have the White House tennis court grassed over
was due to an incident one Sunday morning in the summer of 1989.
Because of a scheduling error, Jean Logan, Assistant to the President
for Public Liaison, and Marvin Edelstein arrived with their respec-
tive tennis partners to play at the same time. Heated discussion
ensued, followed, apparently, by name-calling. By the time my
phone rang, at ten o'clock on an otherwise pleasant Sunday morning,
Jean was in a state.

"He's doing this just to get at me!" she shrieked. "Jews don't even
play tennis!"

Jean, a graduate of the exclusive Madeira School, had led a shel-
tered life, when you came right down to it.

I was attempting to calm her down when my other phone rang.
I put Jean on hold. It was Marvin.

"You tell that anti-Semitic bitch to get her tits off that tennis court," he said.

The situation seemed to require Solomonic action. "I suppose doubles would be out of the question?" I asked. Yes. Marvin had reserved the court first. It was by rights his, he said.

If Jean Logan's ego was delicate as tissue paper, her temper was a hummingbird's wing. She exploded at me, called me an unpleasant name, and told me she was taking her problem "to the top."

"I'm sure the President will be fascinated," I said sarcastically.

I was drawn into no less than one dozen tennis-court disputes that summer. By August my patience was exhausted. At my orders, workers arrived at nine o'clock one night and by dawn all that remained of the tennis court was lawn. If this did nothing to enhance my popularity, I still think I did the right thing. We had a country to run.

Every senior White House official needs an "enforcer"—to use the colorful expression—to make sure that his decisions are implemented. My first executive assistant was Hu Tsang, a thirty-three-year-old graduate of the Kennedy School. He brought to the job a number of attractive qualities, to say nothing of an imposing physical presence. He would arrive each morning at 5:30 and would practice his martial-arts regimen on the South Lawn. It took some time for the uniformed Secret Service guards to accustom themselves to this.

Hu did not have an easy time of it at first. Lleland's deputies, Phetlock and Withers, treated him condescendingly and called him "Rice Bowl." Hu brought this to my attention. I called Phetlock and Withers in and told them I had given Hu permission to use his Tae Kwon Do on them the next time they called him that; presently the nicknaming ceased.

Despite his eventual betrayal of me—for which I have forgiven him—Hu was a superb implementer and an outstanding public servant. I was deeply saddened to learn of his recent conviction, but I am confident that the appeals process will fully exonerate him and that he will someday return to government. It would be a great shame if young people such as Hu were discouraged from seeking careers in public service.

Betty Sue Scoville, the President's personal secretary, had been with him since his first term in Boise, and she worshiped him. Betty was convinced that history would regard her boss as the greatest President of the twentieth century. Once, after she had had too many martinis, she revealed to me that she kept a "little museum," as she called it, of personal articles of his, such as handkerchiefs, a sweatband, pens, a contact lens, cigarette butts, awaiting the day the Smithsonian might want them. I made her promise me not to reveal the existence of her "museum" to anyone. If the press got hold of it, she could expect no mercy from those piranhas.

Everyone who comes to work at the White House must undergo a rigorous security check by the FBI. These take months and cost the taxpayers thousands of dollars apiece. My experience was that they are by and large a waste of time and money and weed out only institutionalized psychopaths and incompetent KGB agents. If the security checks really worked, we wouldn't, for instance, have had the problems we did with Mitch Buxbaum.

Mitch had worked hard on the campaign, and I was enthusiastic when Feeley recommended him for the position of Deputy Assistant to the President and Director of Media Relations and Planning. But, however diligently he had performed his tasks during the campaign, the fact remained that he had put himself through university by acting in pornographic movies. You would think that a full field investigation by the FBI would have turned this up if the *Washington Post* could. When I finally read the FBI report, all I found to indicate that he had made his living by undressing in front of a sixteen-millimeter movie camera was: "Active in college film society." Indeed he had been. The President's refusal to fire Mitch may have been admirable in principle, but it provided elements on the Right with live ammunition which they did not hesitate to fire.

Speechwriters are not expected to have the same moral values as other people in political life. For the most part, they do not attend church as often as non-writers do, and many of them entertain lifestyles which render them unsuitable for public office. Very frequently, speechwriters are recruited from the ranks of journalism, which accounts for a great deal.

The FBI gave our chief speechwriter, Charlie Manganelli, a clean bill of health. I was delighted, since for some time I had suspected his sudden mood shifts had more to do with drug usage than with the vicissitudes of the artistic temperament. The President too had had his suspicions, so that when I told him of the FBI's clearance, he was gratified. He relied on Charlie, and enjoyed his company.

When Charlie developed his drinking problem, I was inclined to put it down to pressures of the job—which were admittedly heavy—and to urge him to seek help. What I did not know at the time was that his drinking problem stemmed from his drug problem. When he casually informed me of this one day during a heart-to-heart talk in the White House mess, I was aghast. I don't think he quite realized the implications. I arranged for him to enter a very private rehabilitation program at Bethesda Naval Hospital. I told the supervising physician that if one word of Charlie's problem leaked out I would see to it personally that he spent the remainder of his Navy career tending to sick seals on Diego García. I was always very fond of Charlie. He still writes me every now and then from his ashram in Mexico, when the mails are running.

3

FIRST FAMILY

Have been detailed to cope with our First Brother problem. Am not sanguine.   —JOURNAL, OCT. 5, 1989

The first time I saw Jessica Heath was at Cinema 1–2–3–4–5–6–7 in Boise. I don't see many movies (except ones with Alec Guinness in them), but Joan enjoys them, so once a month we used to go on a Saturday night. I confess that I found the violence and sex in *Midnight Water* off-putting, but I must admit that the future Mrs. Tucker was, as they say, a bit of all right.

There were those who counseled the Governor not to get involved with an actress, but not me. From the first moment I met her, I knew this was the woman for him: young, vibrant, beautiful, and quite independent-minded. And a temper, too. All for the best, a very modern woman. The Governor certainly would never be bored.

We became friends. She knew she could always count on me, and she could. Herbert Wadlough is nothing if not reliable. On those occasions when she and the Governor were not speaking, she would sometimes call me, and I would go over to the residence and listen. I enjoyed our sessions very much. It does help to get things out.

Though excited at the prospect of moving to Washington, she was also nervous. "Not to worry," I told her. "I'll be there."

It should come as no surprise to those who have seen her films, especially *Minnesota Hots*, that the First Lady was a deeply sensuous woman. That is perhaps a little unusual in First Ladies, and the White House residence staff was slightly scandalized.

Several weeks into the administration Mrs. O'Dwyer, the rather formal, sixty-year-old Irish woman who headed the household staff, came to see me. She was in a state of agitation, kneading her hands together and going on at length about how "irregular" it all was and how the rest of the staff were "beside themselves." She couldn't quite bring herself to say exactly what it was that was causing all the trouble, although she didn't have to. I could guess.

I explained that the President and his wife were still in the first blush of love and that we all ought to be grateful to be working for such a happy couple. The staff, I said, should treat this as a source of contentment, not consternation.

"But at twelve o'clock noon, Mr. Wadlough?" she said. "In the living room—on the floor?"

Surprised though I was to hear this, I cleared my throat and suggested that in the future she and the rest of the staff err on the side of discretion and knock before entering the family quarters. At this she drew herself up stiffly and said if it was discretion that was called for, it certainly wasn't on the part of her staff.

During the first summer of the administration, an unusually warm one, Bill Dale, the Secret Service shift leader, came into my office one day. Bill was one of the best men on the detail, and one of the President's favorites. He clearly felt awkward as he sat in my office telling me "an unusual security problem" had arisen. I told him we were all family here and not to be embarrassed.

He told me the President and First Lady were leaving the family quarters in the small hours of the night, dressed in nightgowns, and splashing about in the new swimming pool on the South Lawn. I gathered from Bill's pained recitation that they were doing more than just splashing about.

Of course, what married people do is their affair. The problem was that the President was telling the agents who trailed them to the pool to "take the rest of the night off." But Secret Service likes—indeed, requires—Presidents to be in their sight at all times. Bill and his men would retreat to the rhododendron bushes and radio to the sniper teams on the roof. The President espied them and became angry. Last night, said Bill, he had climbed out of the pool, wearing only a scowl, walked over to the nearest bush, dripping wet, and ordered him and the others back to the house.

No matter what your instructions are, it is difficult to disobey a direct order from the President of the United States. Poor Bill and his men withdrew a few more yards and kept a nerve-racked vigil until the President and the First Lady emerged and walked like two moonstruck teenagers, hand in hand, back across the lawn into the White House.

As intimate as I was with the First Family, I could hardly tell the President what he could and could not do with his wife.

The next day I had the White House mess order several hundred pounds of ice, and while the President and his wife entertained their guests at dinner, I personally supervised the dumping of it into the pool. At the same time I instructed the engineering staff to bring the temperature in their bedroom to sixty-five degrees. If my methods sound devious, it should be borne in mind that my only concern was the President and First Lady's safety.

Operation Deep Freeze, as I dubbed it, was not a success. The President opened all the bedroom windows and ordered the pool heated. My consternation was great.

Finally I resorted to what will sound like a drastic solution. I proposed to Major Arnold that we put a mild sedative in the two ounces of rum the President habitually took before retiring. Arnold was alarmed by the idea. An hour later the Secretary of Defense was on the line asking me what on earth I was thinking of. The nation could ill afford a logy commander-in-chief in the event of nuclear attack.

In the end a special detail of Secret Service agents disguised as rhododendron bushes was posted every summer night by the pool as a means of establishing a "sterile perimeter" around the President. It was not a popular detail among the agents, but our peace of mind was worth the extra effort.

The President realized that there would be sacrifices and certain privations. Here was a man who liked to go hiking by himself in the high country of Idaho. Now when he did that, 435 people (including communications personnel) went along. But some things he especially resented—such as when the press was critical of his wife's statements.

Mrs. Tucker was a marvelously candid lady, not given to artifice. She was almost incapable of giving a dull interview, and this led to problems, as when she told the *Ladies' Home Journal* that she thought Washington "dull." My heavens, what an uproar! This was followed soon by her declaration in *Time* that she thought that, as a species, whales were "overrated."

For all her theatrical flair, she had a practical streak. She confided to me that she often remembered the hullabaloo poor Mrs. Reagan got into when she ordered $209,000 worth of new china—even though it had been paid for privately. Thus when Mrs. O'Dwyer informed her that the White House bed linen was worn thin and full of little holes, she did nothing about it. Several times the President complained to me that he would wake up mornings "in ribbons." Finally he asked me to purchase an entire new set of linen at his own expense. (Cost: $3,200.) During their time at the White House he was forced to purchase quite a few household items out of his own pocket, including the new drapes in the Queen's bedroom.

The President had nicknamed their four-and-a-half-year-old boy, Tom, Jr., "Firecracker." Mrs. Tucker did not like the name and waged a lonely, futile campaign to get the staff to use his Christian name. He was a bright little boy and a natural ham who took easily to the cameras. The night of the final ballot of the New York convention, he sat on the floor of the hotel suite writing on a legal pad with his crayons. When his mother asked him what he was writing, he told her it was the speech he was planning to give that night. His father was delighted; his mother, appalled at this precocious political inclination. (She envisioned for him a career in the arts.) When I asked Firecracker to show it to me, he agreed, but only if I promised not to "fuck it up." Obviously, he had been spending too much time with Feeley, and I made a note to speak with Feeley about it. It was a drawing of him at a podium. I told him it needed no editing by me. He was genuinely disappointed when it dawned on him that the cause of all the fuss was his father.

But he was certainly a political asset in his own right, and not just photogenically. Contrary to the press reports, it was entirely his own idea to write Soviet Premier Kropatkin to suggest a summit meeting between the two of them. The fact was, he only told one person he was writing the letter, because, as he subsequently explained to his father, he was worried about leaks. The first we learned of it was a frantic 2:00 a.m. phone call from our embassy in Moscow saying *Pravda* had the full text of the letter in the morning's edition, with accompanying text suggesting the son of the President of the United States was more eager to sign an arms accord than his father.

During the storm that followed, the President tried to get from him the name of the person to whom Firecracker had dictated the letter. (I suspected Feeley.) But even under the threat of a paddling, Firecracker stood firm and coolly told his father it was a matter of "national security" and on a "need-to-know" basis. The next day Senator Kennedy made his quaint suggestion that the President nominate his son to head the Arms Control and Disarmament Agency.

When he was not making administration policy, Firecracker was usually getting into trouble. At a state banquet for Prime Minister Thatcher he managed to transfer several raw Chincoteague oysters from a serving dish to Defense Minister Alistair Horne's chair seat. (Horne, a rather formal Briton, was unamused.)

I believe a lot of it had to do with the fact that he was kept under such tight security. Being popular, he generated quite a number of kidnap threats, and as his mother's worry about them increased, she tended to let him out of the house less and less. Toward the end he had a Secret Service detail of six.

It was hardly a natural way to grow up. Sometimes he would pop into my office and ask me to ask his mother to let him go to the movies or spend the night with his school friends. I got her to agree to the latter once, and what a logistical nightmare *that* turned out to be. The Phinneys—the parents of his schoolmate Tad—were very sporting about turning their house into an armed camp for the night.

Despite everything, Firecracker was fond of his Secret Service agents. His teacher was somewhat taken aback when for show-and-tell at school he brought in some empty cartridges and gave a talk comparing the Uzi submachine gun and the M-14. So was his mother. The Secret Service agents adored him, and all kidnap and other threats were investigated with a vengeance.

Firecracker reacted to the tight control on his whereabouts by trying to elude his protectors. This was impossible outside the White House grounds, and pretty difficult even inside, but he became adept at it. He once sneaked out of his room late at night (evidently a family trait). When the First Lady looked in on him and discovered he was missing, she panicked and sounded the alarm. The search involved fifteen Secret Service men, two German shepherds, several members of the household staff, the First Lady, and the President. For almost half an hour the White House reverberated with cries of "Firecracker!" He was finally located, nestled inside a ventilator shaft on the second floor with his hamster, Theodore.

The President's parents had passed on, but his brother, Dan, was very much alive. The President loved his brother deeply, but Dan's lifestyle left a lot to be desired. I always said that if Dan Tucker had finished college, he wouldn't have turned out the way he did, wandering through life aimlessly, becoming involved with so many women, hot-air-ballooning one week, Buddhism the next, singing with a Bluegrass group the next. I know it all sounds like jolly good fun, but at thirty-five a man ought to have some sort of career. And for me his peregrinations ceased being amusing when he decided, in the midst of the general campaign, to buy a half-share in that

Denver drug-paraphernalia business—"head shops," they are called—
named Opiate Of The Masses.

It was bad enough that he ever should have been involved in this
kind of sordid business, but Dan's partner, Mr. Ezekial Brown, who
went by the name of "Pillbox," had a record of drug-related arrests. Of
course we did not find this out until everyone else did, the morning the
Denver Post broke the story. I remember the moment well.

We were in the *Spirit of Greatness*, 37,000 feet over Tennessee,
when the call came in. It was Roger Bond, our campaign press person
in Washington, and he was beside himself. "Oh," he kept saying as
he read from the story, "this is awful, this is just awful."

Feeley was no island of calm on that occasion either. He sputtered
up and down the aisle, saying the man should be behind bars. He
resigned several times that day.

We were grateful, naturally, for the precedent set by Billy Carter.
I believe the American people are decent and forgiving when it comes
to these things; there are a lot of younger brothers out there.

4
OPEN DOOR

State of the Union speech last night. In my view, both historic
and an unqualified success, though early newspaper reactions
disappointing in the extreme. George Will said President's call
to the nation "more of a parking ticket than a summons." Have
been given charge of the National Metrification Initiative. Awesome responsibility.   —JOURNAL, JAN. 28, 1990

There was an unmistakable air of excitement in the days following
the President's address to the nation. Once again there was a sense
of purpose, an aura of new frontiers. I was confident the phrase he

used for his legislative package, "The Great Deal," would kindle the national imagination, and for a while there was talk of a new Camelot on the Potomac.

It was a giddy, busy time of state dinners, weekends at Camp David, and battleship decommissionings. (The President felt he might mollify the Navy, whose budget he had cut so drastically, if he made the decommissionings special occasions by his presence.) We huddled in the Oval late into the evenings. The President talked about his dream of revitalizing the Infrastructure. He spoke too of normalizing relations with Cuba. The air was rich with the pure ether of power, and I took care not to breathe too deeply. I buckled down to work on Metrification, devising a program that would convert American to the metric standard, no easy task. Joan was typically understanding about my late hours. What a good egg she was!

I wanted the President to be free for "creative thinking," as I called it, so I tried to "run interference" for him by taking on myself some of the more nettlesome problems. Such as Vice President Douglas Reigeluth.

"Bingo," as he was called by his friends, was a frisky fellow who had his eye fixed on one thing and only one thing: the top job. And, in my view, he wasn't going to sit around twiddling his thumbs for eight years.

Whenever Secret Service advised us that there was heightened risk in an area the President planned to visit, Bingo would always pipe up cheerfully and say things like "We can't let ourselves be ruled by fear." One had to wonder. I was especially put off by the way he comported himself at cabinet meetings, speaking up whenever he pleased, even interrupting the President—the President!—to offer his views on this and that. It had been a marriage of convenience. He had been foisted on us at the convention, and now here he was carrying on as if his opinions mattered. If you ask me, Vice Presidents should be seen and only infrequently heard.

I also felt that Bamford Lleland was a bit too cozy with him. It was he who suggested Bingo be given charge of the President's Task Force on the Infrastructure. I demurred heavily, convinced as I was that in his lust for influence Bingo would turn it into a personal power base. But I suppose he had to have something to do. To my horror, Lleland suggested he be given Metrification—and on the spurious grounds that it "didn't matter anyway." *My* Initiative. I sent him a stiffly worded memo telling him exactly what I thought of that. I could see that Bamford Lleland and I were not destined to be easy partners in history. The back-stabbing had already begun.

One day the President called me into the Oval and said, "Herb, I want to open this place up, get some fresh air in. It still feels musty from those Reagan years." I did not at first understand the President's meaning, but he often spoke elliptically.

"I don't want to lose touch with the American people," he said. "Don't want to isolate myself."

"Noble sentiment, sir," I replied.

"If I ever start using 'we' instead of 'I,' promise me something." I agreed, of course. "You'll pull the plug."

I promised I'd do the honorable thing, though of course in jest. Then he told me that no matter how busy or important his schedule got, he wanted to meet with one "ordinary American per day."

I was, well, speechless. As admirable an idea as it was, it was hardly practical.

"Just how ordinary?" I asked.

"*Ordinary*, Herb. I want dirt under their fingernails. I want to be able to smell them."

This was certainly an unpleasant prospect. I could not help myself. The words came out before I could check them: "And will we be having barn dances in the East Room?"

He did not seem to "get" my sarcasm. "That's not a bad idea," he mused. I decided not to pursue it. I was confident, anyway, that he would soon come to his senses. In the meantime I was put in charge of Operation Open Door.

Jean Logan's reaction was predictable. Hysteria.

While it was true that Jean had made herself invaluable during the campaign putting together fund-raisers, she was a woman of obvious limitations. It was Lleland who persuaded the President to give her the Public Liaison shop. (Feeley suspected the two were having an affair, but of course that was beside the point.) Feels and I had rather hoped he would give her something out of the way, such as the National Endowment for the Arts.

"You can't be serious!" she screamed at me over the phone.

"Calm yourself," I said. "We have work to do."

She was sputtering. "Where are we going to find them?" Social ambidexterity was not one of Jean's talents. She was a Washington hostess, and, as the popular jingle from the early eighties put it, she was not the sort to reach out and touch someone—unless she had first been introduced.

This was silly. "I don't know, Jean," I said tartly. "Maybe your servants know some."

"Yes," she said, "I suppose they do."

Thus began a distinctly unpleasant period of my life. Jean fought me every step of the way. Our ideas of what constituted an ordinary American were quite unalike. Hers dressed in Laura Ashleys and drove Volvos.

My ordinary Americans were *ordinary*: drab, dull, and fragrant. I saw to that personally. If the President wanted to smell real people, then let him have a good whiff—maybe they might change his mind and cause him to cease this undignified spectacle. I was especially proud of one aromatic chicken-packer from Maryland. "Come as you are!" I told him over the phone.

Jean found my "ordinaries" —as we called them—grotesque, and we tussled constantly. "Why is it," I said one frustrating afternoon after reading the briefing sheets of her next two weeks' worth of ordinary Americans, "that four of them went to Harvard, two to Princeton, one to Yale, one to Stanford, one to Vassar, and the other to Wellesley?"

"You know," she said, twirling her frosted bangs with a forefinger, "I wasn't sure about the Stanford person."

"Jean," I said, "I'm not sure I'm getting through. It's bad enough they all went to college. But to Harvard, Princeton—"

"What's wrong with a good education?" she snapped.

After a month I no longer had the energy to argue. I took her off Open Door (she didn't complain) and turned her work over to Hu

Tsang. For a while there was a preponderance of Oriental ordinary Americans, a tendency I had to correct.

Hu showed real zest for the job. It was he who set up the Office of Human Background, which processed and evaluated the ordinary Americans, weeding out the extraordinary and subordinary ones. Candidates for presidential interviews had to be carefully screened by Secret Service, then by OHB's health, economic, and ethnology experts. Only then could they be pronounced truly ordinary.

The press, in its callous, cynical way, was suspicious of the program at first and called it pure symbolism. The President chafed at this baseless criticism. At a press conference he said, "I hear more common sense from these ordinary Americans than I do from reading most editorial pages." The press shut up after that, and Bob Petrossian, our pollster, reported a one-point rise in the President's approval rating that week.

A few weeks later the right-wing journal *Human Events* reported that the Ordinary Americans program had been penetrated by the KGB. Honestly.

The President thrived on his sessions with his ordinaries. When affairs of state were overwhelming and he had spent too many hours in meetings with soft-spoken, pin-striped men, he would buzz for an ordinary American. (I kept one on standby at all times just across the street at the Hay-Adams Hotel.) They were his link to the America he loved and understood, and he always emerged from his sessions with them refreshed and ready once again to take up the heavy mantle of leadership. In time, I confess, even I became a convert. Truly, the President was a visionary man.

But then two unsettling incidents occurred that marked the beginning of the end of ordinary Americans in the White House.

The President was given a two-page "backgrounder" on whomever he was to see that day. This meant that valuable conversational time was not wasted on such irrelevancies as "So, tell me about yourself."

It had been a trying day for the President: a morning speech to the National Association of Manufacturers, legislative strategy session, appointments with Admiral Boyd of the Joint Chiefs and mem-

bers of the Senate Appropriations Committee. Then a private lunch
with Ambassador Massot of France.

Massot was a pleasant but impossibly long-winded Gaul whose
briefest reminiscence about his days in the Resistance tended to last
an hour. The President was not fond of submitting to these gaseous
sessions with Massot, but, as Massot's son was President of France
and as he placed great value on Franco–U.S. relations, he did. But
he also made sure that Aquinas, his Filipino steward, kept him well
fortified with martinis. (He was otherwise abstemious at lunch.)

Their lunch ran twenty minutes over schedule, and when I brought
in the afternoon's agenda, the President looked tired. The knot in
his tie was askew and his breathing was heavy. A three-martini
lunch, from appearances.

"How was the Ambassador?" I asked.

He rolled his slightly bloodshot eyes. "Glorious. We relived the
siege of Rouen. Who've we got?"

I handed him a backgrounder. "A Mrs. Smith to see you."

"Good. I could use a Mrs. Smith about now. You know, Massot
must breathe through his asshole, he never even stops talking."

"One of these days, Mr. President, you're going to say something
like that in public and—"

"Okay, okay." He usually got impatient with me when I ad-
monished him about his language, but I felt it my duty.

We went over the rest of the day's schedule and I went back to
my own office and busied myself with arrangements for the upcoming European pre-advance trip I was making with Leslie Dach, director of Presidential Advance.

At 2:18 p.m. he buzzed me. I got the distinct impression he was
displeased. "Wadlough," he said, "get the fuck in here."

He shoved a piece of paper at me. It was the OHB backgrounder
on Mrs. Smith. "Read this."

It told a tragic story. Mrs. Smith's daughter was an alcoholic.
Her only son had been killed in Vietnam. Social Security had just
cut the benefits of her husband, who was in the hospital with em-
physema. And two months earlier a tank truck had hit a telephone
pole outside her home, causing a firestorm from which she had
escaped with only her negligee, slippers, and dentures. I grimaced.

How had Hu let this quite un-ordinary woman through the turnstile?

"A tragic story, Mr. President," I said. "I anticipate your criticism. But I'm sure her visit with you was a great comfort."

The President lit a cigarette and rubbed the bridge of his nose. "I talked," he said, "for five minutes. I told her this country owed her more than it could ever repay for the loss of her son. I told her I was sorry about her daughter and offered to help get her into the Betty Ford Center."

"Generous of you, sir. Very generous."

"I sympathized about her husband. I told her about my Uncle Luke, who had it too. And I told her that before sundown the skin of the GS-7 who cut her husband's disability would be hanging from the top of the Washington Monument. It was a pretty inspired performance, Wadlough. You'd have been proud of me."

"I'm sure I would have, sir," I said a bit uneasily, for I saw that something was out of kilter here.

"Do you know, Wadlough, how I felt when I was finished?"

"Relieved, sir?"

"No, Wadlough. Imbecilic."

The trouble lay in the fact that the woman was a Mrs. Cora Smith, of Mamaroneck, New York. The backgrounder was for a Mrs. Sylvia Smith.

"Oh," I said. "Oh, dear."

The President crumpled the backgrounder into a tight ball and threw it in the wastebasket.

"No, Wadlough. Oh, shit."

The worst of it was that Mrs. Cora Smith subsequently sold her story to the *Ladies' Home Journal* and of course the President became the butt of many jibes. He was deeply wounded. Lleland saw it as an opportunity to criticize my handling of Open Door. His henchmen taunted Hu, renewing their "Rice Bowl" epithets. But President Tucker was not a quitter, and he got right back on the horse. Three days later he buzzed for another ordinary American. But one month later the unfortunate incident with Mr. Leverett occurred. Somehow the fact that he was under a psychiatrist's care for exhibitionist tendencies had eluded OHB. I was mortified.

As I look back on it, the whole episode showed the need for

tighter security screening. I made that point at the staff meeting the next day, but Lleland hardly acknowledged my comment or my presence, and the President informed me, through Lleland, that the Ordinary Americans program was henceforward discontinued. The era of Open Door was at an end.

5

CITADEL

Serious incident involving the Chancellor of Germany yesterday. Lleland trying to put the blame on me, but am sure the President understands I can hardly be held accountable for ionospheric disturbances. Still, whole thing a nuisance.
—JOURNAL, JULY 17, 1990

We had been told of the existence of Citadel in a Defense Department briefing a few days after the election. Frankly, I was shocked. The idea of turning the most historic room in the nation into a bomb shelter struck me as in exceedingly bad taste. The military said it was essential, but I privately wondered if it wasn't just another of those expensive toys so beloved by former President Reagan.

The argument for it, we were told, went like this:

When the Soviet Union deployed its new generation of GROK SLBMs (submarine-launched ballistic missiles), the interval between launch and impact—as the military planners blandly put it—was reduced from fourteen minutes to four. As a result, the White House Emergency Procedures, or WHEPs, had to be entirely redrawn.

Pre-GROK, the WHEPs had been based on the principle of being able to evacuate the President from the White House and have him inside the National Emergency Airborne Command Post—"Kneecap"—within twelve minutes.

Another WHEP called for evacuating the President by helicopter to any of seventy-five Presidential Emergency Sites, or PESs, underground command stations from which the President could direct nuclear retaliation. "Rare, medium, or well-done," as one former White House military director described it. Still another WHEP called for the President removing himself to the bomb shelter built during President Truman's time underneath the East Wing of the White House.

The GROKs made all these procedures obsolete. During simulated nuclear alerts they had never gotten a President to Kneecap in less than half an hour. And the problem with the PESs was that the Soviets knew where they were and could "dig them out" even if the President could get to them in time. The bomb shelter under the East Wing could only withstand twenty-five psi—adequate at the time, perhaps, but in the age of GROK no more effective than cellophane.

President Reagan had approved Citadel as the least expensive, most reliable, and most effective means of ensuring "survivability." The moment NORAD (North American Air Defense Command) confirmed an "incoming [missile] with high degree of probability," the National Military Command Center at the Pentagon would notify the President. He, his family, and "essential personnel" would then proceed to the Oval Office, which would then sink forty-five feet into the earth.

Citadel was also equipped with a so-called safety trigger. When the missiles were one minute from impact, Citadel would automatically activate itself.

The mind boggled, but there it was, every distressing detail. It had been built secretly, under the guise of "renovations," during one of President Reagan's three-month summer holidays. Only a handful of us knew of it. Its very existence had the highest classification. Of course I was delighted to be "essential personnel," but the thought of leaving poor Joan and the children to face nuclear holocaust without me was wrenching indeed. Public service makes heavy demands on a man.

One day, right in the middle of a meeting with Feeley, Marvin, Lleland, and me, the President decided to take Citadel "for a spin." He reached into a desk drawer, released the "safety" and snapped a red toggle switch. A few clicks and whirrs and the Oval Office sank into the ground. With a gentle thump it stopped. Then one wall peeled away to reveal a large room with black electronic screens on the walls, a large conference table, and about twenty cots.

"Hey," said Feeley, "can I use this this weekend? I've got some people coming in from out of town."

"Sorry, Feeley," said the President, "this is strictly for essential personnel."

"Well," he said, "you're going to need a press secretary to explain why you're still alive when everyone else isn't."

A year into the administration an unfortunate incident occurred involving Citadel and the German Chancellor.

The President was conducting a meeting in the Oval with Chancellor Schmeer and several high officials when a computer in the National Military Command Center at the Pentagon wrongly interpreted an ionospheric disturbance as a massive Soviet nuclear attack. Citadel was automatically activated. Without warning, the entire Oval Office began whirring and clicking and started to sink beneath the ground.

The President and I exchanged quick, horrified glances. Citadel had never malfunctioned before, so at first we thought this must be the real thing. *Poor Joan*, I thought.

The President dashed to his desk and picked up the phone linking him to the NMCC. "What's happening?" he demanded. I was saying the Lord's Prayer and wondering what apocalyptic briefing he was receiving from the duty officer. His face relaxed.

"False alarm?" he said. Oh thank heavens.

"Then would you mind stopping this thing?" he said into the phone.

He hung up and began pressing the ARREST FUNCTION switch in one of the drawers. Nothing. The lights flickered. A hydraulic vibration accompanied us on our descent. For some reason, despite all that was happening, my eyes fixed on the Charles Wilson Peale portrait of Washington over the mantel. The vibrating caused it to tilt. When we finally came to rest with a resonant *clang*, the picture was jarred to a forty-five-degree angle askew—a metaphor, I mused, of the Tucker Presidency.

Then with an electronic whirring sound the east wall lifted to reveal the Citadel's nuclear command and survival facility.

Chancellor Schmeer and the German Foreign Minister looked at each other. The President was back on the phone, his jaw tightening. "Right," he said abruptly and hung up. He smiled weakly at the assembly of officials, waved me over to him, swiveled so he wasn't facing his guests, and whispered to me, "Get us out of here. I'll try to keep them busy." He swiveled back toward his guests.

"Chancellor," he beamed, "my *profound* apologies." He said he'd arranged a little demonstration to show them the extent of our nuclear deterrent facilities, but that the timing was "a little off."

As the President led the Chancellor into Citadel, Foreign Minister Echt touched my arm and whispered, "It would be best if we do not linger."

"Quite," I said. "We're due at lunch in ten minutes."

"That is not the problem," he said. "The Chancellor has"—he gestured—"*Platzangst.*"

I stared. German is not one of my languages.

The interpreter was hovering between the President and the Chancellor and out of our reach.

"He is uncomfortable without windows."

Well, I thought, *so am I uncomfortable without windows.*

"Elevators. Small places." He gestured, hugging the air.

"Oh," I said, "claustrophobic?"

"Exact!" he said.

"I understand," I said grimly. He went to join the President, who was explaining the function of a console with a number of television screens built into it. I wondered what he was telling them. It was well known inside the White House that the President was not mechanically minded, so much so that the communications people had periodically to re-explain the functioning of his (admittedly complicated) telephone intercom system. The Chancellor, I noticed, was sweating, despite Citadel's cooler temperature. I made quickly for the phone and reached Colonel Ed Swygert, director of the Office of Special Support Services. "What in the blazes is going on?" I said in a whispered shriek.

"We're very embarrassed, sir. We think the problem may have originated at Unimak."

"Unimak?"

"Yes, sir. In the Aleutians. One of our DEW line facilities. The computer—"

"Good God, man," I said, "I don't care if the problem originated in Siam."

"That would be unlikely, sir. We don't maintain any facilities in Siam."

I ground my teeth. "Some other time, Swygert, if you don't mind. Now get us up."

"Sir, we're trying."

"*Trying?* What do you mean, *trying?*"

"Yes, sir. We apparently have a fluid problem."

"If you do not undo this, Swygert, fluid will be the least of your problems."

"Don't worry, sir. We have men on their way down the access hatch. They'll be there in a matter of minutes. You'll be able to exit through that, if it's not inconvenient."

"*Inconvenient?*" I stammered. "You want me to tell the President of the United States and the Chancellor of West Germany they have to crawl through a mineshaft? Have you taken leave of your senses, man?"

He said they were doing everything possible.

"More. You have to do more."

"Yes, sir."

I went over to give the President the news. The Chancellor had loosened his tie and was breathing heavily. The Foreign Minister shot me a nasty look. The President, I was sure, was now making up his explanations of the various Citadel command-post functions. My own vocabulary of Armageddon was limited, but I was reasonably sure there was no such thing as a "prompt hard-target kill capability." It was just as well, since the President was not supposed to be divulging America's nuclear counterforce strategies to foreign nationals, no matter how high up they were. I managed to get the

President aside while Marvin Edelstein and Secretary of State Holt continued chatting with the poor Chancellor. I explained the situation.

"Christ," he said when I told him about the emergency hatch. He looked at the stoutly built Chancellor. "He probably won't even *fit*, for Godsakes."

I told him about the claustrophobia.

"You don't think he's going to go weird on us, do you?" he said. I replied that it was my earnest hope this would not be the case.

He took out his cigarette case. He never smoked in front of visitors.

"Sir," I said, "do you think that's wise?"

"Not *now*, Wadlough." He snapped the Zippo shut. It sounded like the guillotine blade I knew would be descending on certain heads after this was over.

I was back on the phone with Swygert two minutes later. I was in the midst of a fresh threat when with a violent lurch the east wall of the Oval Office began to shut. Seconds later the Oval Office lifted off the floor of Citadel and was propelled upward at an accelerated rate. I had been leaning with one arm on the President's desk. I was knocked down, and as I lay there getting my bearings, I saw the Chancellor, trying, somewhat frantically, to get to the closing wall and back into the ascending Oval Office. As the Oval Office floor came flush with the ceiling of Citadel, scissoring it out of view, I caught a last glimpse of the view and the others. They were watching with faces of serious alarm.

Moments later there was another *clang* and the Oval Office was aswarm with Secret Service agents and military people.

"Where's Firebird? Where's Firebird!" They looked at me accusingly, as if I had eaten him.

"Where do you *think* he is?" I said through clenched teeth. "Buried alive. With the leader of our most important ally. Idiots! Get me back down there!"

Someone hit the down button and the Oval once again began its forty-foot descent into the earth. When I got back down to Citadel, the scene was an unfortunate one. The Chancellor's claustrophobia had apparently overcome him. There were signs of a struggle: several chairs knocked over, Marvin Edelstein's glasses broken, and the

Chancellor staring straight ahead, breathing rapidly and being spoken to in soft, soothing tones by the Foreign Minister.

"Going up?" said the President sulfurously.

On the way back up, everyone stood, as if in an elevator. Major Arnold attended to the Chancellor's medical needs, which were greatly helped by a mild sedative. The Foreign Minister glowered at the Major as he administered the injection. At lunch someone remarked that the Chancellor seemed "subdued." A special effort was made to insulate him from the press.

Citadel was deactivated the next day, and Ed Swygert was sent to our radar facility at Unimak to conduct a month-long "administrative review" of the incident. Though the fault was hardly my own, the President seemed to associate me with the whole unfortunate episode. He did not buzz me for several days.

BOOK TWO
FIRST FLUSH OF POWER

6
ASSIGNMENT: HAVANA

Am finding the Latin temperament trying, but much is at stake.
—JOURNAL, JAN. 6, 1991

On the first morning of the new year the President told me he was going to normalize relations with Fidel Castro.

I welcomed this bold initiative, but our plurality in the election had been marginal, and I worried how the Republicans would react. As usual, the President had anticipated me.

"It can't be one of those Nixon-in-China deals," he said. "If I say anything nice about Castro, the Right'll have my ass for breakfast."

An infelicitous metaphor, to be sure, but he was right. The thing had to be handled carefully. The President wanted "no rhumbas, no kissy-kissy," just a "straightforward signing of bilateral agreements and exchange of ambassadors."

To my surprise, he asked me to accompany Marvin on his exploratory mission to Havana. "You'll be my eyes and ears," he said.

I broke the news to Joan that night over a dinner of her delicious meatloaf. I knew she would take the news hard.

"Dear," she said, "you know that kind of food doesn't agree with you." True enough. On a business trip to Guadalajara years earlier I had been severely stricken. It had been an unpleasant and protracted ordeal, and my personal physician had advised me that another such episode could leave my intestines gravely weakened.

"But, dear," I said, "I can't tell the President of the United States I can't go on a historic mission for him because Latin food doesn't agree with me."

"Yes," she said, fighting back the tears, "but I just can't bear to think of you hunched over the toilet like that, making those awful noises."

Nevertheless, my duty was clear and, though my decision broke her heart, Joan was a brave girl and she was deeply committed to the goals of Thomas N. Tucker. Three days later I left Washington for Havana. In one of my bags was a three-day supply of food and copious amounts of Pepto-Bismol. Joan was not about to send me off unprepared.

To satisfy Marvin's bizarre predilection for secrecy, we flew to Havana via Bangor, Maine. He had arranged to give a speech there— to an unlikely foreign-policy forum, the Bangor Chamber of Commerce. He gave interviews afterward to the local press saying how much he was looking forward to spending the next two days fishing in Penobscot Bay. The locals were quite perplexed. "In January, Mr. Edelstein?" asked the reporter from the *Bangor Daily News*. Caught off guard, Marvin replied that he found the winter weather "invigorating." I was grateful when he finally boarded the unmarked Air Force jet after a ridiculous charade through the streets of Bangor, changing cars twice to make sure we weren't being followed.

We arrived at José Martí Airport at four in the morning, I haggard and badly in need of bed. Instead we were whisked off for breakfast with Foreign Minister Galvan. "Breakfast" consisted of coffee the texture of loose sand, pineapple slices, and eggs which would have hatched the next day.

Foreign Minister Galvan was a decent enough fellow who shared with most Latins a native garrulousness. He spoke uninterrupted for two hours and six minutes. It was clear he regarded the "*initiativo*" as Comandante Castro's idea. As a matter of fact, it had been President Tucker's *initiativo*, and after a while I found it necessary to point this out.

Marvin gave me a smart kick under the table, nearly breaking the skin on my shin.

Foreign Minister Galvan seemed not to hear my protests, but went on merrily, saying that the visits of Castro to Washington and Tucker to Havana would be "instantly hailed around the world as examples of the wisdom of America's new leadership." Marvin was saying nothing, only nodding. This was getting out of hand.

Clearing my throat, I begged the Foreign Minister to understand that President Tucker was eager for substance, not mere spectacle, and that we felt an exchange of ambassadors, not Presidents, would be an appropriate start.

Foreign Minister Galvan blinked a few times, relit his cigar, and said how tired we must be.

Once back in our hotel room, Marvin berated me for "interfering." I drew myself up to full height and informed him that the President had sent me down here to make sure he, Marvin, didn't paint him into a corner. Marvin huffed off to compose his cable. I went off to crawl under the covers, which were damp from humidity and gave off a mildewy odor.

That night we were taken to see El Comandante. Castro was in a gregarious mood, and not hesitant to talk about his "achievements." Dinner dragged as I politely declined to partake of one dish after another. At one point the Comandante himself stopped all conversation to ask, through his interpreter, why I was not eating. I told him that my stomach was unsettled. He frowned and in stentorian fashion summoned a doctor. I insisted that I would be fine as long as I trod a delicate gastronomic routine.

Well then, he said, I must have some of the "excellent" Cuban beer.

When I told him I did not consume alcoholic beverages, he made it plain that I had just insulted all of Cuba. Marvin leaned over and hissed, "Will you just take a sip, for Chrissake?"

Well, when in Rome, as they say. I took a swallow of the stuff. Castro indicated his pleasure, and the conversation resumed.

My memory of what followed is indistinct. I remember that my glass was being constantly refilled, even as I held up my hand to decline. There was also much toasting, I dimly recall; and at one point I found myself being embraced by the Cuban leader. His beard smelled of cigar, and prickled. After repeated toasts to normalization, we were loaded onto a procession of jeeps and taken to a newly completed hydroelectric facility. It was during the Comandante's speech regarding the Czechoslovakian turbines that I became physically indisposed. After that, I remember very little indeed.

We were flown—mercifully—back to Washington the next day,

Marvin in a royal huff and barely saying a word to me. I was grateful, as I had never before experienced what is euphemistically called a hangover. To me it seemed more like a combination of the flu, migraine, and bilharziasis. When he demanded that I put on my disguise before landing at Andrews Air Force Base, I told him that under no circumstances would I put on that disgusting beard. To this day beards summon up the most unpleasant associations.

As I walked through the West Wing, people greeted me like a diseased person, lowering their voices, hurrying out of my vicinity. Even through the fog of my distress I thought this unusual. Here I was, returning from a presidential mission, and plainly the worse for wear. Somehow I managed to reach my office. Immediately Barbara said, "He's waiting for you."

Holding my throbbing temples between my hands, I groped my way to the Oval.

The President was in one of his quiet tempers. "Welcome back," he said curtly. "Mind explaining this?"

Dimly I attempted to focus on the cable he'd handed me. It was a description of our negotiations with the Cubans, signed by Marvin. It made him sound like Benjamin Franklin. I, on the other hand, was made to sound like something out of *Animal House*. Alas, due to my circumstances, I lacked the wit to defend myself.

"Codswallop," I muttered.

The President said, "Is that all you have to say for yourself?"

"A tissue of untruths. He would have given them Florida if they'd asked."

"So you threw up on their new dam. On Castro's pant leg. Dammit, Herb."

I explained to the best of my impaired ability, but it was clear that the President was disappointed in me. For the next few days I made myself scarce, hoping that his displeasure was temporary.

Normalization fever swept through the administration. About a week after my inglorious return we had a meeting in the Oval. The President seemed bemused by all the excitement. "Holt called this morning from State," he said. "Wanted to know when 'we're' going to Havana. Petrossian's in a lather because he thinks there goes Florida.

Reigeluth's delighted. He thinks one of the anti-Castro group is going to blow me away. Remind me, Bam," he said to Lleland, "why did we pick Reigeluth?"

"The Northeast."

"Oh, yes. Right."

It was at this meeting that he told us he had decided against going to Havana or inviting Castro to the U.S. Marvin shifted in his seat and tried to persuade him that reciprocal visits were the thing.

"No," he said, "I won't do that. Castro's a dictator. Dictators like parades—makes them feel legitimate. He doesn't want to be recognized by the U.S., he wants to be respected by the U.S. I'll give him the first, not the second."

The President then told me he wanted me to return to Havana to work out arrangements for The Meeting. I was stunned. In front of the others I asked him why he wanted me to go, considering the mess I'd made of things the first time.

He said that Clay Clanahan of CIA thought my "embarrassment" had been arranged. He grinned. "Marvin here was hot for reciprocal visits. You weren't. Clay thinks this was their little way of making a point. Well," he chuckled, "I too can make a point."

Wadlough, I said to myself, *we're out of the doghouse.* Marvin looked positively miserable.

The President reached behind him, took a desk atlas, and opened it to the Caribbean. He took a ruler and drew a straight line from Key West to Havana.

"There," he said, making a small X. "Longitude eighty-two west. Latitude twenty-three degrees, fifty minutes north . . . hell, make it an even twenty-four degrees. Halfway. Tell El Comandante I will meet him there." He held the point of the pencil in place. Then he added with a slightly devious smile, "Take Leslie Dach along with you."

Feeley, Marvin, Lleland, and I all looked at each other. I said, "Are you sure that's wise?" But the President only smiled.

7
LESLIE

Nothing normal about normalization. Grave doubts crowd in.
Spoke with Joan over telephone. Most annoying when Embassy
operator said, "Be advised there is no privacy over this line."
Joan upset to know our intimate conversation being listened to
by communists.   —JOURNAL, JAN. 16, 1991

Leslie R. Dach, Director of Presidential Advance, was by all accounts the best advanceman in the business but an unmitigated
political liability. He thought nothing of closing off the Brooklyn
Bridge in rush hour to accommodate a motorcade, or of shutting
down an airport on Friday of the Labor Day weekend. When the
President visited the South Bronx, Dach had several enormous ten-
ement buildings razed overnight so the cameras would have an unob-
structed shot of the presidential profile. His motto was "Get the
fuck out of my way." It took on the force of scripture in the advance
office. (One of the secretaries in his office had stitched it in needle-
point on a cushion; I forbade any photographs to be taken of it, for
obvious reasons.)

Leslie managed to insult more or less everyone with whom he
came into contact. Perhaps that is in the nature of advancemen, but
during the campaign it was necessary to devise a computer form
apology which we routinely sent out after an event. It read:

The Governor deeply regrets you were inconvenienced by Mr.
Dach, a member of his advance team. He has spoken sharply to
Mr. Dach about it and has received his assurance that such a
thing will never happen again.

He would like to take this opportunity to thank you for your

assistance in his campaign. He hopes he can count on your continued support, for the good of the campaign and of our country.
Sincerely,

Herbert Wadlough,
Executive Assistant to the Governor

Leslie was serene in his contempt for fools, a category which in his view included most of humanity. But he was so good at what he did that he was untouchable. He made miracles happen, and most politicians like miracles to happen around them. It gives them the illusion of divine aura.

Leslie, Marvin, and I flew to Havana, this time without the disguises. Marvin was still chafing over the President's decision not to turn the meeting into a bilateral orgy and, I suspected, had not quite resigned himself to it. "He's missing a great opportunity, Herb," he told me as the Jet Star sliced through the night 33,000 feet over the Gulf of Mexico. "To turn this into some clandestine meeting in the middle of the ocean . . . What's the point anyway?"

"Marvin," I said, "the President is firm on these arrangements. We have a job to do."

He lowered his voice so that Dach, sitting forward of us, couldn't hear. "What worries me," he whispered, "is *him*. He's a madman, you realize. He'll ruin everything."

"Calm yourself," I said. "Whether the Cubans find him agreeable is irrelevant. And unlikely. No one finds Dach agreeable. Dach is a genius."

"I don't care."

"He has the confidence of the President."

Marvin slumped in his seat. "Then why do I have a bad feeling in my stomach?"

"I am not acquainted with the vicissitudes of your digestive system, Marvin. But if you are having difficulties, I suggest you drink only bottled water and avoid salads. Among Mr. Castro's miracles, the elimination of amoebae is not numbered." With that I turned back to my paperwork.

Galvan was mute with disappointment when Marvin informed

him of the President's decision to meet Castro at 24 North, 82 West instead of 17th and Pennsylvania Avenue. He told us unsmilingly he was not sure El Comandante would agree to the proposal.

"I'm afraid this is not a proposal," I interjected before Marvin could equivocate.

"We will be in contact," he said grimly.

"When?" It was Leslie. Marvin and I rushed to assure the Foreign Minister we were at his disposal, but the insult had already registered. He turned on Leslie.

"When I tell you," he glared. "The Comandante is a busy man."

Leslie regarded him with casual contempt. "Yeah, well, so am I. So is Mr. Edelstein here and Mr. Wadlough—"

"*Leslie!*" I said.

"—so why don't you pick up the phone here and call him? Assuming your phones work, which they don't, from what I've heard."

Oh, dear, I thought.

At this point both Marvin and the Foreign Minister began screaming at Leslie. Their combined remonstrations had as much effect on him as bugs have on windshields. He yawned. "Listen, Ricky, we're not getting anywhere, are we?"

The Foreign Minister sputtered. "*Ricky?*"

"Ricardo, whatever—"

"My name is Galvan! To you I am Your Excellency!"

"Right. Look, why don't you just turn us over to someone who knows what he's doing?"

"*What?*"

Marvin said to me: "You've got to stop this. It's undignified."

But you couldn't stop Leslie. Now he was telling the Foreign Minister to put us in touch with someone who "has influence." Galvan was threatening to have him expelled from the country.

"I'll be at this number for one hour," said Leslie, looking out the window at the beach. "After that you can call long distance." At this the Foreign Minister stormed out.

"I'm hungry," said Leslie. "They have room service in this country?"

"Leslie," I said, "you've probably ruined the whole thing."

"I doubt it," he yawned. "You've got to make things clear at the start. You save yourself a lot of trouble that way."

I called the President on a SECURE line from the American Interests section of the Swiss Embassy and gave him an account of our "progress" so far.

There was a long pause after I finished.

"Do you want me to send Leslie home?" I offered.

"Home? *Hell*, no. I may make him ambassador."

Marvin wrested the phone from me. "Mr. President," he said, "you cannot allow an advanceman to conduct foreign policy."

When he'd hung up, I asked him what the President had said.

Marvin looked at me miserably. "He said, 'Well, I'm President. I guess I can do anything I want.'"

Shortly afterward we received word that our appointment with Castro was set for eleven o'clock that night. The invitation was *exclusivamente* for Señor Edelstein and Señor Wadlough.

He greeted me less physically than at our previous encounter; however, I was grateful, inasmuch as El Presidente had been "in the fields" and was sweating profusely. At first I thought he might turn us down, so keen was his disappointment about the President's Florida Straits Rendezvous With Destiny plan, as it was called. Marvin was eloquent in his unctuousness, however, and in the end Castro agreed to the historic meeting. As he was leaving, he said through his interpreter, "If we are to meet at sea, I hope your President has a stronger stomach than you."

The great event was set for March 14.

The Cuban government refused to hold the meeting aboard a U.S. naval vessel and we refused to hold it aboard a Cuban naval vessel. The stalemate was broken when Canada offered its new helicopter carrier, the *Diefenbaker*. Leslie set about making the Canadians regret their decision, and I spent many hours sweeping up after him, soothing enraged Canadian naval officials. The Captain of the *Diefenbaker* was sorely tried. He agreed to vacate his cabin, and to paint over the entire flight deck with the United States and Cuban flags. He even accepted with consummate graciousness Leslie's frequent insults about the condition of the ship, which was nearly as immaculate as the Queen's own yacht. But when Leslie blithely informed the Captain that he would have to reinsulate the ship "top to bottom" so TV sound crews wouldn't pick up any hum, the Captain ordered him off his ship and for three frantic days refused to allow him back on board. The President wanted the press contingent limited to 200, which set the Fourth Estate to baying about the "trampling of free speech." The conservative press was apoplectic, especially *Human Events*, *National Review*, and *Commentary* calling the President "Red Tom." We could have done without the endorsement from the *Daily Worker*, but as America warmed to the thaw, no one seemed to notice.

The President himself was surprised by the extent of the hubbub over the Cuba opening.

"Did you see this?" he groused one morning, staring at the Bloomingdale's ad in the *Times* for its "Havana '91" fashion line. Across the top of the two-page spread screamed: REVOLUTION—AND THE LOOK IS NOW! "Jesus," he groaned, "what have I done?"

Cigars became the rage around the White House until the President banned them. But even in the shopping malls of conservative, suburban Virginia, where the Che Guevara look had never been much in evidence, one could see the bizarre effect the Cuba opening was having on the public. My own teenage son, Herbert, Jr., stopped shaving and came home from high school one day wearing olive fatigues and jungle boots. Joan was beside herself. Another day she called me at work, something she never did unless it was serious. "He's out back in the yard with that machete. He's cut all the bark from the maples."

The High Seas Summit, as the press dubbed it, nearly fell through two days before it was to occur. I had a call from Mr. Docal, my counterpart in Havana. He was fit to be tied. And for good reason.

Major Arnold had been keeping tabs on the recent outbreak of dengue fever—he'd had conversations with Leslie about it. Now Leslie, acting on his own authority, had blithely informed Docal's deputy that all Cuban officials to come into contact with the President would have to be fumigated by a U.S. Department of Health official.

I told the fuming Docal that there had undoubtedly been a failure of communication, and not to worry.

My next call was to Leslie. "Have you taken leave of your senses?" I screamed into the phone. "You can't expect high Cuban officials to allow themselves to be sprayed!"

"Calm down, Herb. You ever seen a case of dengue? Great big, nasty blotches—"

"Now you listen here, Leslie. There will be no spraying of Fidel Castro, or of *any* Cuban. If I so much as see you with a can of deodorant, I will have you hanged. Do you hear me?"

"Uh-huh."

I don't like to use threats, but they were the only language he understood.

8
24 NORTH, 82 WEST, HIKE

Myself, I consider the High Seas Summit a masterpiece of diplomacy and a great feather in TNT's bonnet. Lleland trying to blame the whole fiasco on me. Am disturbed that Marvin should take his side. Joan a great support throughout historic episode. —JOURNAL, MARCH 15, 1991

I remember the day as if it were yesterday: the clear skies flecked with small clouds, crisp morning breeze, the deep blue color of the Florida Straits, the whop-whop sound of Marine One landing on the huge American flag painted onto the deck of the *Diefenbaker*; the arrival moments later of the Soviet-made Mi-26 HALO containing President Castro and the Cuban leadership. The anthems, the review of honor guards. (I must say that I thought the Cuban guard a bit tatty.) It was an awesome sight to behold.

We were steaming in a circle, surrounded by a small armada of

U.S. and Cuban naval vessels. Off on the horizon was the Soviet guided-missile destroyer *Sovremennyy*. Beneath the waters the nuclear-attack submarine *Chattanooga* prowled the deep.

We were steaming in a circle for a reason. Cuba wanted the *Diefenbaker* to steam south, toward Cuba. The U.S. wanted her to bear north. East was ruled out by us, west by the Cubans, out of deference to the Soviet Union. Marvin had had to come down to Havana with an admiral and a meteorologist. After tense negotiations the idea of steaming in a circle was proposed. The Cubans accepted, but demanded it be in a clockwise direction because, as Foreign Minister Galvan said, they wanted to set the clock forward. At this point the President declared the whole situation "silly" and said all right.

That El Comandante was smitten by the First Lady was immediately apparent. I must say, I had seldom seen her look so beautiful. (The sea has always complemented Mrs. Tucker.) She wore her peach suit with the ruffle neck and ivory stockings; not a sailor's eye was off her the entire time.

El Comandante bowed low and planted a kiss on her hand. She accepted his arm and accompanied him on a review of his Moncada Battalion troops, President Tucker following docilely behind. It was an egregious breach of protocol.

Lleland came over, bookended by the beady-eyed Phetlock and Withers, and complained, but there was hardly anything I could do.

By the time the reviewing was over, El Comandante had discovered that Mrs. Tucker spoke Spanish and was even more taken with her. The President was grinding his mandibles, but forcing himself to smile.

Luncheon was more of a success. There had been a great deal of wrangling over the menu. The Cubans wanted their own (revolting) native cuisine—greasy pork and fried plantains. We pushed for a good, hearty *North* American meal: roast turkey and all the trimmings. They counterproposed chicken, but then an impasse .was reached when the Cubans insisted it be boiled and served with black beans. We counter-counterproposed Southern-frying it and serving it with new potatoes and green peas. Just when it looked like a mealless summit, the Canadians offered to undertake the catering. This was acceptable to both parties, and so we sat down to a lunch of smoked rainbow trout and Melton Mowbray pie, accompanied by Okanagan Valley Pinot Noir and Zinfandel. I am quite partial myself to Melton Mowbray pie, and I was told the Okanagan wines were "drinkable," which is, I suppose, what wine should be.

The President and Castro were seated next to each other, with the First Lady on the Premier's left. Castro began by telling Mrs. Tucker he had seen all her films. This seemed greatly to distress the President, what with the First Lady's celebrated *déshabillé* scenes in *Minnesota Hots*. Except for a few opening pleasantries with the President, El Comandante spent most of the lunch talking with her. By the time dessert arrived, I feared for the President's enamel, so hard was he grinding his teeth.

At lunch's end the President stood and spoke for eleven minutes— about the importance of the day, the need for dialogue and understanding, and ended with his pledge to "forge vibrant links" between our two countries. It was an admirably delivered talk, I thought, and quite appropriate to the occasion.

El Comandante's people had assured us he would speak for eleven minutes as well; that had been all hammered out in advance. He was known to give five-hour speeches, so particular attention was given to this detail. Eleven minutes, Docal had assured me.

As everyone who has watched the live broadcast remembers, El Comandante spoke for fifty-five minutes. Twenty minutes into what became known as *"El Discurso Enorme"* (literally, "the enormous speech") President Tucker's face assumed a passivity that a volcanic eruption could not have disturbed. He did not even flinch when Castro got to the part about America's "history of felonious foreign policy" *vis-à-vis* Cuba.

The networks were furious too, since they were locked into live coverage and El Comandante was cutting into the soap-opera time. In sum, no one was happy—except for El Comandante, whose protracted expatiations inflicted incalculable damage on the administration. There was not much discussion aboard Marine One on the flight back to Key West that afternoon.

BOOK THREE
MID-TERM BLUES

9
MORNINGS AFTER

The President is cranky of late. —JOURNAL, APRIL 4, 1991

The year that followed the High Seas Summit was not a happy one for those working at the White House. The scandal at the Interior Department, the mid-term elections, the Soviet invasion of Pakistan, the President's brother's conversion to Islam—it was one thing after another.

The President was working grueling eighteen-hour days trying to save the Great Deal. But with the loss of so many Democratic seats in the House in the November '90 elections, he had to fight like a bobcat to save this far-reaching legislation from the long Republican knives; nothing so seemed to please those eager, well-scrubbed freshman faces as the prospect of disemboweling it of its most progressive elements.

It was during this period that the President began to despair of his cabinet.

Cabinet meetings had grown so unproductive and depressing that we had to plead with the President to schedule them. We would have to remind him that one of his campaign promises had been a return to cabinet government.

"My cabinet," he grumbled, "gives me a pain."

Secretary of State Holt's perfervid desire for a breakthrough in the Middle East led him to pay little attention to the rest of the world. Thus the news that one third of Pakistan had been rendered radioactive seemed hardly to disturb him, except insofar as it "impacted" on Jordan.

At one meeting he launched into a forty-five-minute disquisition on an opaque nuance made in a speech by Foreign Minister Rubal of South Yemen. The President's eyes looked like eggs in aspic. Feeley, exasperated well beyond his five-minute attention span, crushed his tenth cigarette of the meeting and declared, "Mr. Secretary, with all due respect, this doesn't amount to a sockful of shit."

Holt's face turned the color of an overripe pomegranate. The President reprimanded Feeley, but with a mildness suggesting sympathy. He agreed with the assessment.

Then in September the *Post* broke the story about Interior Secretary Chief Fred Eagle. That was a particularly black day for those of us who had urged the President to take on the Chief at Interior. Indeed, I had been his prime sponsor, believing as I did—and still do—that this country's treatment of our Red Brethren is its saddest chapter.

The press distorted many aspects of the case, but the nut of it was that as a regional commissioner in the Bureau of Indian Affairs he had sold off an ancestral Sioux burial ground to a South Dakota Rooty-Toot Root Beer franchise. It did not mitigate the controversy that the Chief was a member of the Cheyenne, historical enemies of the Sioux.

The President stood by the Chief, though privately he was furious. More than once he made tart comments in my direction, such as "Where do you find talent like that, Wadlough?" It was a period of great stress for the Chief, what with the special prosecutor and the Senate hearings. We squeaked through, but it took its toll on him. He became irregular in his sobriety and would launch into disconnected, hortatory speeches about such matters as space exploration.

It was all we could do to prevail on the President to hold one cabinet meeting every two months. And even those he approached as if they were trips to the dentist.

The fact was that the President had changed in two years. He was less patient. His Great Deal zeal had been frustrated by the Congress, that cacophonous body of do-nothings. Every time he announced a bold initiative, a hundred obstacles were thrown in his way. He wanted things *done*, not "acted on." Anyone who has worked in government will appreciate the difference.

I believe that explains his short-lived proposal, following his moving visit to an inner-city drug-rehabilitation center, to have the government grant letters of marque and reprisal to private individuals, authorizing them to sink or shoot down any ship or airplane carrying drugs into the United States.

Now, letters of marque and reprisal had not been granted since the War of 1812, when privateers were empowered to plunder British vessels. Attorney General Struzzi, a strict civil-libertarian, was visibly shaken by the President's idea, though he understood that Congress would never go along with such a program.

Relations with Congress were, in fact, at a very low point. When Senator Bliffen of Louisiana denounced our Metrification Initiative as "un-American," not one of his colleagues rose to protest this frankly absurd charge.

Tim Jenkins, our congressional liaison person, thought we should lay on more candlelight dinners for Congressmen and their wives. The President did not think highly of the proposal. "We've had so goddam many candlelight dinners," he said, "my eyes are failing."

During a budget session in the Oval he grew heated when told there wasn't enough money to fund a Department of the Infrastructure. When someone suggested he might shave a few more billion off the defense budget, he grumped, "If I cut any more out of the Pentagon, the Navy's going to have to go back to tall ships." Relations with Admiral Boyd of the Joint Chiefs were not very good either.

I had noticed that the President had started to quote conversationally from his speeches. Though disturbing, this was not without precedent. Historians have recorded President Kennedy's tendency to ask his wife, "Ask not when is dinner; ask what is for dinner." And at least TNT had not yet begun referring to himself in the third person.

The President had always enjoyed self-deprecation in his speeches, little touches such as apologizing for "ruining your dinner" in an evening talk. Charlie Manganelli, our chief speechwriter, always included such a self-deprecatory line. But now one day he called me in a state. He'd just gotten a speech draft back from the President, and the President had X'd out the self-deprecatory line, writing in the margin: "Unpresidential—let's drop this sort of thing."

"Herb," said Charlie, "tell me. Is the man going Nixon on me?"

I told him the President was under some stress at the moment.

"Stress?" said Charlie. "Stress? I've got four writers who haven't seen their wives in three months. I spend more time on that plane than I do on the ground. I'm getting too old for this, Herb. One of my researchers—Julie—fainted last week on the West Exec. If the man wants less stress, tell him to stop making so fucking many speeches!"

It was true the speech schedule had been heavy, but the President felt firmly that the worse things were going in Washington, the more important it was to be on the road, taking his message to the people.

Three days later the President looked up from a pile of papers and scowled. "What's gotten into Manganelli?" he demanded.

"Sir?"

"Read this."

It was Charlie's latest speech, the one for the Eleanor Roosevelt Society Dinner. It began: "I don't deserve this honor you're bestowing on me this evening. The way I've been screwing things up lately, about all I deserve is early retirement."

I must admit it was extreme.

"You tell him the President is furious. One more chance, then he goes back to writing ad copy for yogurt."

There it was—the third person. *Oh, dear*, I thought. *Not a good sign at all.*

Jovially, I told him that Charlie was just using a formula that had served him well in the past.

"This is the White House, Herb." He sounded sincere. "I'm just thinking of the office."

"I see," I said.

"You've got to have respect for the office."

"Yes."

"Manganelli has no respect for the office."

"He—"

"What does he think this is? The Kiwanis? They're giving me the Eleanor Roosevelt Medal." He gestured with his hand at the text in my hands as though it were a stray dog that had wandered in.

"Tell him I need a completely new draft. Tell him a completely new approach."

"Yes, sir."

"And tell him to stop quoting John Kenneth Galbraith. I want *new* ideas."

By now it had become obvious that the Vice President had his own agenda. His speeches—which I now insisted on reading before-hand—rarely made *any* mention of the President. A historian of the future, in fact, might have inferred from reading them that Reigeluth was the Chief Executive, such was the proliferation of references to "my vision for America."

Admittedly, the man had a dynamic speaking style and was a first-rate fund-raiser for the party. But when his interview with Ann Devroy of the Gannett newspapers came out, the one in which he said he wasn't sure if he'd run again in '92 because he might want to spend a few years "getting back in touch with the people," we decided we had a bona-fide problem on our hands. We also learned that certain elements at the Democratic National Committee who envisioned a Reigeluth run in '96 were quietly encouraging him to put some distance between himself and Tucker.*

Thus it was decided to send the Vice President on a series of foreign trips to such countries as Mauritius, Oman, and Sardinia.

"Let him get back in touch with *them*," sniffed Lleland. The Vice President took to buttonholing people in the West Wing and telling them he had been misquoted, but it was a bit late for that.

---

* It is not true, as Lleland alleges in his book, that I tapped Reigeluth's phone. I had good contacts at the DNC, and I hardly would have had to resort to such an un-derhanded method.

10
THE MUFFIN INCIDENT

Disturbing incident this morning in the Roosevelt Room. Doubt
such undignified behavior ever displayed there since LBJ's time.
Spoke with Hardesty about the margarine stain. He appalled.
— JOURNAL, JUNE 25, 1991

I sensed the showdown which was coming.

For some months now Lleland and his henchmen had been feeding tidbits of prevarication to the press, saying the President was displeased with my handling of the Cora Smith business, the Cuban business, and so on. I'm surprised he didn't blame me for the weather. While I didn't doubt the President had better things to worry about— and he did—I found these vile canards distressing. And of course Joan was extremely upset by them.

The President, once contemptuous of flattery, now submitted to it; enjoyed it, even. Lleland and Marvin were ample purveyors of it, as were their deputies. Withers, I noticed, had adopted the royal custom of walking backward when he left the Oval Office. I resolved to have a real heart-to-heart with the President. But, to my dismay, every time I proposed we have "a chat," he said he was too busy. "Next week," he'd say, and then forget.

In all fairness to him, it was not a happy time. His marriage was under a strain. (The First Lady and I still had our little talks, and I was able to infer from them that all was not well at home. She spoke of taking a "sabbatical" to make another film. I tried to be both encouraging and discouraging at the same time.)

The President had always had a temper, but as Governor he had taken bio-feedback treatments for it, with happy results. Now, however, he had lost the knack of regulating his heartbeat—where was the time to practice?—and it showed.

During an interview he told columnist John Lofton of the *Washington Times* to "go soak [his] head" in response to his antagonistically phrased question about "destroying America's economy and defense." Lofton went with it, as they say, and appeared on TV shows playing the tape of the President screaming at him and ordering him out of the Oval Office.

A few days after the incident we were in the Roosevelt Room having our customary senior-staff breakfast. Lleland was there, as were Marvin, Feeley, myself. The "Big Four," as we were called by the press.

Feeley had spent a rough couple of days coping with the fallout from the President's ill-advised behavior. He called the President a "jackass."

Now, if anyone other than Feels had said this, I would have been on my feet demanding a retraction. But Feels was—Feels. There was no question of his loyalty to Thomas Tucker. He loved the man almost as much as I did.

But in reply Lleland sniffed, gave the top of his soft-boiled egg a smart whack, and said, "I hardly think that's appropriate. You're talking about the President of the United States."

"Bamford," said Feeley, "why don't you sit on that egg?"

Lleland put down his spoon. "I beg your pardon?" he said.

Feeley repeated what he had said, louder this time.

"I will not tolerate that kind of talk from a *staff* member," said Lleland. He made it sound as if he were talking about the pantry maid.

Feeley laughed. "You're just arrogant enough to think we're working for *you*. Well, Bamford, this isn't the crew of that barge of yours."

Lleland smiled superciliously. "Actually, it's a motor yacht, Feeley. But I wouldn't expect someone of your background to understand the difference."

"I'll tell you what it *is*," said Feeley, flushing. "It's a fucking disaster. All that communication gear—is that so you could stay in touch with E. F. Hutton?"

"Gentlemen, gentlemen," I interjected. The President was due any moment in the Oval Office a few feet away. It wouldn't have been very seemly for him to overhear all the shouting.

"Now look here, Feeley," said Lleland, his lips whitening. (His lips lost color whenever he became annoyed. Feeley said this was common among upper-class Episcopalians and that it was due to centuries of inbreeding.) "You run a sloppy operation and it shows. It showed three days ago. Lofton's a nut and he shouldn't have been there. If you want to take your inadequacies out on me, I'm quite indifferent. But if you're going to take them out on the President, then you will have to go through me. And I promise you that will be an un-*puh-leasant* process." He finished the sentence with a slight raising of the eyebrows.

Feeley leaned back in his chair. "Sloppy?" he said.

"That's what I said," Lleland replied, returning to his egg.

"You know what's sloppy?"

Lleland did not answer as he excavated a spoonful of yolk.

"*This* is sloppy." With that Feeley hurled his English muffin. It flew sideways past my nose, curving in the manner of a Frisbee, missing its target and striking the magnificent oil painting by Bierstadt, "A Look Up Yosemite Valley."

No one spoke. We looked at the Bierstadt. A small trickle of margarine glistened on the surface, just above the Indian village.

Feeley went over and dabbed at it with the corner of his napkin. Edelstein cleared his throat and looked at Lleland. Lleland looked at Edelstein.

"You know," I said, trying to get conversation going again, "I've never really noticed that painting before. It's quite beautiful. I mean, the way the light hits the sides of the mountains." (I have always felt that mirth is a good way of releasing tension.) Feeley started laughing. So did Marvin, briefly. I joined in. But my comment seemed to have piqued Lleland. He called me a fool and stormed out.

After breakfast I went off to talk to Hardesty about having the margarine removed from the Bierstadt before it congealed and required the ministrations of an expert. He kept demanding to know how it got there. Attempting to jolly him, I told him I suspected the Soviets. He was not amused.

When we met with the President shortly afterward, Feeley told him what an unmitigated misery his life had been since the President told Lofton to soak his head.

"Lofton pisses me off," said the President. "He questioned my patriotism."

"Yeah," said Feels, "well, now everyone's questioning your sanity."

A year ago the President would have laughed, but now there was not even a smile, only an abrupt change of subject.

11
LOST ACCESS

Things not working out as I expected. Joan taking it well, but I fear most for the children. It is hard when your father is a laughingstock.   —JOURNAL, JULY 7, 1991

Things changed in the days following the muffin episode. The President stopped buzzing me. On a trip to Omaha my usual seat on Air Force One was occupied by Phetlock. I raised a stink about it and got my seat back, but it was a Pyrrhic victory. Lleland's people didn't speak to me the whole way out and back. I was made to feel like a petulant child who has flown into a temper because his favorite toy was removed. During the flight some cables on the deteriorating Bermuda situation were being passed around. When I asked to see them, I was told they were classified THUNDERSTORM and that I was only cleared for DRIZZLE material. I hotly replied that as a member of the senior staff I had never been denied access to important cables. "What," I said to Lleland, "if the President wants my views on it?"

I did not like his smile. "Oh," he said, "I wouldn't worry about that."

Feeley too was being "cut out of the loop," as they say, and he was not at all happy.

I decided the air was in need of cleaning. When we got back to Washington, I called Betty Sue Scoville, the President's personal secretary, and asked her to set up an appointment for me.

When I had not heard from her three hours later, I called back. She told me the President had asked "what it's in reference to." This was quite bizarre. Impetuously I replied, "The health of the Republic!" It was wrong of me, but it just came out.

Surprised, she said she would "get back" to me. The next day she called to say the President had a "window" in his afternoon schedule.

"Splendid," I said.

"Between three thirty-five and three forty," she said.

Five minutes? Oh, this was iniquitous. I, who had spent hours in the Oval brainstorming with the commander-in-chief, now limited to *five minutes*.

He greeted me warmly enough, but there was an air of distraction that I did not recognize.

"Yes, Herb. You wanted to see me."

I asked him if things were running smoothly. He seemed to avoid my eyes. "I'm having a hard time concentrating," he said.

I asked if he shouldn't resume his bio-feedback sessions, but he became impatient.

"We'll have to limit staff contacts. I'm getting flooded with details. Too many details. I shouldn't have had to get involved with that Jacuzzi matter. I shouldn't have had to deal with that."

In a memo I'd enclosed several Jacuzzi brochures to see which model he wanted.

He said, "From now on everything goes through Lleland."

It was as if someone had suddenly placed several telephone directories on my chest. I had difficulty breathing. He continued avoiding my blank gaze.

"It's temporary. Maybe. And in no way is it a comment on you, Herb. You've done a fine job. A really wonderful job."

It sounded as if I were being fired.

"Herb," he said, "we were wondering—"

We?

"—if in the meantime you might help out in the East Wing. Jessie'd be awfully grateful. You two get along so well."

The East Wing. The First Lady's domain.

" 'In the meantime'?"

"Oh, absolutely. Just till she finds a new chief of staff. Thorndyke didn't work out too well."

"No," I said. "No, he didn't."

"She thinks the world of you, Herb. I don't need to tell you that."

Then why *was* he telling me that? I thought it best to ask flat out: "Of course officially I'll be staying on here—in the West Wing?"

"Uh, yeah." Not what I'd call a ringing reassurance.

With this he began talking about the "chemistry" in the West Wing.

"I'm not happy with the chemistry, Herb. I think a lot of our problems are chemical."

"Chemical?" I said.

"Yeah. Chemical."

I nodded. Then shook my head. "No," I said. "I don't understand."

Uneasily he said: "This friction between you and the chief of staff. It's damaging the Presidency. Throwing food in the Roosevelt Room. Christ, if that ever got out . . ."

"Oh, that. That was just a silly bit of nonsense. No harm done."

"Food-throwing by a top administration official in the Roosevelt Room is not a big deal? Do you realize the history associated with that room? That's where I signed the Omnibus Infrastructural Metrification Educational Assistance Act."

Not to mention Teddy Roosevelt's Nobel Peace Prize on the mantelpiece, I thought.

"A great occasion it was, sir. And a fine piece of legislation."

"I thought so," he said a bit huffily.

"Nevertheless, Mr. President, I have a feeling Mr. Lleland has elevated the muffin business into something it was not." The moment of truth had arrived. The President and I went back a long way. It was time to speak frankly. "Frankly, Mr. President, I'm disappointed he succeeded so easily in persuading you to the contrary."

Now the President made eye contact. I had gotten through to him. "Herb, we all have work to do. My decision stands about access to this office. Thank you."

He picked up a red folder marked TOP SECRET and pretended to be absorbed. It was his signal that our discussion was at an end. The door clicked behind me, but in my mind's ear I heard through-bolts being rammed shut, keys turning, chains being fastened. The mind reeled.

There, waiting to go in, was Phetlock. *Phetlock!* I thought I detected a smirk. I got a grip on myself and made it back to my office.

I walked past Barbara as if in a trance. I sat down at my desk and looked about the walls of my office. It looked so small and plain next to the elegant curve of the Oval. *Steady, Wadlough,* I thought. *Better get used to four flat walls.*

Barbara stuck her head in. "Are you all right, Mr. Wadlough? Can I get you some hot water?"

I told her to hold all calls.

I looked at my desk calendar. July 5, 1991. Eight hundred and ninety-seven days into the administration.

How many more days will I last? I wondered. In the West Wing a man without access is like a man in the desert without water.

The period that followed was among the worst in my life. By the time I got home that night, Joan already knew. I could tell by her face—she didn't have to say anything. She hugged me and said, "You'll always have access to my heart." I almost lost control of my emotions.

"Dear—" I fumbled.

"Don't say anything," she smiled bravely. "How about a cup of tea?"

"You know," I said with an air of gay abandon, "I could use a cup of tea about now."

In the cruel days ahead she was an absolute rock. It could not have been easy. There would be whispers at the church socials, catty remarks behind her back in the supermarket aisles. At least she would not be submitted to the indignity of being seated below the salt at embassy dinners. We were not "regulars" on the Washington social circuit anyway. I have always found socializing tiring and a waste of time that could otherwise be spent reading a good book or watching an interesting program on Public Television.

But Joan was strong, of good pioneer stock. Her ancestors had set out from St. Louis in Conestoga wagons and traveled across the vast, perilous country in search of a better life in the West. Many of them had been ruthlessly slaughtered by the ancestors of our Secretary of the Interior. Thinking about it now made my blood boil.

It would be hard, too, on the children.

Herb, Jr., became sullen and unresponsive. He came home one day with a black eye. He said he got it playing football.

"Football? In July?"

He finally told me he'd gotten it in a fight. A group of boys had started taunting him about my loss of access. There had been shoving. It turned into a melee.

Little Joan suffered too. At slumber parties the other girls hardly talked to her. She would cry herself to sleep at night.

It is not easy to look a nine-year-old in the face and know you have lost her respect.

At the office, meanwhile, the phone didn't ring as much as it used to, and when it did, it was some assistant secretary over at Commerce wanting to know if his superior could use the Indian Treaty Room in the Executive Office Building for a press conference. For over two years I had put heads of state on hold. Now I was getting calls from GS-14s about room availability.

Barbara and the White House mess people did their best to cheer me up. (You truly don't know who your friends are until times such as these.) Barbara kept me well fortified with hot water, and Sanborn, the head Filipino at the mess, saw to it his men treated me like the king I was no longer. My favorite dish, meatloaf and buttered eggplant, was on the menu every day.

In victory, Lleland played the haughty *seigneur*. His myrmidons, Phetlock and Withers, delighted in humiliating Hu. Hu found himself cut out of Cabinet Council meetings. When he asked for an explanation, they sniggered that they were "trying to streamline the decision-making process." Hu's Oriental disposition helped him greatly (these people can absorb a great deal of abuse without showing it), but the poor fellow was made to suffer grievously for my fall from grace.

Phetlock had his minion, Fred Scroggins, the director of the Office of Administration, send Hu a memorandum instructing him peremptorily that his West Executive parking space was being reallocated in order to "facilitate spatial automotive requirements in the office of the chief of staff."

This was what Henry Kissinger would have called "an intolerable situation," an insult of the grossest proportion. And of course it was transparently an attack on me personally.

I decided on a course of what the strategists over at the Pentagon call Massive Retaliation. I had not started this war, but by heavens if it was war they wanted, I would give them one. I might have lost my access, but I was not without ammunition.

Within the hour I had instructed Sanborn to bar both Phetlock *and* Withers (I smiled at this escalation) from the Executive mess. Let them eat in the regular mess, with deputy assistants and speechwriters! I am a reasonable man, but, forced to revenge, I am not without a certain sense of perversity.

I enjoyed a good laugh imagining their faces when Sanborn informed them that their usual table in the Executive mess had been "reallocated due to spatial consideration."

When I told Feeley what I had done, his spirits were greatly buoyed, especially inasmuch as he had just received a "request"— as the arrogant swine in the chief of staff's shop coyly titled their inter-office *diktats*—to submit his phone logs for the previous two months. Lleland had just embarked on one of his hypocritical leak-plugging crusades. So Feels had submitted his phone logs, but only after adding a few creative red herrings. He'd had his secretary doctor his log so that the only names that appeared were those of Nobel laureates in the field of microbiology.

Lleland's reaction to my White House mess maneuver was predictable: dire outrage. He sent me a stiff memo informing me that, as he often lunched with his assistants, it would be necessary to reinstate their access to the Executive mess. I sent him back a memo saying that "a full review of White House mess privileges was being undertaken at the present time" and that he would be informed of the findings "in due course." Ha!

The hell that Feeley was going through is well described in his own memoir, *The Outrage of Power*. We met frequently during this time of crisis at a bar on G Street called the Exchange. It was slightly shabby there—a suitable atmosphere, I thought. A good place for such as us to meet: the sort of dimly lit *endroit* where secretaries and Secret Service agents drank. Occasionally you'd find a GS-17 or Schedule C appointee there, slumming.

In happier times Feeley and I used to meet for drinks (in my case, ginger ale) at Maison Blanche. That was where the Inner Circle met. Now it would have been too embarrassing to go there and endure the smirk of Antoine, the *maître d'*.

I was worried about Feels. His wife wasn't as strong as Joan, and they were part of the social scene. He confided to me his wife had been seated next to the Chilean military attaché, an unthinkable slight in former times. She'd begun drinking before noon and spending too much time at Neiman-Marcus.

"Tell you, Herb," said Feeley one evening after two double bourbons, "it's affecting our sex life."

I winced at this intimacy, but I realized at the same time that he was reaching out to me. I felt helpless, but tried to gather my wits. Perhaps some "man talk" was in order.

"Maybe if you both drank less," I offered. "They say it inhibits the libido."

"Nah," he said. "Can't you see? In this town a man's dick is only as big as his standing with the President."

It took me some time to recover from this remark. But perhaps there was some truth in it. At any rate Joan and I were having no problems on *that* score.

I shall leave Freudian interpretations to the reader. I mention the episode only to show what emotional havoc was wrought by our lost access to the President.

They say you have to hit bottom before things start looking up. I didn't know about looking up, but a week later I hit bottom. I was informed in a memo—a memo!—that the White House mess was being taken away from me and given to Withers.

Sanborn grieved with me. "You must be brave," I told him. "There will be changes. Mr. Withers is not like me." Of course I urged him to serve Withers as faithfully as he had served me, but my heart was not in it.

On my last day as head of the mess Sanborn and his staff went all out. They presented me with a large wooden salad spoon, made in the Philippines, and signed by almost all the stewards. My voice almost cracked as I made a little speech thanking them.

As gratified as I was by this display of loyalty and human decency, the picture was bleak. Thirty-seven days had elapsed since I had seen the inside of the Oval Office. It wasn't that I minded not being in the proximity of power, but, being unable to get through to the President, I was unable to give him the counsel I felt he desperately needed. Lleland and his new ally Edelstein had gotten control of more than presidential access. Yes, they had gotten control of the agenda.

12
IN THE PITS OF POWER

The President is out of touch.　　—JOURNAL, AUG. 12, 1991

The administration was in trouble—with the Congress, with the press, with the people—and neither Feeley nor I could get through the concertina wire (figuratively speaking, that is) Lleland and his cronies had thrown up around the Oval Office.

On August 2 the President announced his ill-fated Territory For Progress initiative, whereby the United States would give back to Mexico 180,000 square miles of territory the U.S. had acquired during the Mexican War. Without going into the merits of such a plan—and there were some, arguably—I think it is certainly fair to say the President was ill-advised to think the country would go along with it, to say nothing of the affected areas in Texas, New Mexico, and Arizona. The whole thing bore Marvin's fingerprints: bold, unprecedented, preposterous.

If the brouhaha that rose up around the White House as a result of this short-lived proposal had any salutary effect, it was that it was a setback for the Lleland-Edelstein Axis. I had come to think of Feeley and myself as "The Allies."

Foreign-policy morale was not boosted by the attack, three weeks later, on the U.S. Naval Air Station in Bermuda. Anti-American incidents were becoming common on the island. The same day Mr. George Murray-Thripton, Mayor of Somerset and owner of a large sweater concern, was assaulted while playing golf. When his unconscious body was found, his golf cart had been spray-painted "US COLLABORATER" (sic).

I concurred in the President's decision not to send a naval battle group, even though I was not asked for my opinion. It was, as he said, "a time for cool heads." I urged him—in a memo—to "take the moral high ground" by directing our base commander in Bermuda to host an "open base" party for the Bermudian public. I believe this approach might have paid off had it been tried. Unfortunately, my memos were not getting read, because they were not getting through. Lleland had directed that the paper flow be routed through his hoplite Phetlock.

The Right was wasting no time, meanwhile. Senator Hyatt denounced the White House response to the Bermuda attack as "unparalleled pusillanimity." Similar bovine voices could be heard ululating in both chambers of the Congress. It was an easy time to be Republican. White House morale was very low. Ed Pollard of the Secret Service reported a forty-percent increase in death threats. I felt very badly for the President.

Lleland's legion of yes men strained to put the best face on things.

Hal Jasper, Director of Communications, would send the President fawning, effervescent memoranda whenever some unimportant newspaper ran a favorable editorial. When the *Post* praised the President for his soil-management study grants, Jasper sent the President a Kremlinesque memo saying he deserved to be hailed as a Hero of American Agriculture. While I did not begrudge the President his due recognition, this was a trifle fulsome.

But it was hardly worse than censoring his news, which they were also doing. When I found out about the news "digests" he was receiving in the morning, I was disconsolate.

Later that month the President's Gallup Poll approval rating dropped to thirty-four percent. Jasper hailed this wretched development on the grounds that since the approval rating had only dropped one point in the previous month, the trend indicated a "slowdown in the disapproval rate." I despaired. I tried to bury myself in work. The problem was that there wasn't anything to do.

Since the President had no need of me in the West Wing, I concentrated on my duties as the First Lady's acting chief of staff. This work I found agreeable, since it was always a pleasure to spend time in Mrs. Tucker's company. How fresh she looked every morning, despite the slight shadows under her eyes which denoted not much sleep.

Together we worked on a number of projects. She was, of course, keenly interested in cinema, and her White House film festival was fast approaching. The visit of the Princess of Wales was only two months off, and naturally I was deeply involved in that. We also interviewed candidates for her chief of staff. We thought highly of one, but he was disqualified after a preliminary background investigation turned up the fact that he had had a youthful dalliance with a picador in Seville. Thus I found myself spending a good deal of time in the East Wing. The East Wing was not the West Wing, but it was still the White House.

On August 14 the green button on my phone console lit up for the first time in an ice age. I almost leaped out of my seat. At last! It was the President calling. With an almost trembling hand I reached for the receiver. Just like old times.

"Yes, Mr. President?" I said crisply.

"Mr. Wadlough?" said a voice I did not recognize.

"Yes?"

"This is Wacca [White House Communications Agency]. Sorry to bother you. We're checking the President's telephone instrument. You're not having any problems with your direct line?"

"No, I am not," I said curtly and hung up.

That week Joan suggested we might think of returning to Boise. The notion was frankly tempting. My family was under considerable stress. Herb, Jr., had been caught by a camp counselor inhaling whipped-cream-dispenser gas with some undesirable teenagers. And little Joan had grown morose and was under the care of a dermatologist who was giving her antibiotics. Joan was taking it on the chin—what a trooper she was—but she had developed a nasty case of shingles.

I had to ask myself some hard questions: was it fair to subject my family to this kind of strain and humiliation? On the other hand, could I just walk away from a public trust? I spent many hours agonizing over the decision. I knew this much: that a struggle for the heart and mind of the President of the United States lay ahead. Washington would be no place for women and children. Over Joan's wonderful meatloaf the next evening I informed her of my decision. She and the children would return to Boise. I would stay and finish the job, to do what had to be done.

She wouldn't hear of it. "My place is here with you, Herbert," she said. "We will have no more discussion about this." What a gal!

A few days later I had a call from Paul Slansky of *The New York Times*, wanting an interview. I tried to put him off, but I hadn't much to do that day, so I assented.

"My sources tell me you're about to move over to the East Wing permanently," he said.

"Bird entrails," I said. "I have work to do here."

"If I could speak frankly, Mr. Wadlough, that's not what I hear."

"Oh?" I replied.

"Then perhaps you could tell me what it is you've been doing the last few months."

"I'd love to, Mr. Slansky, but I'm awfully busy. In fact, I'm due in the Oval Office in a few minutes."

There was a pause. "But the President is in Orlando speaking to the Baptists."

I was caught off guard momentarily. "I am perfectly aware of *where* the President is, Mr. Slansky. It is my business to know where the President is. Now if you'll excuse me . . ."

I am the first to admit that dealing with the press is not my specialty. After I hung up, the anger and frustration began welling up inside me. All those years of service, those hard months of campaigning. To come to this. Well, by George, Herbert Wadlough had not come to Washington to explain to reporters why he had nothing to do.

I knew what to do. It was bold, possibly rash. Perhaps someday the historians would call it the act of a desperate man.

I buzzed Barbara. "Hold all calls," I said. She looked puzzled, since I got so few. "And get me a pot of tea."

"Yes, *sir*," she said. She knew something was up. With that I sat down to write what would prove to be either my epitaph or my passport back to power.

THE WHITE HOUSE

MEMORANDUM TO THE PRESIDENT

FROM: HERBERT WADLOUGH
DEPUTY CHIEF OF STAFF

RE: THE SITUATION

It has been many days since our last meeting. While I sympathize with your desire to streamline presidential access, I am concerned that you have deprived yourself of valuable counsel and that in doing so you have isolated the Presidency.

Let me be frank, Mr. President. You are out of touch. The signs are everywhere. Sinister elements are attempting to seize your heart and mind. I fear they have succeeded. I fear, too, that they have their own agenda.

The hour is late, but there is still time. I urge you, for your sake and for the sake of the country, to open the door once again.

Let the fresh air of dialogue and reason once again circulate inside the Oval Office, before you are overwhelmed by constricting cobwebs of catastrophe.

I rather liked that last line. I felt it added a sort of literary touch.

I sat there watching the memo as it lay in my OUT tray. Several times I was tempted to seize it and tear it up. *Who are you, Wadlough,* I thought, *to address the President of the United States in such a fashion?* His friend, that's who.

But my heart was heavy as pig iron. An hour later, when Barbara came in to collect the memo, it was a relief. *It's history now,* I thought. The rest of the day I buried myself in work. The First Lady had an upcoming swing through four cities that required my urgent attention.

Three days went by with no response from the President. They were hard days. It was difficult to concentrate. Had the President felt betrayed by my memo?

Finally I could not endure it any longer. I called Lleland.

"Well," he said after keeping me on hold for four minutes, "how are things over in the East Wing?"

"Quite well, thank you very much," I said coolly. "It's not so far as you think. Same time zone."

"The President was talking about you this morning at breakfast."

"Was he?" I said without interest. An obvious trap.

"He said, 'Herb's doing a bang-up job over there in the East Wing.' "

"The President is very gracious. Now about my memo . . ."

He claimed to have no knowledge of it.

"Then might I suggest you delve into the matter?" I said.

"Get right on it. And Herb?"

"What is it?"

"I don't want to get out front, but if you ask me, the East Wing job is wide open. I think the President would sign off on it in a second."

"As a matter of fact, I did *not* ask you."

"Anything I can do, you let me know."

Two hours later Barbara handed me an envelope delivered by

one of Phetlock's people. It was my memo to the President, paper-clipped to a covering memo that read:

> The Chief of Staff has read your memorandum to the President (attached), and appreciates your having taken the time to express your concern about this important matter.
>
> Sincerely,
Jamieson R. Phetlock
Assistant to the President and
Deputy to the Chief of Staff

Feeley was very empathetic toward me during this trying period.

"Maybe I should leak it Phetlock's on drugs or something," he said one night over several bourbons at the bar on G Street.

Ordinarily, I would have found such a notion outrageous. Now I only said wanly, "Who'd believe you?"

He beerily eyed Nancy, the bosomy barmaid. "For all you know, he might be on drugs."

"No," I said. "That would be wrong."

He stirred his bourbon with his finger. "You heard about Lleland, right?"

"No," I said. "What?"

"He's been invited up to Monhegan."

"Oh?"

"For the weekend. With his wife."

Lleland invited to the Summer White House. I slumped against the bar rail, and suddenly I felt a great weariness.

13
DAYS OF RAGE

Apparently I am the last to be informed of my own resignation.
Intolerable!   —JOURNAL, AUG. 15, 1991

The next morning at 7:45 I sat down to do what had to be done and wrote my resignation. It was not an easy task. I had been with Thomas Tucker for over twelve years, more than one fifth of my life. That is a long time. The memories crowded in around me as I sat with a nice cup of steaming hot water, writing in longhand. How ironic that the fountain pen I used was affectionately inscribed: TO HW FROM TNT. It was the sort of detail you'd find in one of those novels they sell at airports. I agonized over the wording, and by 10:30 a.m. it was done. I gave it to Barbara to be typed. I knew she would be stricken by the news. I stood there by the window of my office, looking out at the Darlington Oak planted by President Lyndon Johnson.

I had always liked the view from here. I would miss it. But there are trees in Idaho, and the air is good there, much better than in Washington. I'd had sinus problems ever since moving here. An odd sense of calm came over me. I'd always imagined that the end, when it came, would be more wrenching than this. I was aware of someone in the room with me.

"Mr. Wadlough?" It was Barbara. I hoped we would be able to avoid tears.

"Just one thing, sir. Did you want to make this effective immediately, or leave it as is?"

Good. She was taking it calmly. I'd always been impressed with Barbara's grace under pressure.

"Barbara, I know this must come as a shock to you," I said as gently as I could. Without going into the gruesome details, I explained that the situation had become untenable and that for family reasons I had decided to return to Boise. To soften the blow, I told her she could come back and work for me there.

She began to thank me rather effusively. Since I am uncomfortable with such expressions of gratitude, I smiled and said she needn't thank me, and that I would be glad to have her.

"Actually, sir," she said, "I'll be staying on here."

"Here?"

She explained she had been "offered" a job as assistant to the chief of staff's personal secretary. In response to my mute stupefaction, she said that ever since July she had assumed my departure was a matter of time and had begun making "contingency arrangements."

"Indeed," I said. "Does anyone *else* know about this?"

"Only Margaret [Lleland's secretary], Mr. Phetlock, Mr. Withers, Mr. Lleland, of course. Mr. Tsang. Mr. Jasper—"

"Stop," I gasped.

She asked if she could get me anything. Even in betrayal she was solicitous.

"No," I managed.

"Then shall I put through the memo?"

"This is not 'a memo,' Barbara," I expostulated. "This is my resignation!"

"Yes, sir. It's very well written."

I sighed. "Thank you, Barbara."

"I assume we should route it through Mr. Lleland?"

This was insupportable.

"*Through Mr. Lleland?* For your information, I have known the President for twelve and a half years. This is between him and me, and I am not going to *route* a highly private letter to him through— that man!"

Regaining my composure, I managed to conclude the discussion in a dignified manner. I resumed staring at the trees on the South Lawn, wondering what had become of Loyalty. I summoned Hu.

"Hu," I said after telling him of my decision, "you have been a good and able assistant. If you would come to Boise with me, you'd be my right-hand man at Dewey, Skruem."

He shifted uncomfortably in his chair and said he was "unworthy" of my praise.

"Nonsense," I replied heartily. But my reassurances did nothing to allay his nervous demeanor. After a few minutes of excavating, I mined from him the revelation that he had already accepted a position at OMB.

This was scandalous.

"Am I the *last* person to be informed of my own resignation?" I exclaimed. "This is outrageous!"

Hu became abject in his apology.

"You needn't bother with that," I told him. "And as far as I'm concerned, you can report to OMB today. Out. Out!"

What further nasty surprises awaited me that day? I wondered. Suddenly the South Lawn no longer looked stately and green, just hot and parched.

I checked the President's schedule. Lunch with Jacques Cousteau. "Senior staff time" from 2:00 until 3:00. (That was the euphemism for Lleland.) Senators Dole, Hills, Garn, 3:00 to 3:30. (Another one of those ineffectual "reconciliation" coffee sessions.) Infrastructure Task Force, 3:35 to 3:40. 3:45 to 3:50, Commission on the Millennium. National Security Council, 4:00–4:15. That would run long. 4:30–4:45, Chairman of the Federal Reserve Board. 4:50–4:52, photo opportunity, Miss Connecticut. A lot of beauty-queen photo opportunities lately. 5:00–5:30, private time. 5:30–5:45, Ambassador Kutyadikov of the Soviet Union. 6:00, depart for reception, Organization of African States. 6:30, return residence.

Frightful scheduling. No wonder he couldn't concentrate. I would probably be brought in between Miss Connecticut and the Soviet Ambassador. We had a lot of ground to cover. Maybe he'd cancel the Ambassador—better him than Miss Connecticut. He had an eye for the ladies.

Barbara buzzed me to say that Peter Nelson, the *Post*'s political correspondent, was on the line.

"What does *he* want?" I said.

"He wants to confirm you've resigned."

"*What?*"

Hopping mad, I picked up the phone.

"Peter!" I said, bubbly, "what utter nonsense is this my secretary is telling me?"

He told me two "senior" West Wing sources had already confirmed that the President had accepted my resignation.

"Well, I don't know who your sources are. But I'm certainly not going to comment on something as ridiculous as that."

"Then will you confirm you're being appointed to Mrs. Tucker's staff?"

"I beg your pardon?"

"Are you going over to the First Lady's shop?"

"Mrs.—?" I couldn't speak.

Gathering my wits, I told him to address all further inquiries through Feeley's office.

"I'll put you down for a 'will neither confirm nor deny,' then."

"Now see here, Peter," I said hotly, "I have nothing more to say on the subject. You're not going to trick a quote out of me."

I immediately called Feeley and told him what had happened.

"Yeah," he said languidly. "I heard."

"But I only sent it in an hour ago. It hasn't even been accepted!"

"I think it has, Herb."

"This is outrageous!"

Feels urged me to calm down, then said, "Listen, I gotta get back to you. He's just vetoed the B–1B [bomber] again and the place is going batshit."

I was still sputtering when the green button on my console lit up. I punched it without even putting Feeley on hold.

"What?" I said without thinking.

"Herb, old friend."

It was the President.

"Why, hello. Sir."

"Great to hear your voice."

"Uh, great to hear yours, sir."

"How've you been?"

"Fine, Mr. President."

"Great. Busy as hell, I'll bet."

"Well, actually—"

"*I've* been busy as hell, I can tell you."

"I can imagine—"

"How come I never see you anymore?"

"I—"

"I miss you, Herb."

"I miss you too, sir."

"I'm *really* going to miss you."

"But—"

"I understand, Herb. The pressure here is killing."

"Nothing I can't handle, sir."

" 'Course it's not like you're going back to Idaho."

The President cleared his throat. "You won't be far, anyway. I want you to stay in touch. Keep me informed."

I said I would do my best.

"And Herb?"

"Sir?"

"I can't tell you what this means to Jessie. The world."

"Mr. President, I think we need to have a talk."

"Anytime. But right now I've got to go. You wouldn't *believe* my afternoon."

"Yes I would. How about five o'clock? You've got a window between Miss Connecticut and Ambassador Kutyadikov."

"Details. I really don't track the details, Herb. Check with whoever does my scheduling. You know, things have gone to hell since you left. How's the commission going?"

"The commission?"

"Yeah. Listen, gotta go. Speak soon."

I must have been holding the silent receiver against my ear for a full minute when Barbara walked in. My head felt numb.

She began puttering about with papers on my desk.

"Barbara, have I been involved with a commission these last few months?"

"No, sir."

"You're sure?"

"Quite sure."

"Nothing? That AIDS thing? The citrus farmers?"

"No, sir. Those were last year."

"Then bring me a cup of tea and get Mr. Lleland on the line."

Just after three Lleland returned my call.

"*Great* news, Herb. The President is delighted."

I was in no mood to be patronized.

"I'm in no mood to be patronized," I said. "This is your handi-
work."

"Nay, nay, old chum."

"Stop calling me 'old chum.' I didn't go to Harvard."

He found this amusing.

"Never mind that. Why have you done this thing? Apart from
your normal treacherous inclinations, I mean."

"I wasn't aware the position of chief of staff to the First Lady
was to be sniffed at."

"I am not *sniffing* at it."

"I would have thought you'd be grateful for the opportunity to
make a difference."

"Don't quote campaign slogans at me!" I was growing heated.

"Look at it this way," he said. "We'll be co-equals."

"You're enjoying this, I take it."

"What I most enjoy about this job is the chance to serve the
President."

"Borscht!" I exclaimed. You'd have thought he was taping the
conversation. The thought gave me a mischievous inspiration.

"You can turn off your taping device, Bamford," I said. "I find
that a highly distasteful practice of yours, by the way."

His voice was suddenly hard and emphatic. "What are you talking
about? I don't know what you mean."

"Your administrative habits are of no concern to me," I continued.
"But their potential for bringing disgrace on the office of the Presidency is reckless in the extreme."

With that I hung up, cradling the receiver gently for the first time
that day.

14
FLOTUS BLOSSOM

Working with the First Lady a pleasure, but seem to spend half
my time resigning.   —JOURNAL, SEPT. 9, 1991

My change of positions was announced—officially—the next day.
The press managed to treat me with reasonable humanity. The
Washington Post ran a story about me on their "Style" page with only
one vicious and untrue quote in it, fed to them, no doubt, by Phetlock
or Withers:

" 'The feeling around here was he'd be more intellectually at home
over there in the East Wing,' said one knowledgeable White House
source."

That night at the bar on G Street I asked Feeley, "How much
crow must a man eat?"

He grunted. "It's been added to the mess menu."

The thought of those fine Filipinos having to answer to that
arrogant whelp Withers grieved me.

"Well, I've had my last serving," I said.

"Thought you'd have developed a taste for it by now," he said.

I said I didn't find that humorous.

"Just kidding. Relax. 'This place could turn us all into assholes.'
Remember?"

"Vividly," I muttered.

It was apparent from my first conversation with the First Lady
that she had been duped into thinking I wanted the job as her chief
of staff. Not that it wasn't an honor to work for Mrs. Tucker. I
loved Mrs. Tucker—platonically, of course. But the thought of their
having dragged her into their sordid office intrigues made me
boil.

"I was so glad when they told me you wanted the job," she said. "You should have told me, Herb."

"Well—"

"Tom hated the idea of giving you up. He just thinks the world of you."

So. The President was involved too. Such should have been beneath him.

"Yes," I said, "well, you know how I feel about him."

She curled a lock of her blond hair around a finger. "If his other people cared about him the same way you do, he wouldn't be having the problems he is." She laughed: "Giving away Arizona!"

"*And* New Mexico. *And* Texas."

We found ourselves giggling like schoolgirls. I enjoyed the First Lady very much.

But for the little blue shadows, she seemed not to have aged in the more than two and a half years since we had arrived in Washington. She was then just thirty-six, the second youngest First Lady in history, and in my opinion more beautiful even than Mrs. Kennedy. Even in her most chic evening gown there remained about her the aura of the country girl; of summer health. It was impossible to imagine her getting ill. Perhaps it was her dimples.

Shortly after moving in, the President had begun calling her "Flotus Blossom." FLOTUS is the acronym used by the White House advance office for First Lady of the United States. (The President is POTUS.) The name had caught on among the house staff. Naturally, I did not encourage it, but as nicknames are inevitable, it was a pleasant one. Much more agreeable than my own, "Auntie Herbert."

It was not long before I experienced my first crisis as her chief of staff.

Mr. Jerome Weinberg, the Hollywood impresario and producer of *Minnesota Hots*, had for some time been trying to get her to do another film. I had experienced Mr. Weinberg on a number of occasions—he was a frequent guest at the White House. I was sure this was standard Hollywood chatter; you know, "Baby, we gotta make another picture." Of course it was out of the question. But Mr. Weinberg was persistent, and would send a script practically every week. The First Lady would sometimes tease the President by saying that she was tempted. It made the President very nervous.

In late September, with only a month before the visit of the Princess of Wales, she told Maureen Dowd of *The New York Times* that she was "seriously thinking" of signing a contract with Mr. Weinberg to appear in a film entitled *Beirut*. My Lord, what a fuss it caused!

I didn't for a moment take it seriously, though everyone else did. She told me the morning of her interview with Miss Dowd that she and the President had quarreled the night before. I think her remark was just a way of making the point that he'd better not take her for granted. As a matter of fact, I think the President *did* sometimes take her for granted. I never admitted it at the time, but when I read the story that morning I thought, *Well, good for her*.

In almost no time at all, blame for the resultant hullabaloo was laid at my feet. The snipping and slander began afresh. I took a phone call from Ann Devroy of the Gannett papers. "They're saying in the West Wing you're not even competent to handle the East Wing job," she said. "Any comment?"

"I should say not," I said.

Lleland called. "The President is very upset," he said. "He wants this undone."

I told him the President should take the matter up directly with the First Lady. Her film career was her own business.

Ten minutes later the President buzzed.

"Herb," he said, "I've got half the world on my ass as it is. I've got a cabinet full of hysterical dykes, an alcoholic Indian, a Vice President I have to keep sending to Micronesia. I don't need this."

I heard the sound of a newspaper rustling in the background.

"*Beirut!*" he roared. He was upset. He went on shouting for about a minute. "No more interviews," he said. "Not with the women's magazines. Not with *Democrats Today*. And call Weinberg and tell him to get someone else for his goddam movie. Tell him he's had his last free meal at the White House if he doesn't."

"You want me to threaten Mr. Weinberg?"

"Idiot!" He was ranting. He had never used such language with me. "I want you to *fix* this!"

Calmly, I told him we were treading on difficult terrain here. The First Lady was not likely to take it kindly if I told one of her friends he was no longer welcome in the White House.

He sighed. "She's been difficult lately."

I said: "She's under a lot of strain. She had a very busy week last week."

"Herb, we *all* had a busy week last week. I don't see what's so fucking exhausting about having a couple of Congressmen's wives in for tea and cucumber sandwiches."

This was intolerable. He could abuse me as much as he liked, but I would not allow him to speak this way about the First Lady. "Now just you wait," I thundered. "For your information, in the last week she's given three speeches in three different states, toured two medical centers—one of them an infectious-diseases ward. On top of which she had those *unspeakable* women in for tea so their *unspeakable* husbands will vote for your *unspeakable* programs. Cucumber sandwiches my foot!" Oh, I was hot.

There was a pause. He said, "Are you out of your mind?"

"No," I said. "I have just given you a piece of it."

"I'm the President of the United States." He sounded genuinely wounded.

"And you have become, Mr. President, the asshole you feared you would."

"Wadlough," he said, "you're fired. Fired! Immediately! Got that?"

The White House protocol is that one submits one's resignation immediately upon being fired. (Only underlings are "fired.") I did, but I couldn't lie to Mrs. Tucker, so I told her I'd been fired.

"The hell you have," she said.

I told her it was the right thing to do, that I had exceeded the bounds of propriety. I was, in fact, ashamed to have used such language.

"It's good for him," she said. She was especially attractive when she was defiant. To my great horror, she picked up the phone and in a sweet tone of voice asked, "Would you get me Mr. Tucker, please?"

When he came on, she said, "Yes, my chief of staff just told me he's resigning." She winked at me and smiled. I began to perspire. "He said it was because of 'family considerations.' Um-hum. I don't believe him. I think this is your nasty doing. Un-hum. I haven't finished. I've become very fond of Herb, he seems actually to care about me and your son. Your son, Thomas—you might remember him from before the election? So I've decided that unless you can convince Herb to stay on, I'm going on strike."

She was enjoying this. It was a Grace Kelly performance, very soft-spoken, bemused, totally in control of the situation.

"I'll tell you what that means," she said after listening for a moment. "It means I am going to New York. This afternoon. I'll have to cancel a few things."

Pause.

"Darling, this isn't long distance. I can hear you without shouting."

Pause.

"Well, I don't honestly care about the Nicaraguan Foreign Minister. I'll ask Annie Reigeluth to fill in for me."

Pause.

"I leave it all in your strong, capable hands. I'll be at the Sherry Netherland. And take your time convincing Herb. Don't hurry—I can't get enough of New York. The Secret Service agents seem to like it too. Maybe I'll ask Jerry to fly in, he's very excited about the movie. He's got Jackie Gleason to play Ariel Sharon. Bye, darling."

When I got back to my office, Mrs. Metz, my new secretary, told me Lleland was trying to reach me urgently. I know it was mean-spirited of me, but I couldn't resist letting him wait a minute or two for my call.

"The President is deeply, deeply upset," Lleland said in a hospital-waiting-room tone of voice. "He wants to do what's right." And so he went on, detailing the "gravity" of the situation. I have to admit, I quite enjoyed it.

"Bamford, old boy," I said, knowing the familiar address would annoy him, "I completely agree. The situation between the President and the First Lady is not all it could be. And I think you should make it a top priority to have good relations with my successor. But I want you to know I appreciate your involving me in the President's thinking."

Heavens but that felt good—Lleland was always flattering people by telling them he wanted to "involve" them "in the President's thinking." Suddenly, for the first time in months, I found myself in a very good mood. I buzzed Mrs. Metz, my secretary.

"Take a resignation letter, Mrs. Metz," I said, putting my feet up on the desk.

"Mr. *Wadlough*," she said with her faint trace of a Hamburg accent. She was an admirably efficient woman of the most correct demeanor. We *understood* each other.

"Not to fear, not to fear," I said. I was positively ebullient. It was quite unlike me, actually.

I was puzzling over the wording of the second paragraph when the phone rang. She picked it up. "It's him," she said, impressed.

"Ah. I'll take it."

"Herb!" He was bursting with bonhomie. "What's this about your resigning?"

I told him I was only following protocol for those who have been fired.

"I don't know what gets into me," he said with a forced laugh. "But you know me well enough by now not to take me seriously when I do something like that. Ha! I must have had you going there."

"Yes. Out the door."

"Ha!" He cleared his throat. "Herb, I need you here. Fact, I wish you hadn't left the West Wing. You had a real . . . touch. But since Jessie wanted you over there with her, well—" he gave the kind of grunt men share between themselves to signify the futility of arguing with women—"even this office has its limitations. Ha!"

"Um-hum." It was the sound his wife would have made. It seemed to rattle him.

"I beg your pardon?" he said.

"Just a throat condition, Mr. President."

"Oh," he said uncertainly. "You want me to send Major Arnold over to have a look at it?" His concern for my health was overwhelming. He then went into one of his coughing fits. "Chest cold," he said between hacks.

"Yes," I said. "You ought to cut down on those chest colds."

"Good old Herb! Can't fool *you*, eh? Now about this resignation of yours. I'm just not going to accept it. You're too valuable." He started coughing again.

"I'm not submitting it to you," I said dryly. "I work for the First Lady."

"Damn lucky to have you." Cough.

"I've enjoyed working for her. She doesn't surround herself with devious and supercilious people."

"I know. She's great that way." Cough.

I was not getting through.

"I am extremely fond of Mrs. Tucker," I said formally. "She brings dignity and grace to the office."

"Boy, doesn't she? She's a classy lady." Cough.

If this was to be a duel of innuendo, I would match him nuance for nuance. "A wise woman," I said. "She has a keen grasp of human nature."

He stopped coughing.

"Herb, let's cut through this bullshit, shall we?"

Having gained the high moral ground, I was reluctant to quit it right away. But it was the voice of an old friend on the other end of the telephone, no matter how meanly I had been treated.

We talked—for the first time in months. It was like old times. I did not hold back. I told him the Gadsden Giveaway business was "dunderheaded."

He was defensive. "The Mexicans love me," he said defensively. "They think I'm the greatest President since Kennedy."

"Then why don't you run for President of Mexico next time around? You're bound to do better in Chihuahua than the Southwest."

"Hell with the Southwest," he said. "Bunch of Republicans anyway."

But this wasn't the canny young Governor I once knew. It was Lleland and his "Let them vote Republican" attitude. I could swear the President had even picked up a faint trace of Boston accent, that unpleasant, hair-lippy, nasal sound.

So: Lleland's control of the Presidency extended to ventriloquism. This was indeed pernicious. I hadn't realized the full extent of the

President's captivity. It was for that reason and no other that I finally agreed to stay on. In a way, I knew it would disappoint the First Lady—I think she was rather set on the idea of going to New York. But this was serious business.

15
FIRST FRIENDS

The President very distracted lately. I worry.
—JOURNAL, SEPT. 24, 1991

By early fall of our third year in office, a number of pressures were coming to bear on the President.

The leadership of the Democratic party was anxious for him to declare his intentions about running for the second term. His *New York Times*/CBS Poll approval rating of twenty-one percent (a historic low) had the party bigwigs scared. House Speaker Ferraro visited the Oval Office on September 28 and asked him seriously to consider not running. The President was not receptive to this advice, and relations between him and the Speaker became strained from here on in.

The situation in Bermuda by now had taken a nasty turn. During the riots of September 22–28 several more sweater concerns along Front Street were torched. The British Governor General, Viscount H. J. F. P. Rennett, had declared another state of emergency, and a detachment from the 52nd Gurkhas—the Queen's Own—was en route. In Washington the President was under considerable fire from hawkish elements of both parties to show the flag, but had persisted in his conviction that the disturbances were "purely Bermudian." With the Reverend Jesse Jackson championing the side of the black Bermudians as well as pressing his third presidential candidacy, President Tucker was of course anxious not to alienate black voters. He had also come into office vowing "No more Grenadas," which would have made it very difficult for him to intervene, even if he had been inclined to do so.

I was deeply concerned, naturally, by these developments. I have always been keenly interested in foreign affairs. But at the time I was even more preoccupied with domestic matters. The strain between the President and First Lady had become aggravated.

One morning when the First Lady was away, I called Mrs. O'Dwyer, the housekeeper, into my office. I had a difficult question to ask, and felt embarrassed posing it.

"Are things between the President and First Lady as . . . er . . . conjugal as they used to be after they first arrived, Mrs. O'Dwyer?"

She told me it was none of my business.

I told her I understood that my question sounded indiscreet, but that it was not idle curiosity that compelled me to ask it. Moreover, I informed her, I was not accustomed to being spoken to that way by housekeepers. I do not enjoy interrogating elderly Irish ladies, but this was an affair of state.

"I don't care *how* yer used to bein' spoken to," she said defiantly, but when I pointed out that there was no shortage of housekeepers, her tongue loosened up.

"Well," she sniffed, "if you mean are they doin' it on the floor, the answer is no. Beyond that I don't care to say."

I found this irksome in the extreme. "Mrs. O'Dwyer," I said forcefully, "if you think I am asking you this question for reasons having to do with other than the harmony of this administration, you are most grievously and pathetically mistaken." I gave her a good strong look just for good measure.

It was like squeezing a third cup out of a teabag, but I managed to get out of her the fact that of late the President and First Lady had not been sharing the same bedroom. This was deeply disconcerting intelligence.

"Mrs. O'Dwyer," I said, "if word of this gets out, the consequences to the Presidency and the nation would be difficult to imag-

ine. I trust you and the staff won't go noising this about." At this
she became indignant and began remonstrating in a strenuous manner. I wrote it off to the Irish temperament.

As of yet, no one suspected what was going on in the boudoir of
power; or rather what was not going on in the boudoir of power.
The First Lady had maintained an exemplary civic profile. There
had been no more talk of movie-making, and the press never failed
to remark on how radiant she looked and on what an attractive First
Couple she and the President made. She was, if truth be told, the
one positive note in an administration beset by divisions and crises
both petty and grand.

But toward October she was tired (as she had every right to be)
and in need of greater stimulation than the endless round of congressional wives' teas that the Legislative Affairs shop was forever pressing on us. This is not to say she did not personally like many of the
congressional wives, but such settings were not her milieu.

"It's odd," she said to me one afternoon after they had departed,
"how many of them used to be their husbands' secretaries. I bet
they don't do it as much as they used to—on the sofa and over the
desk, between appointments with constituents. I guess it's not as
much fun in bed."

I must have blushed, because she looked at me in that girlish way
and laughed. "Oh, Herb," she said, "you're such an old lady."

It is not that I am embarrassed by discussion of sexual matters,
although I certainly think they have their time and place. But after
what Mrs. O'Dwyer had told me, I was wary of the subject. Perhaps
I should have pursued it, but at the time I couldn't find the words.

She did not form many very close friendships with Washington
women, except with Joan Bingham, the Georgetown socialite and
Democratic activist, a vivacious, enthusiastic woman with whom the
First Lady often had private lunches at the Four Seasons restaurant.
The two women had the same sense of humor, and Mrs. Tucker
was fascinated by Mrs. Bingham's work with South Africa and the
Institute of Sperm Motility.

But her closest friends remained those she had made in the Hollywood and New York film worlds. They were a gay bunch, and
as her ennui with the world of politics grew, their visits became

more and more frequent. Mr. Henry Hoguet, Mr. Alexander Onanopoulos, and Mr. Ramon "Billy" Angullas-Villanueva were es-
pecial favorites of hers. Often they came as a group. Mr. Hoguet's
play *Tender Gender* was at the time receiving very favorable reviews.
Mr. Onanopoulos dealt in fine art, and Mr. Angullas-Villanueva,
the Spanish painter and set designer, was much in the news at the
time, owing to his murals, controversial even by modern standards.

The President enjoyed their company—he was not a classical
homophobe of the Kennedy school. He was, however, mindful of
appearances, and Mr. Villanueva and company certainly were flam-
boyant figures. During weekends at Camp David they would wear
caftans most of the day instead of more customary attire. Once or
twice the President joked, semi-seriously, that they might be taken
for representatives of the PLO.

One Sunday afternoon, returning from Camp David, television
cameras recorded the President, the First Lady and Firecracker dis-
embarking from Marine One on the South Lawn. They also recorded
Mr. Villanueva, conspicuous in mauve suede trousers and carrying
his sulfur-crested cockatoo, Perseus, in its Victorian bamboo cage.
The President did not pause to speak with the waiting reporters.

Early the next morning Lleland's secretary, Faye Blaine, called
and said he wanted to see me at three o'clock. I told Mrs. Metz to
tell her that would be inconvenient. The First Lady was having a
reception for the Motion Picture Association that evening and I was
being besieged by hysterical Capitol Hill staffers frantic to wrangle
last-minute invitations for their principals. Word had gotten out that
Polly Draper, the actress, would be there, and the more hormonal
Senators and Congressmen were desperate to be invited. In any
case, I was unavailable at three o'clock.

Mrs. Metz reported that Lleland's secretary was "insistent." I said
her insistence was of no concern to me. She buzzed me back and
said, apologetically—Mrs. Metz was in all respects exemplary—and
said that Ms. Blaine would not desist in her insistence. This was
too much.

I picked up the phone and said, "It may come as a great surprise,
Miss Blaine, notwithstanding that the sun rises and sets only at the
pleasure of Mr. Bamford Lleland IV, but I am occupied with the

affairs of the First Lady this afternoon. Consequently, a three-o'clock appointment is not only inconvenient, it is out of the question. It is therefore my earnest hope that you will carry that message back to His Eminence and arrange with Mrs. Metz, who is empowered to speak for me on this and all such matters, an alternate time. *Good morning to you.*"

She hung up angrily. The arrogance of those people. I may not have been a West Winger any longer, but I was not about to be summoned over there like some browbeaten summer intern.

His Eminence called me fifteen minutes later. "Herb, old man," he said. This was his chummy tone, one he did not wear well and which almost always portended treachery or some other nastiness. "What did you tell Faye?"

Dryly, I said, "Exactly what I have a feeling I am about to tell you."

"Well, don't worry. I won't tell the President about it."

Really. "You may send the President an inter-agency report on the matter, for all I care," I said.

He didn't like that. "I'm calling about those queers."

"Those what?" I said.

"The First Lady's friends."

I stiffened. "I haven't the faintest idea whom you mean."

"Don't be coy. That scene yesterday on the South Lawn. It's un-presidential. We're going into an election, Wadlough, in case you haven't looked at your calendar."

I sat up straight. "If it's signals you're worried about, why don't you get rid of that floating embarrassment of yours?"

The remark hit home. Just a week earlier *Newsweek* had broken the story about his sending the *Compassion* to Mexico to have her decks replanked. (It was cheaper to have it done there than in an American yard.) Labor had taken a dim view of this, and George Bush was mentioning it in his speeches.

He took umbrage at my remark. "I didn't call to submit myself to abuse from a member of the President's *wife's* staff. The President wants the problem *taken care of*," he said very quietly. "And he wants *you* to take care of it." He hung up.

I didn't believe him for a moment. He was always telling people

the President "wants it taken care of" when it was Bamford Lleland
who wanted it taken care of. However, a White House chief of staff
is the second most powerful man in government, and is not to be
taken lightly.

What to do? I wasn't about to burden the First Lady with it. She
might believe Lleland and think her husband was trying to bar her
friends from their home, and that would only damage an already
strained domestic situation. I decided to discuss the problem with
Feeley, even though that meant I had to confide the Tucker marital
problems to him.

"It's worse than you think," I said as I swore him to secrecy. "I
am reliably informed they're not sharing the same sleeping arrangement."

"They're not fucking?" he said.

"Please," I said, "endeavor not to be revolting."

"Jesus. Used to be they couldn't keep their hands off each other.
Remember the swimming pool?"

"*Yes.*"

"I always wondered . . ." he said. "I bet she's great in the sack."

"You are speaking of the First Lady!" I said heatedly. "I will
thank you not to share your disgusting speculations with me."

When he had calmed me down, I asked him what I should do.
Feeley had a mind for dilemmas. Also, his insight into this matter
would be sharpened by his dislike for Lleland, which had grown
exponentially.

He stirred his coffee with his index finger, a habit he had picked
up on the campaign trail, where the coffee is never hot.

"I can solve your problem," he said. When he smiled and kept
stirring, I became impatient.

"This isn't a novel," I said. "Stop being dramatic."

"Okay. We leak it that Villanueva is having an affair with Lleland."

I was annoyed. "I thought you wanted to help."

"I do. Listen, it's terrific."

"It's preposterous."

"It doesn't matter if no one believes it. All we have to do is get
it to where he has to deny it and everyone will assume it's true."

"You've been reading too much Allen Drury. Or Gordon Liddy, for that matter. Either way, I don't care to continue this conversation."

But he was quite taken with his idea, and trying to get him off the subject was like whistling after a bird dog hot on the scent of a rabbit.

"They were all on that fucking boat of his over Labor Day weekend, weren't they? On the way up to Monhegan."

"I don't remember."

"Yeah. Him and the other one. The Greek, Onawhatsis."

"*Onanopoulos.*"

"Yeah. Remember Lleland was all bent out of shape because she included them?"

"No, I don't remember. Can we change the subject?"

His eyes had that conspiratorial shimmer. "Where'd they pick up the boat? That town near Lleland's summer house."

"Provincetown."

"Provincetown! That's right. What a *zoo* that was! Never seen so many antique shops. In a beach town, for Chrissake."

"I really don't know, Mike."

"Perfect. It's perfect."

For a few moments he was lost in devious reverie. Then, as if speaking to himself, he said, "Can't you just fucking *see* Lleland? '*I am not a homosexual.*' " He laughed and slapped his hand on the counter.

"Michael," I said in a firm tone, "you've been under a strain. I shouldn't have brought this silly thing to you. Forget it. As if you don't have enough to worry about."

He wasn't listening. "You never know, come to think of it. Didn't he go to boarding school?"

"*I* went to a boarding school. Do you think everyone who went to a boarding school is gay, for heaven's sake?" He had me so flustered I was swearing.

"No," he said thoughtfully. "Not everyone."

I signaled for the check. "This conversation is over," I said. "What's more, it did not take place, as far as I am concerned."

"Absolutely. We need to hold this tight. I wouldn't even tell Joan."

"I have no *intention* of telling Joan," I protested. "Why should I tell Joan about a conversation that didn't take place?"

He winked—*winked*—at me. "You got it," he said, and left.

BOOK FOUR
DISARRAY

16
PEACOCK AND PETUNIA

Just returned from New York. Bizarre assignment. Feeley has
lost his mind.   —JOURNAL, OCT. 7, 1991

On Friday, October 4, I was woken by the White House operator
at 5:30 a.m. and told the President wanted to see me at 6:15 in the
Oval. It had been a long time since I had received such a summons.
Obviously, it was important. I wondered if it involved national
security. I enjoyed very much working for the First Lady, but I
missed the old West Wing and its headier concerns, its moods, its
crises, its air of excitement, of puissance.

When I arrived, he was in his pajamas behind the desk, smoking
and drinking coffee. He was wearing his commander-in-chief frown.
I knew right away it was national security. Perhaps the Bermuda
situation had exploded.

"Jane and the kids fine?" he asked with a smile that resembled a
squinting into harsh sunlight. I decided not to remind him that my
wife, whom he had known for almost thirteen years, was named
Joan.

"Couldn't be better," I said brightly, despite the hour. "She sends
her best."

"Good," he said through clenched teeth. "She's a good woman,
Jane. Ought to bring her around here more often."

I also saw no point in reminding him that he had last spoken to
her four days ago at a reception for East Bloc diplomats.

"She's a great admirer of yours," I forced myself to say. This was
excruciating.

"Yes. Well, you give her my best."

"I certainly will." I was earnestly hoping the President would get to the point. Had I been woken out of a warm bed at 5:30 a.m. for small talk about my wife, whose name is not Jane?

"Things aren't going so well," he said.

I nodded. "The Congress is being difficult."

He shook his head. "No. Upstairs."

"Oh." It was the first time he had brought up the matter of the First Marriage. "Well, you've been working hard. I think she misses you."

"She could be more affectionate, you know."

Tread lightly here, Wadlough, I said to myself. I found myself looking at my shoes. I said, "Perhaps if you could carve out a little quality time. Say on weekends."

"She's got her friends on weekends. They're up there all the time. You know what the Secret Service has code-named Billy and Onanopoulos? Peacock. Peacock and Petunia.

"Jesus," he said. "I thought I was in Istanbul. These caftans they wear all the time. What would Ike say?"

I agreed it was best the former President was no longer around to see it.

"I don't see why they can't wear ordinary clothes."

I said I did not understand either.

"Lleland thinks they're bad for my image," he said.

I said so I gathered.

"He thinks I shouldn't have them at Camp David anymore. But Jessie loves them. So what the hell."

So—that swine Lleland had *not* been acting on presidential authority when he told me to ban them from the White House. Probably I should have told the President about it. But looking at him, chain-smoking in his pajamas at 6:30 in the morning, lonely for the wife he loved, despised by the Congress, held in historically low regard by the American people, I decided not to burden him with it. As much as I loathed Bamford Lleland, the President had made him his chief of staff and relied on him, trusted him. *Let it go, Wadlough*, my better nature urged me. And so I made my disastrous decision.

"I've been busier'n a cat shooting peach pits trying to keep from getting eaten alive by those hypocrites"—he waved in the direction of the Capitol—"and I may have been a little inattentive lately. So I understand about her wanting some company weekends. We've had a few—disagreements, you might say. But we'll survive."

Two days later I was working feverishly on arrangements for the First Lady's appearance at the Festival of Hydrangeas when Mrs. Metz told me Colin Socks of the *New York Post* was on the phone. I promptly told her I did not take calls from that scandal sheet, and went back to work.

Half an hour later Joan was on the phone. She was agitated.

"What's wrong, my dumpling?" I asked.

She said she had just received a call from Socks. I was livid. He had told her he had urgent need of speaking to me, and had told her, darkly, that it would be to my "advantage" to return his call.

"Are you in trouble, Herbert?" she asked. It broke my heart. I reassured her all was well. How dare that sensation-mongering yellow journalist call my wife at home! She had been in the midst of baking a pound cake and it had come out too heavy. I boiled.

I called Socks and gave him a large piece of my mind. But lecturing an Australian journalist is like trying to house-train a wombat.

Straightaway he got to the point. Was there anything to the "rumor" of a "relationship" between Billy Angullas-Villanueva and myself?

If he had asked me whether I had strangled my own dear mother, my reaction would not have been different. I was unable to speak.

"You there?" The voice seemed to come from another dimension. I shook my head and pulled myself together.

"Now you listen to me, Socks," I said. "If I so much as hear one nanogram more of this revolting canard, I'll see to it you're deported back to that penal colony you came from and put to work mucking out sheep stalls for the rest of your life."

He seemed delighted. "Fantastic," he said. "You'll have me thrown out of the country?"

"This conversation is concluded," I said. I hung up; then stared at the walls for twenty minutes.

Presently I was aware of Mrs. Metz, as if through a fog.

"Mr. Wadlough? Mr. Wadlough?"

After reassuring her that my pallid demeanor was the result of not having slept much the previous night, I picked up the phone and said to the Signal operator, "Get me Mr. Feeley." I stared at the ceiling. The President was in Gary, Indiana, that day.

Three or four minutes later there was the crackling on the line that meant an airborne patch to Air Force One. A voice said, "This is Frigatebird, Crown. Go ahead." The Signal operator said, "Mr. Wadlough, I have Mr. Feeley. Be advised this is a radio call and there is no privacy." I was glad for the reminder; I'm sure the Russian Embassy would have been delighted to know of the wretched business.

"Herb, what's happening?" came a cheerful voice.

"Never mind that! I've just had a call from the *New York Post* wanting to know"—had to be careful—"about a certain rumor."

"Yeah?"

I reminded him, as obliquely as I could, of our little talk and his brainstorm about planting the rumor about Mr. Angullas-Villanueva and Lleland.

"Well, they think it's me. *Me!*"

There was a pause. "Son of a bitch. They got to us first!" He started laughing.

"That is not funny," I said. "This is horrible."

"Hang on," he said. "Don't do anything until I get back."

"Roger," I said miserably.

I was waiting for him in his office when he returned. I'd been unable to concentrate on the Festival of Hydrangeas. He came in trailing secretaries and pieces of paper. After he shut the door, he said, "I've got it all figured out."

"What," I said, "what do we do?"

"Nothing."

"Don't tell me 'nothing.' This isn't 'nothing.' This is the worst thing that's ever happened to me! What about Joan!" I put my head in my hands.

"Listen," he said, "the *Post* isn't going to print it—I'm almost sure—so we just ignore it."

"But—"

"Think like the enemy. They want you to deny it. And the second you deny it, everyone knows it's true."

"Oh," I said. "Oh. What if there are press queries?"

"Queries?" He began to laugh. "Queries!"

"Dammit, man!" I said.

The next day at 12:14 p.m. I was in New York City, sitting in a booth at a restaurant called Mortimer's, waiting for the arrival of Mr. Ramon "Billy" Angullas-Villanueva, fretting over Festival of Hydrangeas details.

I had claimed a bad cold, put on one of the wretched disguises left over from my trips with Marvin, and come to New York aboard a commercial aircraft—my first commercial flight in years.

I had come to warn Mr. Angullas-Villanueva of this scurrilous campaign of Lleland's against me—and him. Lleland was obviously out to kill two birds with one stone. The faintest whiff of scandal would mean the end for me at the White House, and the end of Mr. Angullas-Villanueva's visits there as well.

I had told Mr. Angullas-Villanueva I needed to speak to him on an utterly confidential basis and asked him to meet me in a "quiet, out-of-the-way place." He had suggested Mortimer's, which I now realized cast some doubt on the man's sense of discretion. Mortimer's, in the heart of the upper East Side of Manhattan, was clearly an "in" restaurant. I did not recognize the people there by name, but they seemed very much "in," the kind who used to be seen at the White House during the Reagan administration.

I had worn my red tartan plaid jacket, the one I wear only on weekends. It was a bit on the loud side, but I assumed it would allow me to blend in with the chic New York set. Oddly, the *maître d'* had looked at it with an unmistakably condescending air. I resolved to tip him only ten percent.

I had been seated in a table in the rear—at least Mr. Angullas-Villanueva had *some* discretion—where it was dark. With my glasses on, it was difficult to see.

Presently I heard the distinctive stentorian voice.

"Jerbert! My God, what a horror you look!"

. . .

Because of my inability to see clearly, I was caught unawares by the hug and the kiss he planted on me. I am not in principle against physical expressions of affection between men; but even with Father I shook hands, and I am uncomfortable being kissed by other than my wife, Joan, or my daughter, Joan. Or by my mother and sister, Ernestine.

I let him do the ordering, inasmuch as he was obviously familiar with Mortimer's cuisine. He also, I might add, seemed familiar with the waiters. An unfortunate moment arose when he introduced me to one of them as the man who "run de whole Hwhite House." It was necessary to remind him of my desire not to be recognized.

Mr. Angullas-Villanueva's neck kept periscoping every time someone walked in, and it also became necessary to restrain him from introducing me to a half-dozen fashionable acquaintances of his.

"But you must," he reproved me. "He practically run de Met."

I ate my "*paillard*" of veal—an unadorned but reasonably edible fillet of overpriced meat—and listened to his soliloquies on the *beau monde* of New York. He was an exuberant conversationalist, and I surrendered in silence to his narratives, feeling so awkward about presenting my own. But at length it could not be deferred any longer, and with a great heaviness of soul I plunged in.

"A rather indelicate situation has arisen," I said.

Immediately he interrupted. "I *lave* indelicate thituation!" he said.

Then try this one on for size, I thought. I then told him about my call from Socks.

"It's too divine!" he said.

I had not counted on this.

"You're not . . . upset?"

"I cannot wait to tell *everyone*! They will tell to me, 'My God, Billy, what taste you jave!' " He gripped my arm. "No, Jerbert, I'm sorry. I don't mean it against you. But it's so—" He began laughing again. "They are so dreary in Washington. So *serious*."

With that he summoned "Johann," our waiter, and told him to bring *anise*. I confess I was so shell-shocked by now that I actually drank the unpleasant liquor set in front of me. (It tasted of licorice.)

With considerable heaviness of heart, I brought the subject around to the President's problem. I explained that naturally the President would place no credence in the rumor, but that I felt it essential he absent himself from the White House for a few months until things had quieted down. He listened, and nodded.

"Jerb," he said, "you are right. We cannot go on as before. But we will always jave de memories, yes?" He put his hand on my arm and winked.

I attempted a laugh, but really the whole business was very unsettling. Outside the restaurant he gave me another kiss—on both cheeks this time. (I believe this is the European custom; and I would point out that on the Continent, men kiss all the time.) My stomach finally quieted down for the first time in twenty-four hours on the shuttle flight back to our nation's capital.

17
SLINGS AND ARROWS

Wound in stomach appears not to need stitches. Things not going well.   —JOURNAL, OCT. 15, 1991

Four days after my meeting with Mr. Angullas-Villanueva, the First Lady asked me to stay after the morning staff meeting. She appeared more tired than I had ever seen her, except on the campaign trail. The bluish circles beneath her eyes were more accented. I confess to wondering how a man married to such a woman could bear to sleep in another room, even the Queen's bedroom. I decided I would urge her to take some time off, what with the busy holiday season looming ahead.

After the others had left, she turned to me and, in a voice suddenly cross, demanded, "Did you tell Billy not to come see me anymore?"

I was caught completely off guard. "Ah," I fumbled. "It's rather complicated." I should have known I couldn't trust Mr. Angullas-Villanueva. Lord, what a mess.

"Well?" Her arms were folded, her eyes boring right into me. As best I could, I explained about the call from Socks. I said I suspected Lleland or his people were bruiting it about, and that I'd gone up to New York to try to spare Mr. Angullas-Villanueva—and myself—the humiliation of being linked romantically in the press.

She listened intently. When I finished, she began laughing. She laughed for some time. I was even tempted to join in, but I detected something wrong with her laughter. It was—well, it was uncontrolled.

"You?" she said. "And *Billy?*" She went on laughing.

"Yes," I said, "it's rather unlikely, isn't it?"

Presently she dried her eyes. They were moist, and dark as thunderclouds.

"You bastards!"

"I beg your pardon?"

"You and Lleland and him—my husband. You made this up?"

"Madam," I said, "I assure you—"

"So you could drive my friends away!" She was standing and looking rather menacingly at me. I got up and edged backward.

"No, no, no. The President *likes* your friends. I like Mr. Villa—"

"Damn you, Herb!" With this she picked up a large chintz pillow and struck me. Struck me! On the side of the head. And with surprising force. My glasses were knocked off.

"Mrs. Tucker!" I couldn't see much without my glasses, but I managed to make it behind an armchair and crouched low. "Please! This is undignified!"

"Undignified! I'll tell you what's undignified. Making up this ridiculous lie to hurt me, to hurt Billy." There was a whoosh over my head which I soon recognized as another pillow being hurled in my direction.

No oil will calm these roiling waters, Wadlough, I said to myself. I began to back toward the door. Mrs. Tucker was only an agitated blond blur.

"I'd never do anything to hurt you. I'd rather—"

I felt a thump against my abdomen and it became necessary to double over in order to facilitate breathing. As I did this, she began to belabor me with the wretched pillow on either side of the head. Deducing that this was not the time to explain I was not in a conspiracy against her with Lleland and her husband, I decided to try and make my escape. I turned and, still hunched over, stumbled in the direction of a dark rectangular shadow I took to be the door. But after a few steps my head came into contact with an object. It yielded after causing only moderate cranial discomfort, but as it did I found my feet caught up in something. There followed a crash and a rending of fabric and I fell to the ground.

The blows resumed, this time augmented by sharper pains about my calf and shin, which I took to be her shoes. (I was grateful she was not wearing high heels.) My immediate concern was for a prompt egress, but I did give some thought to the fact that I had in all likelihood upset the Japanese screen, a very fine example of Yosaku Era workmanship which had been presented to the President and First Lady by Prime Minister Kundo. The Smithsonian had appraised it at $12,000.

I thought I might buy some time by appealing to her feminine instincts.

"Mrs. Tucker, the screen!"

"Fuck the screen!" she said. She was still drubbing me with the cushion. In an attempt to protect myself, I put my head through the screen with a further tearing of silk.

I grasped the base of a lamp in an attempt to pull myself up, but the lamp came down, and with it, me. I felt screen remnants in my eyes, so the First Lady's outline was now even less distinct. My hope at this point was that she would tire out. Unfortunately, she kept very fit.

I regained my bearings by dead reckoning. I found the wall and groped my way along it, keeping my head low so that my upper torso would absorb the brunt of the blows. It was with considerable relief that I felt the door molding. Then I found it was the hinged side, which gave the First Lady the advantage of leverage. She swung the door against me, pinioning me between it and the wall. This did, however, make it impossible for her to continue striking me, for which I was grateful. I could hear her exertions on the other side as she leaned against the door, attempting, I would guess, to inhibit the flow of oxygen into my lungs. She was in part successful, although by this point my breathing was irregular anyway.

"I helped you," she said. She was crying. "They were out to get you and I protected you. And you do this. You and *them.*"

My heart went out to her. "Oh, Madam," I said, "I'm not with *them!*"

"I trusted you."

She stood back from the door. It swung back.

I was on the verge of making one last plea when I was propelled backward through the open door. My legs gave out from under me and I fell over. The door slammed shut.

I lay there a few seconds, trying to take stock of my injuries. I did not feel at all well.

I felt arms assisting me. It was Hurley, one of the Secret Service agents on the First Lady's detail.

"You all right, Mr. Wadlough?" he asked.

"Yes, fine, thank you," I answered. "How are you doing, Joe?"

"Can't complain."

With Joe's assistance, I made it back to my office. I would have had to grope my way there without him.

"*Gott!*" Mrs. Metz exclaimed. "What is it? Terrorists? In the residence?"

I didn't want the household staff buzzing about this. "I lost my balance and had a fall."

"You are bleeding." She dabbed at my lip with her handkerchief. I gave myself over to her ministrations. My left shoulder felt swollen and stiff. My entire left leg, which had borne the brunt of the kicking, was in pain, and my face felt hot and sore. I flushed most of the Japanese screen particles out of my eyes, and took an aspirin.

"The President wants to see you right away," said Mrs. Metz with a stricken look when I got back from the bathroom, and she reminded me that I had asked her to send my spare set of glasses to be repaired. She was putting a few finishing touches to me when she said, "Your jacket is ripped behind."

"Never mind that," I said. "Hurry up."

"Your lip is bleeding again. Wait." I felt a wet handkerchief on my lip followed by an astringent, searing pain, and an overwhelming smell of her perfume, a scent of which I was not fond.

"What have you done, woman?" I cried.

"It will stop the bleeding. And clean the wound."

The phone rang. It was Betty Sue Scoville, the President's secretary.

"Yes," said Mrs. Metz. "He is coming, coming."

She led me down the stairs, past the family theater, through the long, vaulted, red-carpeted hallway on the ground floor. I was just as glad not to be able to see the looks on the faces of those we passed. Senior staff with ripped jackets, bleeding lips, and reeking of German perfume are an uncommon sight in the White House. We went through the door at the west end of the hallway and through the Rose Garden colonnade, the one visible on the back of twenty-dollar bills.

"Don't let any reporters see me," I hissed at her as we went in the door of the West Wing next to the press room.

"We will go this way."

She took me back through the door and to the right, past the windows of the cabinet room and toward the outside of the Oval Office. The Secret Service gets apprehensive when people even walk on this part of the colonnade. I saw shadows approaching us. Mrs. Metz explained that we desired to avoid the route past the press room. I recognized the voice of Bradshaw, one of the agents on the PPD (Presidential Protection Detail).

He led us through a door into Betty Sue Scoville's office, next to the President's. Betty Sue was surprised.

"Mr. Wadlough," she said. "What's happened to you?"

"Never mind, Betty."

She picked up the phone. "Mr. Wadlough's here, sir. Yes, sir."

Turning to me, she said, "You can go in now." Something in her voice worried me.

I had the ladies lead me to the door. "Open the door and point me in the direction of the President," I said.

"The statue," whispered Betty Sue. "Look out for the statue."

I nodded. The President had acquired a sculpture by Frederick Hart called "Javelin."

The door clicked open. "He's right ahead of you," whispered Mrs. Metz.

"Good morning, Mr. President," I said, striding purposefully toward the desk.

He was gruff, in no mood for pleasantries. "What the hell happened to you?"

"Oh, this?" At that moment my right knee came into excruciating contact with the corner of the Roosevelt desk. I had overestimated the distance. I stifled a moan and staggered back.

"Ah—I—fell. Sir."

"Fell? Well, sit down."

I felt my way backward and sat down.

"Where are your glasses? And what's wrong with your lip? Did my wife do this to you?"

"We had a staff meeting this morning."

He sniffed. "Jesus. Are you wearing perfume?"

"I can explain that," I replied.

"My wife just told me she is going to divorce me."

Oh, dear. I wondered if a President had ever campaigned for reelection in the midst of a divorce, but to my best recollection such a situation was unprecedented.

"She seems a little upset at the moment."

"Upset? You skinless hot dog, she's threatening to divorce me!" I was not familiar with the President's expression, but his tone of voice was clear. "Do you realize what this means?"

"An uphill campaign, sir?"

The President became vehement in his remonstration. No useful purpose would be served by repeating it here.

Our interview did not last long. I assumed the First Lady would no longer be requiring my services, and it certainly wasn't likely the President did. I suggested that perhaps the time had come for me to take my leave. He agreed. I told him that, despite recent developments, it had been an honor to serve in his administration. He did not keep me long.

I would have liked one last look at the Oval, the room where I had spent so many happy hours; but without my glasses it was just a gauzy mist. Taking my final leave of the President, I turned toward the door, erect and with a dignified, purposeful bearing. I missed the door, however, and became impaled on the Frederick Hart sculpture. I will spare myself recounting the details.

18
PEACE BREAKS OUT

Resolve to concentrate on Metrification Initiative.
—JOURNAL, NOV. 7, 1991

Major Arnold dressed my wounds, the javelin puncture being the most serious. Mrs. Metz retrieved my glasses from the residence, and I called Joan and told her I would be home early. I didn't go into details, but Joan knows me better than anyone. She said she'd make meatloaf that night, which was her way of saying, *It doesn't matter*. What a woman!

Feeley called, very worried. The First Lady had arrived in New York—on the Eastern Shuttle—and the press was demanding to know why they hadn't been advised, why she was there, etc., etc. "Buying shoes, getting a divorce," I said without interest. "Who knows?"

He arrived in my office in less than two minutes, panting and out of breath. I told him he really ought to cut down on his smoking. "Fuck that," he said. "What's going on?"

I explained.

"You can't resign," he said. "Not now."

I told him it wasn't a question of resigning.

"I'll fix it," he said.

I think I told him that I wasn't really sure I wanted my job, or

any White House job, back. He told me I was being hysterical, and
to leave everything in his hands.

That night on the news the First Lady's "surprise arrival" in New
York was played prominently. She was holed up at the Sherry
Netherland hotel on Fifth Avenue. Feeley was shown at a press
briefing saying it was just some early Christmas shopping. The
Greater D.C. Merchants Association spokesman was shown saying
it was an insult to all the fine stores in Washington. The whole thing
was a sorry spectacle. I was surprised that news of my "resignation"
wasn't included—I'd have thought Lleland would have had it announced even before my wounds were seen to; no matter. But, for
the first time since arriving at the White House, I felt comfortably
numb, beyond the care of such concerns and intrigues.

The next morning I asked Mrs. Metz to help me put things in
boxes. As we worked, the phone rang without stopping: press queries
about the First Lady. Mrs. Metz held them off with exemplary
Teutonic firmness. Throughout my ordeal she maintained the most
correct bearing. Another woman might have given in to emotions,
but not Mrs. Metz. I came to regard the German character very
highly on account of her. (Of course she was a naturalized U.S.
citizen. It was not our practice to employ foreign nationals.)

Lleland called. "Sorry to hear you're leaving," he said. "You'll
be missed. But we can use the parking space."

The conqueror's smirk, the knife twisted in the wound. My West
Exec parking space . . . they had tried to take it from me when I
moved over to the East Wing. I'd fought them like a beast uncaged,
and won. Who would get it now? Phetlock? Withers? I closed my
eyes—it was too painful to consider. I'd become accustomed to the
space.

If Lleland wasn't magnanimous in victory, I decided I would be
in defeat. I told him it had been "interesting" working with him and
wished him luck with the Bermuda Crisis, the Inflation Crisis, the
Budget Crisis, the Deficit Crisis, the Confidence Crisis, the First
Lady Crisis, and with the campaign, which wasn't far enough along
to have become a crisis but which almost certainly would before
long. He reacted as though I were being cynical, but I wasn't.

Then an odd thing happened. I was summoned to the Oval.

Maybe a goodbye photo, I mused on the way over. The President was very good about that sort of thing.

The President greeted me cordially, but formally—the way he did heads of uncooperative states. He seemed almost embarrassed. I tried to put him at ease by apologizing that I hadn't put through my resignation letter yet, but that I would before the day was out.

He told me he didn't want it.

He said he'd given the matter some thought, and that he wanted to offer me my old job back. The West Wing job. Deputy chief of staff.

This was startling. "But why?" I said.

He told me the National Metrification Initiative was faltering, and that he needed someone with my "instincts" to take charge of it.

I did not know what to say. The President had never really expressed much interest in Metrification. (Of course, he was deeply committed to it. He was determined that America should begin the twenty-first century "fully metric," as he used to say.) Though I do think I had a certain—call it knack—in this important national initiative, I suppose there were others who could have done the job. I was, therefore, puzzled that the President, with so much on his mind—including, possibly, a very public divorce—should have his mind on this.

Just then Betty Sue Scoville walked in. "Mr. President," she said, "it's the First Lady."

His hand darted for the phone when she said, "She's apparently calling for Mr. Wadlough."

He looked at me; I looked at him. Neither of us made a move.

"Should I put her through?" asked Betty, puzzled.

The President frowned and nodded. I walked to the phone by the fireplace and picked it up. "Madam?" I said cautiously, as if the receiver might electrocute me.

"*Herb*," she said. It was a sweet, caring voice. "Are you all right?"

Most curious. I thanked her for asking, and said that I was quite well. She wanted to know about my stomach wound. I told her it was healing nicely. The President was listening intently.

She began to apologize for the day before. I said that it was nothing, really, just a few scratches. But she went on to explain that she'd been feeling out of sorts and had overreacted.

It was perplexing. Mrs. Tucker was a woman of some whimsy—theatrical people are this way—but this was positively, well, schizophrenic. (I do not mean to imply that the First Lady had psychological problems. It was simply strange behavior.)

She said there was someone there who wanted to say hello. Firecracker, no doubt.

But then on came a familiar voice.

"Jerb!" it said. "Is you?"

I looked over at the President; his eyebrows were knotted.

"I am *furious* with her!" Mr. Villanueva continued. "She say she beat you up."

I was at a loss.

"She don't understand. I tell her dat you jave tell me not to come to Washington. Sure, but now she tell me she think you are making plot against me. Jessica, you are so estupid sometime. I want you to say you are sorry again to Jerb. Here, say."

The First Lady came back on, apologizing once again. We chatted. She said she *was* furious with whoever was spreading the rumor about me and Mr. Villanueva. She said, "Is my husband involved? Is he behind this?"

The President was *in extremis*, trying to figure out what was going on. I said, "Certainly not."

She seemed to believe me.

I asked her if she was coming back to Washington soon. She said she didn't know.

I told her the President missed her. He nodded vigorously. She said if he really missed her he'd spend more time with her and Firecracker.

It went on this way, me pleading with her to come back, she demurring. The President began writing things down on paper—talking points, as we call them in politics—for me to tell her. On one slip of paper he wrote, TELL HER MY COUGH WORSE.

It was certainly the most taxing phone call I have ever experienced, but twenty minutes later I had her promising to call him as soon as she hung up. I almost made a fatal mistake when she asked me to transfer the call to the Oval Office. I nearly handed him the phone. But I pulled myself together and said that it would be much more "dramatic" if she called him directly on his private line.

When I hung up, the President practically embraced me, he was so happy. I said I was only too glad to help and that I should withdraw before the First Lady's call came through.

"Go ahead and write the book," he said cheerily as I made my way to the door.

I didn't understand. "What book?" I said.

But then the phone rang. As I closed the door behind me, I wondered what he had meant by that.

19
CAKEWALK

The President has got it into his head to take walks in the park.
—JOURNAL, DEC. 8, 1991

We were a happy family once again. The First Lady returned from New York, and I plunged into Metrification. I took the keenest pleasure in expelling Phetlock from my old office, two doors down from the Oval. I informed Withers I would be needing my old parking space. I am not a vengeful man, but I would be dishonest if I said this was not a happy homecoming for me. This, I mused, must be how it had felt to retake Paris in 1944. Lleland grunted that it was "nice" to have me back. My security clearance was upgraded from DRIZZLE to TYPHOON.

I told the President that I would like to have the mess back again. Immediately, it was done. Sanborn assembled the staff for a full-dress review. I had difficulty suppressing a tear when they presented me with a wooden fork to match the spoon they had given me when

I departed. It was inscribed, in their quaint handwriting, WELCOME HOME MR WADLOUGH. All was well with the world.

Except that the President seemed not to confide in me as he had in the past. I couldn't put my finger on it, but he seemed to be keeping things from me.

I thought it might have to do with the distraction of his continuing domestic situation. On the whole, things were happier between the President and First Lady, but she was taking quite a number of trips to New York that pre-Christmas season. These were announced as shopping trips—to the continuing distress of the Greater D.C. Merchants Association. The truth was that the peace between them was an uneasy one. The First Lady had also been dropping remarks about how much she wanted her husband not to run for a second term.

The President was more often than not depressed. His attention span diminished and he grew unresponsive, even in the (rare) event of good news. When he was told the Senate had passed his handgun-reform legislation, the Bullet Control Act, he looked up from his briefing papers, murmured, "About time," and went back to work. Considering that he was the first President to get action on this most pressing social need, this was an understated response, to say the least. Considering it was his only major legislative victory since taking office, it was even more surprising. That he seemed to take no joy at all in this important achievement worried me. He was also smoking heavily. Major Arnold was frustrated, and kept telling me he didn't want to be the first Presidential doctor to be blamed for a case of lung cancer. "These are difficult times for him," I told the Major.

He was also starting to rebel against the tight security. He had never been comfortable in the fishbowl. Now he kept saying things like "I should be out there talking with my people." Feeley worried he might use that phrase, "my people," in a press conference. Unfortunately, the number of death threats coming in from his people, as well as the egg assaults on his limousine, precluded his being out there.

Then, on the afternoon of December 5, it happened. He got it into his head to take a walk in Lafayette Park, across from the White

House. At first I didn't know why; then I remembered he had been reading biographies of Harry Truman lately.

Rod Holloway, chief of the Presidential Protection Detail, called me. Rod has a calm disposition, and I had never heard him so alarmed. The egg that had struck the President's limo three weeks earlier had been thrown from the park.

"You've got to do something, Mr. Wadlough. He's serious. He told me he only wanted two agents."

"Two?"

"I don't think he understands. He also wants it 'spontaneous.' No advance."

That meant the Secret Service wasn't to "sanitize" the area before the President arrived.

"What time does he want to go?"

"Six."

I looked at my watch. It was 5:42 p.m. Good Lord.

"We have work to do, Rod," I said.

I immediately called Marvin. I explained the problem and told him he had to make up a foreign-policy crisis. (I almost added, "You shouldn't find *that* very hard.")

He refused. "Out of the question."

"I don't have time to argue with you. We need a crisis."

He was sarcastic. "What did you have in mind? Mechanized divisions in the Fulda Gap, or something in a Sino-Soviet border clash?"

I said, "Fine. When I'm called before the investigating commission, I'll tell them your scruples wouldn't permit you to prevent his assassination."

That got his attention. When he started telling me it went against his better judgment, etc., etc., I cut him off. "Never mind the preamble. Call him at exactly two minutes to six. Get on the line and stay on the line as long as you can. Tell him it looks like war."

"I can't do that!"

"Marvin," I said, "your President needs you. He doesn't realize it, but he needs you. You may be the only one standing between him and a deranged killer."

"I don't like this," he said. "It's not right." I got the distinct feeling he was taping the conversation.

"Never mind. What are you going to tell him?"

He sighed. "That we have a report of a sinking in the Strait of Hormuz."

It sounded awfully routine to me. "Can't you do better than that?"

He became abusive. "What do you want me to do? Blow up Leningrad?"

"All right, all right. Strait of Hormuz it is."

Rod Holloway and I then went to work like first-generation immigrants. My office became the temporary command post. He rounded up every available agent. We would have raided the Vice President's detail, but at the time Reigeluth was representing the American people at a "cultural conference" in Muscat, Oman.

Counter Assault Teams were rushed to the rooftops of buildings lining the park. Rod was very nervous having to do without his usual helicopter coverage.

The next problem concerned the troop of scruffy and mentally unsound hoi polloi who keep their constant vigils in the park with their signs calling for the elimination of the atom and fornication. (While I sympathize with both those goals, I believe in trying to accomplish them through the democratic process.) Rod wanted to "neutralize" them, whatever that meant. But there wasn't time.

It was now 5:59. Marvin should be one minute into telling the President that war was about to break out in the Persian Gulf. The first wave of agents had arrived in the park. The CAT teams were in place; one of them had caused a commotion in the lobby of the Hay-Adams hotel when they were mistaken for terrorists. Major Arnold was on his way to the ambulance that would wait around the corner of H Street with the motorcade. We wanted to keep the whole operation *"en famille"*—as the French say—so we hadn't alerted the D.C. police. Instead, Uniformed Secret Service agents on motorcycles were poised along the Pennsylvania Avenue intersections between Lafayette Park and George Washington University Hospital. We wanted intersection control in the event of "takedown," as Holloway kept ominously calling it.

At two minutes past six Holloway pressed his earpiece. He listened; grimaced. "It's Firebird," he said. "He's moving."

I blanched. "He can't be. He's on the phone with Marvin."

Holloway just shook his head and was out my door. I rang Marvin.

"What *happened?*" I demanded.

"It didn't work."

"Why? What did you tell him?"

"Exactly what we discussed. I told him we had a report that a tanker of uncertain registry had been attacked and sunk in the Strait."

"*And?*"

"I said it was an extremely grave potential situation. Or a potentially extreme grave situation, I forget which."

"Never mind. And?"

"He said he didn't care."

"What do you mean?"

"His exact words were, 'Fuck the Strait of Hormuz. I'm going for a walk.' Then he hung up."

I dropped the phone and ran out the West Wing door. The Marine guard was standing stiff as a barber pole, but his face showed a residue of great surprise.

"Did the President come out this door?"

"Oh, yes, sir, he did, sir. Just now, sir. He's just walked out the gate. Sir." He pointed toward Pennsylvania Avenue. It was dark. I shivered with the cold and realized I was in shirtsleeves.

There was a wind blowing from the north. The streetlights shone brightly. Washingtonians were going home—to their wives, to a cocktail; to play with their children and have supper. For a moment I stood there and it suddenly hit me how removed the President was from life's comforting, ordinary rituals. I thought of all the men who had walked out the door I had just come through, flushed with self-importance at the thought they had just been with the President of the United States. Suddenly it seemed not so strange or even alarming that the President should want to do something denied to the most powerful man in the world: take a walk in a park. Why not let the Strait of Hormuz conflagrate itself? It could wait the length of time it took a man to refresh himself with December air.

Still I struggled against the temptation to go after him. What if . . . ? I didn't want him to die surrounded by Secret Service agents and emergency-room technicians, people he did not know. Heavy with presentiment, I turned around and walked back to my office.

We were surprised the next morning that there was nothing about Operation Cakewalk—as we'd dubbed it, ironically—in the papers. The President was in better spirits than he had been in six months. He teased Feeley and joked good-naturedly about the incompetence of his cabinet. In the midst of a discussion about my plan to change the Mile One marker near the White House to the Kilometer One marker, he said to me, "*Nice* people." He described an encounter with a lady in the park who told him she had voted for him and would again in '92.

"You know what she said? 'Any President who'd take a walk in the park is just what this country needs.' " His eyes glassed over. "Know what she said? 'Don't give up, Mr. President. We're pulling for you.' "

Oh dear, I thought. *This will mean more walks.*

As I was leaving, he said, "I want her invited to the next state dinner." He told me her name: Charlotte Quillan. "She's in the book."

When I got back to my office, I called Rod Holloway and asked him for his assessment of last evening's operation.

He exhaled purposefully. (Secret Service agents don't sigh.)

"I'm just glad it's over, Mr. Wadlough."

"I'm not so sure," I said. I asked him how many agents he'd deployed in all. About seventy, he said.

I was impressed. I told him the President had remarked on how many people there were in the park so late on a cold winter's afternoon.

He smiled and said that as a matter of fact *everyone* in the park was a security agent.

"Rod," I said, "does the name Charlotte Quillan mean anything to you?"

Indeed, he said. She was "one of ours."

Good God.

I asked him if they'd had a long conversation. He said they'd "conversed for approximately four minutes."

It was most annoying. I said, "Rod, you know how I feel about the agents fraternizing with Firebird."

"Under the circumstances, Mr. Wadlough, it was hard to prevent."

"Yes, I suppose it was. But I don't see why she had to strike up a conversation with him. All he wanted was some fresh air to clear his head."

"Actually, he approached her."

"Oh," I said. "Any particular reason?"

Rod cleared his throat. "She's—attractive-looking, you might say."

"Attractive? How attractive?"

"Well, she's about five nine, a hundred and twenty pounds, blonde, green eyes. Full figure."

"All right," I said. "I get the picture."

Rod said, "She's single, you know."

"So?"

He was uncomfortable. "She's a little unconventional by our standards."

"What do you mean, unconventional?"

"Well," he said, "she doesn't fit the mold."

"I *know* what unconventional means, man." I was getting alarmed.

"She has a kind of vivacious personality."

"Vivacious?"

"Lively."

"I *know* what vivacious means. What do *you* mean it means?"

"Well, outgoing."

"Let's speak frankly, shall we, Rod?"

"She gets around."

I moaned.

"She's extremely capable. And she's definitely not a security risk. She gets polygraphed every six months, just like everyone in her division."

"I want her transferred, Rod."

He looked at me with surprise. "Is that necessary?"

"Necessary? He wants her invited to dinner!"

Rod was not happy when I prevailed on him to have her transferred to the Secret Service office in San Francisco. We arranged to
move her up two GS pay grades as consolation. Though my decision
may seem Draconian, bear in mind what the consequences would
have been for the nation if the President had found out that the
"people" he'd met on his little constitutional through Lafayette Park
were in fact Secret Service agents; or, worse, what the consequences
would have been had he been attracted to the "vivacious" Miss
Quillan. Myself, I shuddered to think.

20

EDWARD VIII

> Wonder sometimes about Feeley's judgment. Am badly ne
> glecting Metrification.   —JOURNAL, JAN. 4, 1992

The atmosphere around the White House in the days following the
New Year could only be described as depressing. The Bermudian
United People's Insurrection, or BUPI, had seized control of three
more sweater concerns. The Southampton Princess Hotel was the
scene of fierce fighting, with room service being cut off to 900 guests,
and the leader of the revolutionary forces, Makopo M'duku (*né* Cedric
Pudlington), was threatening to turn Bermuda's golf courses into
"re-education camps." We were deeply concerned. But each time
Admiral Boyd of the Joint Chiefs implored the President to "show
a little flag," the President reminded him of his campaign pledge:
"No more Grenadas."

The President was not a happy man these days. Things were not
going well *upstairs*, so I gathered, for neither he nor the First Lady
was confiding in me as they had in the past. He was genuinely hurt
by the repeated suggestions Democratic leaders were making in the

press—in the press!—that it would be better "for the party" if he
didn't run again.

I did know that this was in fact the main bone of contention
upstairs. The First Lady really did not want him to run. One morning he grumbled that she had told him the night before that he was
the worst President since Jimmy Carter. I tried to cheer him up by
saying that was just the First Lady's way of teasing him, but he
gave me a very unpleasant look and buried himself in his TOP SECRET
folder.

Mrs. Tucker was at that time busy with her plans to have Christo,
the Bulgarian conceptual "artist"—and for my money a queer egg
if ever there was one—cover the White House in pink plastic. It had
created a small scandal, and her new chief of staff, a man of as yet
unobvious talents, was barely coping.

The President was also drinking a little more than usual. At lunch
he would take two martinis. While it was not for me to say how
much the President should drink, that, coupled with the four glasses
of (American) wine, seemed to make him a bit logy. We endeavored
not to schedule his SNGC (Simulated Nuclear Global Crisis) sessions after lunch owing to his tendency to doze off.

It was during this period also that he had taken to writing his
own speeches. The unsuccessful Notre Dame, U.N., and San Francisco World Affairs Council speeches were written almost entirely
by him.

Let me say this about President Tucker's rhetorical skills. I think
he was one of the best ad-lib speakers on the circuit; but he was not
entirely at home with the written word—if they were his own written
words, that is.

Charlie Manganelli was most upset by the criticism of the U.N.
speech, with its unsuccessful tropes ("the nuclear family of bombs";
"up and atom," etc.), because Lleland was telling everyone Charlie
had written it. (One of Lleland's less endearing traits was to claim
authorship of any well-received speech and to disown the clunkers.)

Attempts to dissuade the President from creating his own oratory
were unsuccessful. Sometimes when we were on Air Force One en
route to a speech and the President was napping, Feeley would filch
his speech text and work furiously to correct some of the more

egregious infelicities of phrase and grammar. The President seemed
never to notice that his text had been tampered with, but this was
a less than desirable *modus operandi.*

By early January the pressure to announce whether he was a
candidate was intense. But he refused to say. Then, on January 4,
my phone buzzed. It was Feels. The President had just instructed
him to get ten minutes of network air time at nine o'clock on Monday.
This was Saturday.

Feels was upset for two reasons: the President wouldn't tell him
what he wanted it for, and he would be cutting into *Tumor Ward,*
the highest-rated TV show on the air.

Immediately, Washington began to buzz. Extra operators had to
be brought in to handle the switchboard overflow. There were a
disturbing number of private individuals who called in to say they
hoped he would *not* be a candidate. I instructed the operators to
give those calls short shrift, but to take the names of those who called
urging him to run. I thought it would be nice to give the President
a nice, thick sheaf of names. It didn't end up being very thick, but
it was certainly a sheaf.

The *Post* headline the next day read

TUCKER ASKS AIR TIME
AMID REPORTS HE WILL
WITHDRAW AS CANDIDATE

The more reserved *New York Times* story was headlined:

PRESIDENT TO MAKE
'MAJOR ANNOUNCEMENT'
THURSDAY NIGHT

SPECULATION HIGH

White House Aides
Deny Reports He Will
Not Be a Candidate

"This is terrible," said Feeley.

I took a call from Vice President Reigeluth, aboard Air Force
Two, en route from Zimbabwe to Lagos.

"Don't you think I ought to get back home, under the circum-stances?" he said.

"*What* circumstances?" I replied.

He seemed as surprised by my question as I had been by his. "Uh, November-wise," he said. It was not a secure line; no con-versation taking place over airwaves is.

I assured him there was no need to return, and that he was doing an absolutely first-rate job representing the President overseas. I even told him the President had mentioned his name the other day in the Oval Office. That always cheers up Vice Presidents.

Yet Feels and I simply weren't sure what the President would do. President Tucker had surprised the nation before. He'd done it in Boise with his call for a nuclear free zone, in '88 in New Hampshire with his call to harness acid wind, by his cockamamie suggestion that we give back 180,000 square miles to Mexico—well, he was adept at the art of political suspense. In my book the odds were even he'd run again. Of course Mrs. Tucker would be very upset if he did, but we would have to cope with that down the road.

Then I got a phone call from Charlie Manganelli. I girded my loins (figuratively speaking), thinking it would be an unhappy call about the President's writing his own speech.

It was. He was furious. Sixty million people watching and he was going to "stick his dick in his mouth again." On and on it went. Finally he calmed down. Then he told me something that piqued my curiosity. One of the researchers had told him Betty Sue Scoville had ordered up a copy of the abdication speech of His Majesty King Edward VIII.

"I guess that clinches it, huh?" he said.

"I don't know," I equivocated, thinking fast, "he's always been fascinated by the between-wars period in Britain."

"*Bull*shit," said Charlie.

I decided to level with him. I said this mustn't get out. I made him swear not to reveal it to a soul. Then I rushed to tell Feeley. He was puzzled.

"*Who?*" he said.

"Edward the Eighth, you ignoramus. The one who abdicated the throne of England for the woman he loved."

He reflected on this. "Jesus Christ."

I told him I wished he wouldn't use the Lord's name like that. I don't like nagging, but it's something I feel very strongly about.

He drummed his fingers on the desk. "I just bought the condominium in Alexandria," he said.

Frankly, I was appalled. "I'm sure the nation will mourn your mortgage payments," I said tartly. "How can you think of that at a time like this?"

"Do you know what my payments are? These nineteen-percent rates—"

"Never *mind*," I said. "We've got to do something."

He agreed, but neither of us could think what.

Several times that morning we looked in on the President and asked if he'd like some help with his address to the nation. Each time he waved us off.

Just before noon Feeley called me. "I asked him when we'd see the text. He said, 'You won't.' So I said, well, when do we get it for the Teleprompter? And he said he was taking care of that. He's being weird, Herb. I don't like it."

I called Betty Sue and asked her about this. It was true. He'd told her to have a Teleprompter typewriter brought to the Oval. He planned to type it himself.

"Are you certain?" I said.

"Yes. He said, 'This time there won't be any leaks.' "

"But he can't type, Betty."

"You want to tell him that?"

"No," I said, and hung up.

Feels and I lunched together in a quiet corner of the mess. We felt miserable and defeated. The President was about to make the most important speech of his political career, and we were helpless to help him.

"Fuck it," said Feels. "It's *his* speech."

"I wish you wouldn't talk that way," I said. "At least not in the mess."

He groaned and went on. "He wants to make a fool of himself in front of sixty million people, let him."

But—what if he was going to run? A badly botched announcement would cripple the re-election effort.

"Suppose the sentences don't even end?" said Feels. "Like in San Francisco."

Well, that would be a problem.

"Jesus," he said. "There's got to be a way to get a look at it."

But we couldn't think of a way.

As I got up to leave, I mentioned I'd offered to baby-sit Firecracker that night. I sometimes did that; he was my godson and I liked spending time with him, especially since he was old enough to learn something of religion. (I feared his parents were neglecting that part of his upbringing.) Joan and the children were still in Boise. The President and Mrs. Tucker were going to the symphony at the Kennedy Center.

That afternoon Feels and I walked into the Oval to make one last attempt at convincing the President to let us help with the draft. There he was, banging away, hunt-and-peck style, on the Teleprompter typewriter.

"No thanks!" he said cheerily, ripping the paper out of the carriage. "All finished." He took the narrow roll, opened the right top drawer of his desk, dropped it in and closed it.

"Sir," I persisted, "ask yourself: is this prudent?"

He said to me, "Ask yourself, Herb: am I being a pest?"

Pest. It was discouraging.

It was 6:30. I was working on a Metrification pep talk I had to give at the National Bureau of Weights and Standards when the door opened and Feels walked in. He was carrying a shopping bag and grinning.

21
TREASURE HUNT

Up whole night searching for First Rodent, then nearly electrocuted this a.m. Exhausted.   —JOURNAL, JAN. 5, 1992

"I have a terrible feeling about this," I said. Feeley and I were riding up the elevator—the one built for FDR—to the residence.

"Will you relax!" he hissed. The door opened. Firecracker, already in his pajamas, took a running leap and hurtled into us. He caught me by surprise. His knee took me in the groin and my glasses were knocked off.

The First Lady appeared in her evening gown, putting on her second earring. "Mike!" she said. "What are you doing here?"

Feeley grinned and said that he and I had some work to do, so he'd come along. We'd do it after Firecracker was in bed.

The President appeared. He was in black tie.

"What, two sitters?" He said to Mrs. Tucker: "I hope you don't have to pay them double."

There were warm family smiles all round that made me hate myself even more.

We bantered for a few moments, then Firecracker blindfolded his father with his cummerbund and made him walk an imaginary plank—a little ritual they had. Rod Holloway appeared and said, "We're ready, sir." The First Lady told me to make sure Firecracker was in bed by eight.

As soon as they had left, Feeley went to work.

"Let's play a game," he said. "Treasure Hunt!"

Firecracker wanted to play soldiers instead. He supplied us each with a rubber pistol and shot at us for the next half-hour. We had to make repeated assaults on his bunker beneath the Lincoln Bed.

"That was great!" said Feeley, wheezing. "Now I want to play Treasure Hunt."

But Firecracker didn't want to yet. For the next fifteen minutes we played hide-and-seek, during which I was shoved behind the firescreen in the Queen's bedroom.

"Boy," said Feeley, "that was fun. Now listen, Firecracker, I really want to play Treasure Hunt."

"That's a dumb game," he said.

Feeley said: "Don't you want to win a TV?"

That got his attention. "What *kind* of TV?"

"A small color TV that runs on batteries. The kind you can put under the covers of your bed and watch all those great shows that come on after your bedtime."

"Is it a Sony?"

"Gimme a break," said Feeley. "You know how much those cost?"

"Two hundred sixty-five dollars," said Firecracker, "for the Trinitron XM."

Feeley lit a cigarette.

"You shouldn't smoke," said Firecracker. "Major Arnold says it's not good for your health."

"Yeah, he's a smart guy, the Major. You want the TV?"

"What do I have to do for it?" He was a canny seven-year-old, and rightly suspicious of Feeley.

"Find the treasure, that's all." Feeley's tone of voice had suddenly grown very businesslike. "You bring it to us, and then you put it back."

Firecracker thought about this a moment. "If it's a treasure, why do you want to put it back?"

"That's just the way you play. But you get to keep the TV."

"I want to see the TV first."

"No, you've got to *win* the TV, see?"

"Um-um." He shook his head. "Dad says you can't trust anyone around here."

Feeley laughed at this disturbing remark. We looked at each other. Feeley said to Firecracker, "He doesn't mean *us*. He means those turkeys he works with, like Mr. Lleland."

But Firecracker stood his ground.

"Okay," Feeley relented. "You get to see the prize first, but you don't get to keep it until you find the treasure."

Firecracker agreed. Feeley reached into his briefcase, ostensibly stuffed with the work he had to go over with me, and produced the miniature TV set. If it seems like an expensive bribe for a seven-year-old, bear in mind that this seven-year-old lived in the White House and went on helicopter rides every weekend.

His eyes widened. He flicked it on. Nothing happened. He frowned.

"No batteries," he said.

"Shit," said Feeley. "They swore it had batteries."

"Let's have some milk amd cookies," I interjected. I dragged Feeley aside while Firecracker probed the TV. "Will you watch your language," I said. "It's bad enough what we're doing. You don't have to give him lessons in obscenity."

"Yeah, yeah," he said. "Those assholes said it had batteries. God-dammit. . . . "

We walked back into the Yellow Oval Room. Firecracker had plugged in the cord and was watching. He was mesmerized.

Feeley grinned like a pusher and whispered, "He's hooked."

That, it turned out, was the problem. Firecracker had flicked on a re-run of a movie called *E.T. Comes Home*. There was no peeling him away.

"Firecracker," said Feeley, now down on all fours, "it's time to play Treasure Hunt."

"Later," said Firecracker.

At the first commercial we redoubled our efforts. "How about a really big hot-fudge sundae?" I said.

"Yeah," said Firecracker. "With Oreo ice cream."

"Great idea!" said Feeley. "Right after we play Treasure Hunt, we'll go get the sundae. Hot shit!"

"You go get the sundae first. Uncle Herb and I'll watch *E.T.*"

Feeley was not accustomed to the deviousness of children. "Listen," he said, "I thought we had a deal."

But the commercial had ended and the trance descended on him. Feeley went rummaging around for the *TV Guide*. I found him in the next room, saying, "God-*dammit*."

"What's the problem?"

"Movie doesn't end until ten."

I called Secret Service, which told me the President was due back from the Kennedy Center at 10:45. That would give us forty-five minutes to get the text. Feeley's secretary was standing by in his office, ready to type Feeley's revisions into Teleprompter text.

We spent the next three commercials trying to convince Firecracker to play a quick game of Treasure Hunt now—as opposed to after *E.T.*

"Look," said Feeley, who was starting to sound more and more like a United Auto Workers negotiator, "you're supposed to be in bed by seven thirty, right? It's eight fifteen. You want to go to bed or play the game?"

"Mom said I can stay up late."

"She didn't tell *me* that," said Feeley. "Herb, did she tell you that?" It was a good cop/bad cop routine. Before we took office, I had imagined myself in earnest, heated negotiations with Soviets over nuclear weapons. Now I was dickering with a seven-year-old over ice cream. "All right, all right," Feeley said, "you go to bed and we take back the TV." He reached over and flicked it off in the middle of *E.T.* Firecracker did the logical thing: he began to cry.

"Smart move," I said to Feeley as Firecracker went on bawling. "Why don't you go out and get us all a *nice, big, hot-fudge sundae?*"

Feeley shook his head. Firecracker interrupted his crying long enough to say, "Steve's ice cream, not Swensen's."

Steve's was in Georgetown; Swensen's was only a few blocks from the White House. Grumbling loudly, Feeley left.

He came back half an hour later, drenched. (It was raining hard that night.) And in a murderous, purposeful frame of mind.

"Here." He thrust an enormous container of high-density ice cream at Firecracker.

"Did you get marshmallow topping?" Firecracker saw by Feeley's expression that this was a perilous line of inquiry and plunged into his sundae, which seemed to have everything on it except marshmallow.

We sat there, we two, watching the film. Feeley paced, chain-smoked, made phone calls from the Lincoln sitting room. I frankly became rather absorbed in the film, which I found very touching.

Promptly at ten Feeley came into the Yellow Oval Room, where we were watching. "Jesus," he said, disgusted. Firecracker and I were in tears.

He started roughhousing with Firecracker, tickling him, and finally Firecracker agreed to play Treasure Hunt. Feeley pulled out a roll of blank Teleprompter paper and told Firecracker that the map to the treasure was written on paper just like it and kept in the top right drawer of his father's desk in what Firecracker called the Egg Room.

I checked my watch. It was 10:10. The President and First Lady were due back in thirty-five minutes. We would have to work fast.

The switchboard put me in contact with the site advanceman at the Kennedy Center. He informed me Firebird and Fantasy were already at the reception for Kenneth Fuchs, the composer whose symphony had premiered that evening.

When I rejoined them, Feeley and Firecracker were arguing over whether or not Theodore, Firecracker's hamster, should be included in the hunt. When I reminded Feeley that we had about half an hour, he dropped his objection to Theodore. Crouching next to Firecracker, he told him that the best pirate was a *fast* pirate, and that if he got back in five minutes he'd get a bonus.

"Money?"

Feeley stared at him. "Yeah."

"How much?"

"Go! Five minutes." Firecracker shot off down the red-carpeted grand staircase.

"Drink," said Feeley. He went to the bar and poured a large Scotch.

Two minutes later the phone rang. It was the Secret Service.

"We have movement on Firecracker. He's heading into the Rose Garden."

"Not to worry," I said, trying to sound avuncular.

"It's forty degrees outside, Mr. Wadlough. Shouldn't he be wearing a coat?"

I felt terrible. I was telling the agent to send Firecracker back when Feeley wrested the phone out of my hand and told him it would be all right. "Kids," he said to the agent. "They're indestructible."

I felt like a negligent mother.

A minute later the phone rang again. It was the uniformed Secret Service post outside the Oval Office.

"We have the President's son, sir."

"Oh, yes," I said. "Don't worry about a thing."

"Very fine, sir. One of the female agents has him. We're taking him back up right now."

"No!" I yelled. "Let him go."

The agent was surprised. "We assumed—"

"We're playing a game," I snapped. "It's the only way to get him to bed. Put him on."

A minute later I was speaking to Firecracker.

"This is great, Uncle Herb!" he squealed.

"Yes," I said, Feeley making frantic hand signals at his watch. "Okay, now, you know what to do."

"Wait a minute," he said, "Theodore wants to talk to you."

I listened a moment or two to the sound of hamster breath. Feeley, listening in on another phone, was shaking his head.

"Goodbye, Theodore," I said gloomily, for by now I had a bad feeling about all this.

Firecracker got back on. "Does Uncle Mike want to talk to Theodore?"

Feeley shook his head vigorously.

"He can't come to the phone, Firecracker. Firecracker, if your mom and dad get home before you're back, we're all going to be in a lot of trouble."

"Okay!"

"There's a good fellow," I said. Feeley, elbows on knees, face in hands, was rocking back and forth.

The phone. "Thompson again, sir."

"Yes?" I said. "What is it?"

"He's going through the President's desk, sir."

I affected a laugh. "Just like his old man, eh, Thompson?"

"Well, sir, strictly speaking—"

"Chip off the old block, eh, Thompson?"

"Isn't the President going to be upset?"

"I'll handle it, Thompson."

"If you say so, sir."

I was leaving a wake of *If you say so*'s. I told Thompson to keep the line open—I wanted to know the instant Firecracker was on his way back. Feeley was on the other line to the Kennedy Center, monitoring the President's movements. "Fuck," he said with more than usual emphasis. "They're pulling out."

That gave us maybe seven minutes.

"Thompson," I said, "tell Firecracker his parents are on their way home."

He came back on. "He's on his way. At about sixty miles an hour, I'd say."

We waited at the top of the staircase, checking our watches every thirty seconds.

"Where is he?" said Feeley. "He should be here by now."

I called, asking for the guard by the door to the Rose Garden. He reported Firecracker had gone by two minutes ago. I calculated—in meters per second—that he ought to be coming up the stairs any moment.

But he didn't. And Feeley was frantic.

"Maybe we should go look for him," he said.

At that moment Rod Holloway and another agent appeared at the head of the stairway. Feeley and I had just time to exchange fraternal expressions of horror when I heard the President's voice.

"What's the matter with you guys?"

We just stood there. The First Lady took stock and said in that tone of voice unique to mothers, "What's wrong?"

Our expressions must not have been reassuring. "Is it Tommy?" she said.

She rushed off in the direction of Firecracker's bedroom. I saw my life, political and otherwise, pass before my eyes.

The President, Feeley, and I stared at each other.

"Do I need to be filled in on something?" the President asked.

The First Lady reappeared. She looked very serious, something like the way she did just before the episode of the Japanese screen.

I closed my eyes, a voluntary reflex left over from elementary school when the other children used to beat me up because I had glasses and was overweight.

"We seem to have a problem," she said very calmly.

22
THE HUNT FOR THEODORE

I closed my eyes and tried to think of some way of explaining to the First Lady why her only son had disappeared. I felt physically ill.

Then she said: "Theodore is missing."

I thought it prudent at this point to remain mute. Feeley, perhaps quicker than I in certain situations, said, "I know. We've looked all over the place."

"Do you want a drink?" said the President. Feeley and I offered to help look for Theodore, but the President said not to worry, that he was always disappearing, then turning up.

The First Lady said that Firecracker wanted to say good night to us. She scolded us for the late hour.

We had to walk past the elevator to get to Firecracker's room. I noticed that the door to it was ajar and realized what had happened.

Firecracker was under the covers when Feeley and I went in. We sat down beside his bed. We saw a glimpse of hair, then his head cautiously peeped out from the covers.

"That was *close*," said Firecracker.

"Jesus," said Feeley. "I thought we were screwed." I gave him a smart elbow in the ribs.

"Theodore," Firecracker said.

"We'll find him," whispered Feeley.

The door opened, light wedged into the room. "Bedtime," said his mother.

"Can Uncle Herb and Mike say prayers with me?"

She said it would be all right, as long as we didn't linger. She half shut the door behind her. When Firecracker was sure she was gone, he reached down into the recesses of his bedsheets and pulled out a crumpled roll of Teleprompter paper. He grinned. "I got it!" he whispered.

Feeley said *"Fantastic!"* He took the prize and held it as if it were a page of Gutenberg Bible. Myself, I was not sure exactly how fantastic it was, since we now had a serious problem on our hands: how to get the speech back.

"You gotta get Theodore," said Firecracker. "He doesn't like the dark."

"I'll have him back here in five minutes," said Feeley. Suddenly the door opened. In unison, we all began saying different prayers aloud. Feeley, who had not seen the inside of a church in over thirty years, started reciting the pledge of allegiance. When we'd mumbled our way through to the ends, we turned around and saw the President standing in the doorway.

Outside Firecracker's room, he said, "Is that your idea of *prayer*, Feeley?"

Feeley grinned. "Whatever does it for you."

We said good night and took the elevator back down. I had a feeling it was going to be a long night, with finding the First Rodent only the beginning.

Feeley went off to his office with the speech text to do his editing.

Thompson was at his post outside the Oval Office.

"Thompson," I said, "have you seen a hamster hereabouts?"

He remembered that Firecracker had had one with him. The silk rope was across the doorway to the Oval. I peered in, checking the base of the curtains where a hamster might be lurking. But Theodore was nowhere in evidence.

"What does it look like, sir?" Thompson inquired.

"Brown, small, and furry, Thompson. I suppose you see a lot of them around the Oval Office."

"We had some mice a month ago."

"Thompson," I said, "I am not interested in mice."

We looked in the anteroom off the Oval Office, in Betty Sue

Scoville's office, and in the corridors. We also checked the Roosevelt Room. No Theodore.

I was worried. Thompson's next helpful suggestion was to bring in one of Secret Service's German shepherds.

"Suppose it eats him? What then, Thompson?"

At that point Feeley arrived. He looked excited. In his hand was the Teleprompter copy.

"What are *you* doing here?" he asked matter-of-factly. For the sake of the subterfuge, I explained to Feeley, in front of Thompson, about the missing hamster.

"Right," he said. "Have you checked the Oval?"

"No," I said. "Of course we can't go in there. Can we, Thompson?"

"That's right, sir. Not without permission. Technically speaking, sir, even I'm not allowed in there."

Feeley started working on him. He understood, of course—those were the rules. But up in the residence a little seven-year-old boy was sobbing his heart out over his best friend, who was lost.

Thompson was nodding, agreeing it was terrible, all right.

"Yeah," said Feeley. "I hope the President doesn't find out."

"About what, sir?" said Thompson.

"Oh—that we weren't allowed in to see if his son's pet was in there."

Thompson looked uncomfortable. "I could check with my superiors," he said.

"No," said Feeley. "That'd only make it worse. Then everyone would find out Firecracker had been up past his bedtime. We'd get in trouble. *You'd* get in trouble."

"Me, sir?"

"Well, you let him in there."

"But you said—"

Feeley shook his head. "It wouldn't matter. Like you say, the rules are no one's allowed in." He went on, painting a dire picture of the inevitable debacle—he and I reprimanded, Thompson transferred to the Turkish Embassy. And poor Firecracker crying himself to sleep for days—weeks.

At length Thompson, eyes searching the hall, said, "It's for a good reason."

"Oh, yeah," said Feeley. "The best."

"He's a nice kid."

"A *great* kid. And he's always talking about you."

"No kidding?"

"Oh, yeah. In front of his father too."

Thompson smiled. "Well, isn't that nice?"

Feeley winked at him. "Doesn't hurt."

Seconds later the rope was down.

"Here, Theodore!" we called. "Here, boy!" I wasn't sure if hamsters responded to voice commands.

Feeley went over behind the President's desk. I noticed he was keeping his eyes on Thompson.

Then, while Thompson was looking behind the firescreen with his back turned, Feeley reached into his pocket, drew out the Teleprompter text, slid it into the top right drawer, and closed it. "No," he said. "He's not here."

I told Thompson to alert all the guards on duty to be on the lookout for a small brown rodent. It was getting late.

When we were alone, I said to Feeley, "Well?"

Feeley shook his head. "Thank God we got to it first."

"Bad?"

He closed his eyes and shook his head. "If he'd given that speech, there wouldn't have been a re-election campaign. Everyone over at the campaign would have jumped out the windows."

"You mean?"

"Yeah," he grinned. "We're running."

Thus it was that Feeley and I were the first to learn of the President's historic decision to run for re-election.

"Jesus, it was awful. Six pages, and only five sentences. It wasn't English," he said. "It wasn't any known language. And some of the lines. 'I have not yet begun to run'? God . . ."

When I asked him if the President wasn't sure to miss what he'd taken out, he shook his head and said he doubted it, because only a drunk man would have written such a speech and a drunk man wouldn't remember what he'd written.

I left him muttering in the corridor and went off to resume my search for Theodore.

By 1:30 a.m. I had twelve Secret Service agents combing the White House and immediate grounds for Theodore. Feeley was tiring of the whole thing and wanted to obtain a substitute hamster— in fact, he had been on the phone rousting some poor Smithsonian functionary out of bed, asking him where he could get a hamster at that hour. I vetoed the idea on the grounds that Firecracker would spot the deception in two seconds. Feeley threw up his arms and said *he* was going to bed.

"Fine," I said, piqued. "Never mind about your promise to Firecracker. Never mind about telling him you'd have his hamster back in five minutes. I'll stay here and mop up after you. As usual."

"Look," he said wearily, "tomorrow's going to be bad enough. I've *got* to get some sleep. The rat'll probably show up in the morning. They've got great homing instincts." By two o'clock he'd started referring to Theodore as a rat.

At three I was still directing the search when my phone rang. I let it ring four times. Was it the President telling me the game was up? Or Joan calling from Boise, worried that she hadn't been able to reach me at home?

But when I picked it up, the White House operator told me Firecracker was on the line for me. *"Where's Theodore?"* he was whispering.

I explained the situation to him. He took it like a man. I promised not to abandon the search and indeed I went on with it until nearly four, but then, exhausted, I too was compelled to give up. The next day was going to be an eventful one, and I reasoned that I ought to have at least two hours' sleep to be ready for it. Nonetheless, I felt wretched about Theodore. The drive home was full of unpleasant visions of squashed and otherwise deceased hamsters.

The phone began ringing at 6:30 a.m. The press. They were in a state over the President's expected withdrawal, foaming at the mouth even more than usual and desirous of the usual irrelevant details. ABC, for instance, demanded to know what he was having for breakfast. After less than two hours' sleep, on top of a trying evening, I found this an especially vexatious question.

"How in blazes should I know what he's having for breakfast?" I said. "What an intolerably *stupid* question."

By seven I had had a dozen such calls and was in a foul mood. Aida, our maid, arrived to cook me breakfast. Joan hated the thought of me having to make my own breakfast, so she'd arranged for our maid to come early.

I was in the shower when Aida brought me the cordless telephone.

Filled with excitement, she said, "It's de President for you, Mr. Wadloo!" With that she thrust the thing through the shower curtain, nearly electrocuting me.

"Agh!" I screamed, leaping naked out of the shower. In so doing, I banged into the edge of the sink and fell to the floor. Aida stood there regarding me. The phone clattered to the shower floor. I rubbed my hip.

"You wan' speak to him?"

"Unh," I groaned. "Unh." My head, resting on the tile, was only a few inches from the phone. Through the splashing I could hear, "Hello? Hello? Mr. Wadlough, are you there?"

Aida turned off the water. I reached over and took the phone. "Yes?" I gasped.

"Please hold for the President," said the operator.

The President came on. "Sorry to bother you this early, but Firecracker's all bent out of shape about his hamster. He keeps saying you or Feeley knows where it is. That's all I can get out of him. You have any idea what the hell's going on?"

Think, Wadlough, I said to myself. I got out something vague about how we'd promised Firecracker to help find Theodore. I said I'd take charge of the search as soon as I could get there.

As soon as I got to the office, I assembled an ad-hoc emergency task force consisting of Mrs. Metz, Mrs. O'Dwyer, and myself. All agents and household staff were alerted. Groundskeepers were alerted. The custodial staff was told to disarm all rat traps in the White House basement.

There were questions. Were there any cats on the premises? Was there an effective hamster bait? I needed answers, and time was running out.

I called Feeley and briefed him. From his grunts I could tell he was having a busy morning and was not concentrating on my briefing. Among Feeley's many talents was his ability to rise above catastrophes of his own making and leaving others to cope with the wreckage. In politics, this is no inconsiderable skill.

The inevitable happened. News of Theodore's disappearance leaked to the press. At the noon press briefing there were questions. I demanded a transcript.

This exchange had occurred:

Q: How long has the hamster been missing?
Feeley: I don't have anything for you on that.
Q: Is Libya involved?
(Laughter)
Feeley: Can we get on with this?
Q: How old is the hamster?
Feeley: When Congress gets back after the Christmas recess, we'll submit the revised immigration legislation—
Q: Can you describe the hamster?
Feeley: For Chrissakes—
Q: Are the Russians involved?
Feeley: Not to our knowledge.
Q: Has the FBI been called in?
Feeley: I understand Herb Wadlough has been tasked with finding the hamster. He is orchestrating the search effort. Can we get on with the briefing?
Q: What are Wadlough's qualifications?
(Laughter)
Feeley: The President has every confidence in Mr. Wadlough. He has the highest regard for his hamster-locating abilities.

Reading it, my finger trembled. I called Feeley.

"This is *outrageous*," I said. "It makes me sound like the White House zookeeper!"

"Herb—"

"It's humiliating," I said. "I'm a substantive person."

"Of course you are."

"Don't humor me," I said. "I'm in no mind to be humored."

"Relax," he said. "After the speech tonight everyone'll have forgotten about the fucking hamster."

The calls started to come in from the press. I prepared a brief statement which I instructed Mrs. Metz to give out. The only thing that kept me from despair was the knowledge that a seven-year-old boy was depending on me. But though the search continued in earnest throughout the day, Theodore could not be found. I began to fear the worst. At 5:30 I met with Firecracker and told him that everything humanly possible was being done, but that as yet Theodore had eluded us. It was a poignant meeting. Once more I was impressed with his manly bearing.

The broadcast was scheduled for ten o'clock. (NBC had refused to cut into *Tumor Ward*, so it had been moved back an hour.) The President had graciously asked me and Feeley (as well as Lleland and Marvin) to join him in the Oval Office at 9:30. I think he felt badly about having excluded everyone from his decision-making process and wanted to make us feel part of the historic occasion.

We sat around making small talk. The President was in an upbeat mood.

At 9:45 one of the White House technicians told me he needed the Teleprompter copy.

"Mr. President," I said, "it's time."

"Ah," said the President. "The great moment." He smiled at us and opened the right top drawer. "Now you'll understand why it was necessary to keep such a—*Ow!*"

He pushed back in his chair, knocking over the table by the window and upsetting the pictures of the family in their silver frames. He was clutching his right hand.

A Secret Service agent rushed forward. Feeley and I collided with each other coming around the edge of the desk. Someone knocked over a television light. There was shouting, the kind of confused commotion that usually attends an assassination attempt.

All eyes went to the open drawer from which the President had so violently recoiled. There was a movement, a rustling of papers, then a glimpse of a wriggling brown body and some twitching whiskers.

If the President ever suspected our involvement in the affair, he never let on. Perhaps he did, but recognized that Feeley's changes had greatly helped his speech. More likely he was preoccupied with the First Lady's reaction to his decision, which, it was obvious, he had kept secret even from her.

Major Arnold was greatly exercised over the possibility that Theodore might be rabid. He and I exchanged sharp words when he informed me that the hamster would have to undergo the rabies test. I gave him to understand that while I valued the President's health above that of my mother, I would under no circumstances permit the Air Force to decapitate the President's son's hamster.* A vigorous debate followed in the corridor, during which it became necessary to remind the Major that the matter was closed, and that if he could not grasp this fundamental precept, he might refresh his understanding of the Constitution in the calm and quiet of one of our missile-tracking stations in Greenland. I did not enjoy having to put it that way, but it had been a trying day, and I was not disposed to trifle.

23
TAKEDOWN

I think this is the end of our little walks in the park.
—JOURNAL, JAN. 10, 1992

The First Lady did not take the President's surprise announcement at all well.

I received a call from Mrs. O'Dwyer the next morning at eight, when the President and First Lady usually took breakfast. She was in a state.

"Mis-ter Wadlough," she said. I always got the feeling she held

---

* When I told Major Arnold that, I was of course using a figure of speech, but that fact is not reflected in the Major's memoir, *The Bowels of Power*.

me personally responsible for the goings-on in the residence. "I'm very sorry if they're not getting along, but I won't have the crockery being thrown about. It's not their house, after all, is it? It belongs to the—"

"Mrs. O'Dwyer," I said peremptorily, for I was in no mood for one of her lugubrious sermons, "what exactly is going on?"

She hooted and told me that, to judge from the sound of it, the President and First Lady were experiencing marital trauma.

"What are they saying to each other?"

"I am not in the habit of eavesdropping."

"Well, are they shouting?" I said. "Can you hear *that*?"

"I can tell you this, Mr. Wadlough: she isn't a bit pleased that he's running again. And if you ask me—"

"I did *not* ask you, Mrs. O'Dwyer."

"Well, it isn't proper. She may be a young woman, and I can't speak for what being in the film world does to you. All the world may be a stage, but I've been here since Mr. and Mrs. Nixon and I've never witnessed such displays as these, and I don't care to witness any more."

"*Thank* you, Mrs. O'Dwyer." *I'd be glad to see to it you don't, you impossible woman*, I thought.

Gloomy premonitions crowded in on me. I'd known Mrs. Tucker would not be pleased by his decision to run again, but, as anxious as she was for him to quit politics, she was a strong woman and a good wife and I was sure she'd "stand by her man," as the country-western singers put it.

She and Firecracker left for New York that morning on the 10:30 New York Air flight. She could have been flown by Air Force Jet Star. *Oh*, I thought, *that is* not *a good sign*.

She spent the next three days at the Sherry Netherland. She would not accept the President's phone calls. This was a tense period for the senior staff, and a difficult one personally for the President.

Christmas was over, so we could hardly announce that she had gone on another shopping trip. Feeley told the President it would seem "too Republican." We put out the story that she was simply on a "private visit." I made several secret trips up to New York, carrying messages back and forth between them. At the President's insistence, I wore a disguise—that same vexatious, scratchy beard I had worn during one of our Cuban trips. My hair had also been sprayed gray. Not recognizing me, the First Lady's Secret Service detail wrestled me to the ground outside her suite at the Sherry Netherland Hotel, putting me in a foul humor.

The First Lady was unresponsive to my entreaties, but at no point attacked me physically, which I took to be a good sign. Her anger with her husband was pronounced. She felt betrayed by his decision to run again. I said that throughout history a number of great leaders had kept matters of state secret even from their wives. She was unresponsive to this argument. When I said that Thomas Tucker had a chance to be remembered as a great President, but only if he had another term in which to fulfill his greatness, she became antagonistic in her response.

In fairness, I could understand her position. On the other hand, the prospect of her making a film during the re-election campaign was unappealing in the extreme. I argued with her forcefully. Let me be frank: I begged her to return.

I think if it had not been for the events of January 9, she might not have returned to the White House.

Bamford Lleland writes in his memoir: "The timing of Hamchuk Hartoonian's attack on the President was so favorable, in terms of the marital crisis, as to be propitious. Herb Wadlough, who in addition to his role as White House baggage handler and food taster had also been given the job of trying to cajole Mrs. Tucker back to Washington, was positively jubilant over the incident, since it solved his immediate problem. We chided him afterwards, congratulating him on his 'coup' in masterminding the attack. As usual, poor Herb failed to see the humor in the remark."

I do not propose to comment on these smug, untrue, and libelous remarks, except to say that among my failings is a failure to find anything "humorous" in attempted assassinations of the President of the United States by Commandos of the Armenian Genocide. At Harvard, perhaps, such incidents are considered "good sport."

I was, in fact, returning from one of my undercover missions when the attack took place. I was aboard the 6:30 p.m. New York Air flight to Washington. (My Air Force Jet Star had developed a mechanical problem on the ground in New York, so I had been forced to return on a commercial flight.) At 7:02 the pilot's voice came on and announced, with what I thought was indecent calm, that the President had just been shot. I wish I could report that the atmosphere aboard the 727 was stunned and grief-stricken, but all I recall is the fellow next to me asking if I knew any good hotels in Washington.

I presented myself to a stewardess in the front and told her I was White House deputy chief of staff and had urgent need of a telephone. She looked at me dubiously and asked for identification.

Since I was known to the guards at the White House, I'd long ago gotten out of the custom of carrying my White House *carnet*. Grumbling that I was surprised she did not know my name, I offered her my driver's license.

She looked at it, then at me, then back at it. It was then I remembered I was *incognito*.

She was now regarding me with some alarm. I told her to summon the pilot immediately, whereupon she told me to return to my seat. I became somewhat indignant—understandably—and demanded to speak with the captain.

It is true, as the press accounts of the incident related, that I yanked off my beard at that point. It is not true, as those same reports allege, that I became "hysterical." Certainly I was forceful—anyone in my position would have been. At any rate, moments later I found my arms being pinioned behind me by several burly passengers and the co-pilot was speaking to me in tones indicating that he thought he was addressing a person of deranged mind. Thus I was incommunicado until we arrived on the ground and the White House driver Mrs. Metz had sent to meet me made my identity clear to the FBI agents who had been sent to arrest me.

On the drive to the hospital I called the First Lady. The White House operator told me she was already en route to Washington.

The scene at George Washington University Hospital was chaotic, the security tighter than I had ever seen it. Sniper teams were already in place on the rooftop. A helicopter was circling. I made my way through a long corridor toward the emergency room. Outside were agents with German shepherds and drawn Uzis. A nurse was arguing with one of the dog handlers. A large black man on a gurney who appeared to have been shunted aside in the general excitement, and who, from the sound of it, had ingested no small amount of controlled substances, was expressing his dissatisfaction with the arrangements.

I moved as if in a daze through the emergency room. The operating area is in the back. I saw Colonel Frye, the President's military aide. I recognized Rod Holloway, wearing a surgical gown. Major Arnold was also there. Rod brought me up to date.

The President had decided, without any warning, to take one of his walks in Lafayette Park. He'd allowed only one other agent besides Rod to accompany him. To the horror of the two agents, he decided to go talk to the permanent protesters on the Pennsylvania Avenue side of the park. He'd just engaged a few of these specimens in conversation when Hartoonian sprang out from behind and began firing. Jake Thompson, the second agent, brought down the swarthy Armenian with one shot, but not before the assailant had gotten off three rounds with his Smith and Wesson .41 magnum.

One of Hartoonian's shots hit the President, passing through the left bicep muscle and grazing his side. From there it passed through two placard-carrying supporters of the Equal Rights Amendment. Extremely unfortunate. The other round pierced the roof of a D.C. city bus, exited, and lodged in the northeast cornice of the Old Executive Office Building.

An agent led me into an examining room they had converted into a recovery room. I heard a nurse's voice: "Please, Mr. President. I must ask you to put that out. It's dangerous to smoke in here."

The President was propped up in bed. His upper right arm was bandaged. An IV was dripping into his ankle. His left arm was folded behind his head. His eyes looked a bit glassy—from the anesthetic, I guessed. A cigarette hung at a forty-five-degree angle from the left side of his mouth. By way of response to the nurse's entreaties, he winked and asked for a cup of coffee, black.

"Got to stay alert," he said.

"Yes," I said, "in case of attack."

"In case Reigeluth tries to have me declared dead." He shook his head. "Where is he anyway?"

"On his way back from Manitoba, sir," said Colonel Frye. "Air Force Two will wheels-down at Andrews half an hour from now."

"Well, tell him to turn around. I'm all right."

"Mr. President," I said, "we can't do that. It wouldn't look right."

"Well, tell him no interviews. I don't want him impressing everyone with how calm and in control he is in a crisis. This is *my* crisis, dammit, and I intend to enjoy it."

I went off to check with Feeley and see how the press end of things was going. He had been answering questions for an hour.

"Half an hour," he said. "If she's not here in half an hour, it's going to be a fucking disaster. That's all they want to know. *Why isn't she at his side?*"

I told him she was on her way.

"What? In a blimp? He was shot two hours ago. He could have had a goddam liver transplant in this time."

I said that, all things considered, we were lucky she was even coming.

He said that from a women's-vote point of view it couldn't be worse. The President's wife off in New York pursuing a film career, and two ERA supporters seriously perforated. "On the other hand," he allowed, "this is going to mean a jump in the approval ratings of fifteen points."

I chided him for thinking of such a thing at a time like this. But Feels was pure politics.

He went on to say we would have to "control" the medical reports. "I don't want this thing played as a scratch. This was a close call with death."

"It does appear to be a flesh wound," I said. "But those poor ERA ladies—"

"Herb," he said, "this is *our* crisis. We earned it." He said we should talk to Dr. Lawrence Saladino, the attending physician.

Saladino, a cheerful and highly competent ex-Navy doctor from Brooklyn, told us that, as far as he was concerned, the President could leave the next morning. The arm and chest wounds were "essentially superficial," he said.

"Superficial?" said Feeley.

Dr. Saladino nodded and described how lucky the President was.

Feeley frowned. "And you're saying he could leave *tomorrow*?"

"Sure," said the doctor. "He'd be more comfortable there anyway."

Feels looked depressed and said darkly he was sure Saladino was a Republican.

I told him we should be giving thanks to the Good Lord it wasn't more serious. He did not respond to this line of thought.

"The way it's going," he said, "ERA is going to get more out of this than we are."

In the elevator he said to me: "Pray for complications."

Feeley tried hard to persuade Major Arnold to get the President transferred to Bethesda Naval Hospital, where he thought the military doctors might be less "release-happy," as he put it. Major Arnold was all for transferring him, but the President, who had taken a liking to Dr. Saladino, refused—despite the political advantages, which Feeley made quite clear to him—and said he wanted to go home.

The First Lady arrived a few minutes after nine. Feeley had pre-positioned a White House photographer outside the President's door, so the first moments of their reunion were recorded in the famous photograph. It is just as well, since the second moments were of a less tender nature, what with her berating the President for his historic decision to run again. But at least she was back in Washington. The late Hamchuk Hartoonian had accomplished that much, as well as the subsequent passage of the Equal Rights Amendment, of course.

24
STRATEGIC APPEARANCE
LIMITATION TALKS

This will be my last campaign.　　　—JOURNAL, JUNE 4, 1992

Perhaps it was indicative of the hard, uphill slogging of Campaign
'92 that Feeley kept saying the Hartoonian attack had come "too
early." While I rebuked Feels for making such macabre statements,
I sympathized. Our approval rating, which had shot up so sharply
in the weeks following the incident, giving us a critical lift during
the New Hampshire primary, dropped back to their previous level.
I might add that it is untrue, as Lleland says in his "memoir," that
I urged the President to conduct the campaign in a wheelchair.

The possibility that the President would not be renominated by
his party was, historically speaking, embarrassing and did nothing
for morale in the West Wing. I have always felt that in times of
distress it is best to keep busy; thus, I called 6:30 a.m. staff meetings
and instituted the WSOAs, or Weekly Summary of Activities, whereby
all presidential appointees below Assistant-to-the-President rank
submitted 500-word descriptions of what they had done that week.
Both the 6:30 staff meetings and the WSOAs proved extremely
unpopular. One (anonymous) person submitted a detailed accounting
of that week's bodily functions. After two weeks I discontinued them
after determining they were not significantly improving morale.

Vice President Reigeluth, meantime, was opening his paper each
morning to read the latest developments in the White House's attempts to replace him. This was seriously disheartening for him.
For several weeks he refused to go out on the campaign trail, and I
was given the job of getting him back "on the reservation."

I found him hostile to my entreaties. Four years of Air Force Two had made him a bitter man. He complained about the goodwill trips to Mauritius and Ecuador, saying that he had been "cut out of the action" and treated like "an unwanted brother-in-law." He said he had had three cases of amoebic dysentery in as many months on the road.

I said he had suffered for his country, and that the President was deeply grateful. I told him that democracy came at a heavy cost, and that we must all do what we could to maintain it. At this he became more hostile and told me he was thinking of resigning the Vice Presidency. He said people were advising him that that might be best anyway for his political future.

Though I suspected this was bluster, I realized immediately that something had to be done to calm the man down. I promised that I would speak to the President about the overseas travel. I also held out the tantalizing opportunity of his meeting with the President in the Oval Office "sometime in the very near future." The prospect seemed to cheer him somewhat, and he said he would "seriously consider" making a campaign trip to New Jersey.

Between the Vice President and the President's brother, who had lately forsaken Islam for the Bhagwan Satgananda Uy—known to his followers as "Baba"— I was kept busy. I despaired of my Metrification duties.

The only cheering note was that the First Lady was back with us—for the time being, at any rate. She and the President had made a truce following the Hartoonian incident. But she made no secret of her opinion of his running again. We feared greatly that she might give one of her interviews, but she didn't.

One Saturday morning I was briefing the President on the new sauna at Camp David when she breezed in and announced to her husband that she had just agreed to do Mr. Weinberg's new film, *Irregular Spaces.*

She was very excited. I also think she was a little nervous about the prospect of going back to films; she had been away from them for ten years. The President made a rum effort at greeting her news with enthusiasm, but I could see he was crestfallen. He asked how soon "principal photography" began. He seemed very up on the lingo.

"September fifteenth," she said.

"I need to go check on tomorrow's departure," I said. I didn't want to be around for what was about to follow.

The President buzzed me later in the afternoon.

"Herb," he said, sighing heavily, "I think it's pretty appalling what's happened to political wives."

"You do?" I said.

"Yeah. They're not the ones running for office."

"Strictly speaking, I agree. However—"

"I think it's gotten, well, grotesque the way political wives are dragged around."

"Well," I said, "it's a team—"

"Told to look adoringly at the candidate while he's making some fucking speech about farm supports."

"Still—"

"Put on the *Phil Donahue Show* and asked what their husbands like to eat for breakfast and who he's going to appoint to the Supreme Court."

"And yet—"

"It's demeaning. Especially for women who had careers *before* they were married."

"But—"

"I'm going to do something about it."

"You are?" I said.

"Yup. I've decided I'm going to campaign alone. Solo."

"Oh," I said. "But don't you think—"

"Jessie agrees with me, you know. She thinks it's an idea whose time has come."

"I see. Frankly, sir, I don't think it's a good idea."

"If the people who run for office these days were *half* as liberated as they say they are, someone would have done it by now. Gotten up there and said, 'My wife has better things to do than go around making me look good.' "

"She is popular out there, you know."

"Listen, she *wants* to help. I told her she could do as much as she wanted or as little. 'Either way,' I said. 'You decide.' "

"And what," I said fearfully, "did she decide?"

"We decided something like half a dozen appearances would cover the major events."

"*Six?*"

"Six is half a dozen, that's right."

"That's not very many, Mr. President."

"Well, I said that'd be fine."

"Yes," I said, sinking into a slough of despond. "I see."

"You and Sig and Feeley and the others will need to get with her"—he sighed—"and work out a schedule. Oh, and she's making a film."

"Yes," I said glumly.

"You heard?"

"I was in the room, Mr. President, when she announced it."

"Oh. So you were. Well, I think the announcement should come from the White House. You better check with Aronow [Chief White House Counsel], see if there's any conflict or whatever."

"Uh-huh."

"And Herb?"

"Sir?"

"If she changes her mind, wants to get more involved, encourage her, okay?"

I was somewhat surprised when Mrs. Tucker did not show up at the meeting I'd arranged. Instead she sent her agent, a Mr. Liebman of International Creative Management.

"Good morning, gentlemen," he said. "I took the liberty of telling my office I could be reached here. You don't mind? Good. Shall we begin?" Feeley took an instant dislike to him. I reserved judgment until he began calling me "Herbie," at which point I decided I disliked him too.

The meeting lasted almost two hours, during which he took four calls. I became quite exercised when he had the temerity to ask us to leave the room for one of them. We were in the *White House*, if you please, and he wanted *us* to leave the room. Honestly. I would have spoken to him sharply, but I didn't want to upset him, so, nearly dragging Feeley by the collar, we waited in Mrs. Metz's office until his call "from the coast" was finished.

"Thank you, gentlemen," he said when we filed back in. "You know how it is." I did *not* "know how it is," but I let it go.

We reached an impasse over the presidential debate in October. Our side did not consider it a campaign appearance if the First Lady merely came and watched her husband debate George Bush.

"My client is going to be in the middle of a shoot in October," he said. "If we're going to come all the way to wherever this debate will be held, we'll have to consider that an appearance. My advice, gentlemen, would be to get the President's sister to go to the debate and to save my client for more conspicuous events, such as this Al Smith dinner you seem so anxious for her to attend."

It was an extremely frustrating meeting. We got our six appearances, and not so much as one drop-by or mix-and-mingle extra. We were exhausted. Sig and Feels had their jackets off and ties loosened. Mr. Liebman was cool as a dill pickle. In all my dealings in government I never met someone more difficult to bargain with than he. Frankly, I don't understand how movies get made if that's what you have to go through every time.

"May I use your phone?" Mr. Liebman asked when we were finally through. I was sorely tempted to show him the way to the phone booth, but I am not a vindictive man.

He asked the operator for the First Lady.

"Jess?"

Jess? Was this how he addressed the First Lady?

"I got your six-picture deal. Pay or play. Are you kidding? They *love* you. They want to get into bed."

"*What?*" I thundered.

"Figure of speech, Herbie. No, I'm here with your Mr. Wadlough. Yes, a very nice gentleman. Listen, they have restaurants in this town? I heard it's all microwave. Yeah? Come on, I'll buy. You gotta car?"

I tried to shut out these abominations and concentrate on Marine One seat assignments. He left us with a valedictory "*Ciao.*" I, for one, was not sorry to see him go.

BOOK FIVE
PITFALLS

25
INJURY

Miss Joan, but feel it important to be with President for last peaceful days before general election begins. Is pleasant here, despite allergies.   —JOURNAL, AUG. 30, 1992

As Labor Day and the official start of the general presidential campaign approached, the President was in low spirits. At my urging, he spent the last week of August at the Summer White House on Monhegan Island, refreshing himself for the grueling ordeal that lay ahead. I was anxious that this period be a pleasant one for him, free of any friction with the local inhabitants, so I quietly arranged for a Department of the Environment grant whereby each Monhegan resident received $500 for answering a quality-of-life questionnaire.

A nearly disastrous incident was narrowly averted when I discovered that Lleland had invited the President for a two-day cruise aboard the *Compassion*. In a moment of weakness the President had accepted the invitation. The thought of the President being photographed aboard this floating embarrassment on the eve of the campaign was nightmarish. When I confronted Lleland, he told me the "salt air" would do the President a "world of good." This so annoyed me that I told him I suspected he was merely trying to inflate the resale of his yacht by lending it the presidential aura. Our conversation ended abruptly and heatedly, and for several weeks he refused to acknowledge my existence, even during meetings in the Oval Office. But I was successful in persuading the President to eschew the salt air aboard the *Compassion*.

By now the President had his doubts about Lleland anyway. He had been given a job of trying to convince Senator Kennedy to withdraw from the primaries and had failed rather spectacularly, when the Senator not only didn't withdraw but publicly asked Vice President Reigeluth to be his running mate. *Quel fiasco!* as the French say.

I had been instrumental in convincing the Vice President not to accept the Senator's offer. (It is not true, as the former Vice President wrote in *Jet Lag: My Four Years Aboard Air Force Two*, that I suggested to him the IRS might be interested in his 1984–1987 tax returns.) At any rate, as a result of my ministrations, I was in good odor with the President.

I wanted the President's time to be his own during that one week of peace with his family. To that end, I accompanied him—amidst much grumbling among the other senior staff, who were not invited to go along—and stayed in one of the cottages on the fringe of the presidential compound.

During this period I acted as a kind of "buffer" or "conduit," and made sure that all paper flowed through me to the President. In the interests of the presidential tranquility, I attempted to keep that flow down to a trickle. This is a difficult task, inasmuch as the average daily number of document pages that flow to the President is 204.6. I was able to reduce that to five. I took some pride in that accomplishment, though I was harshly criticized for it by the press and by certain senior members of the staff, one of whom told the *New York Times* I was a "constipating influence."

The President had asked me to supervise the digesting of news reports during that week inasmuch as he desired to catch up on his book reading. I directed the White House News Summary Office to be especially terse; working together, we managed to reduce the day's *New York Times* to a concise fifty words, and the *Washington Post* to twenty. Actually, I felt the *Times* could have been tightened even further.

I saw no point in disturbing the President's "quality time" by keeping him advised of the hourly Republican denunciations. Given the choice between being informed of the latest reckless charge by George Bush or hunting for periwinkles among the seaweed-covered rocks with his son, I had no doubt as to which the President preferred. Yet the world pressed in on him.

Bermuda was also much in the news on account of the August

27 dynamiting of the Mid-Ocean Golf Club and its subsequent effect on tourism. The little gray fellow from CIA who gave the President his daily briefing looked even more harried than usual when he arrived the next morning. And when Chase Manhattan raised its prime lending rate to twenty-one percent on the last day of the month, there was strong pressure for a statement from the President. Rather than trouble Charlie Manganelli, who was taking advantage of the President's vacation to undergo another detoxification at Bethesda Naval Hospital, I drafted a statement myself and gave it to *The New York Times*. Frankly, I was rather pleased with it at the time, since it went straight to the heart of the problem and put the banks where they belonged—on the defensive. But, in retrospect, perhaps I overstated the case by proposing that we nationalize the banks. I had not been informed that Treasury Secretary Lindsay had come out against bank nationalization at the June 27 cabinet meeting, and that the President had concurred. The whole incident, overblown though it was, points out the need for greater coordination within government.

We had tried to keep the press entirely off the island by getting the Monhegan assessors to pass a temporary ordinance against their presence, but the town selectmen were obstinate. (I privately resolved that these wretched people had seen their last Department of the Environment grant.) So the press was there, though only twenty of them. They spent their time seeking out the more eccentric and discontented Monheganers, who gave them boozy harangues about how the noise caused by the presidential helicopters was causing the lobsters to molt.

I did not actually spend much time with the President during this period, but late in the evening of the next to the last day the President called and asked me if I would like to walk with him. I was already in my pajamas, but of course I said yes. He met me outside my cottage, "Poopdeck," and handed me a flashlight. Accompanied by only six agents, we set off. I could smell bourbon on his breath. But this was, after all, his vacation.

To my consternation, he headed toward the shore, instead of following any of the quite lovely paths that wind their way through the pine forest. The President was fond of taking people for "walks" along this shore. In truth, these peregrinations required the talents of a mountain goat. The route went over boulders, under two gigantic driftwood tree trunks, through slippery seaweed-coated gullies, culminating in an exceedingly unpleasant stretch of foot-wide walkway cut into a cliff face twenty feet above the water. It was difficult enough during the day; at night it resembled the set of one of those Alistair Maclean World War II movies. Whenever the President announced he was going for a walk, Secret Service alerted the medical staff and positioned agents in a Zodiak rubber boat at the foot of the cliff walk. A year earlier the President had taken the Sri Lankan Prime Minister on one of these walks. That was the reason the Honorable Mr. Chiribindigar had left without signing the mutual-defense treaty, although I understand the Prime Minister has since regained full use of his left arm.

I was grateful for the three-quarter moon. It permitted me to see about three feet in front of me. My night vision is not good at all, and when I exert myself, my glasses do have a tendency to fog.

"Remember," said the President, leaping from one rock to another, "no hands." He maintained it was only challenging if you didn't use hands. Frankly, I would have found it challenging with crampons and rope.

He did not say much. I sensed in him some gloominess or apprehension. And why shouldn't there be? He recognized the obvious: that it would be a hard, uphill campaign. The four years had taken some physical toll. He looked older than fifty-two. His face had lines that hadn't been there on inauguration day. His cough was worse too, though he had "absolutely promise[d]" to give up smoking by Labor Day. I earnestly hoped he meant it this time, though the start of a campaign was not an easy time to give it up.

"Herb," he said to me as we paused atop a slimy boulder, "I don't know about this election."

I sensed he wanted reassurance. I am not a "yes man," but there are times when a counselor best serves his principal by saying soothing things. I told him that the entire staff was "in very high spirits." This was not exactly the case, but it was all I could think of at the moment.

"High spirits," he repeated. "You must mean Manganelli." I had

had to tell him about Charlie's problem after the incident at the convention. It was a measure of the man's generosity of heart that he kept him on as his chief speechwriter.

I laughed, and he skidded on some sea moss and fell between two rocks. The agent looking down on us from above said something into his walkie-talkie and all of a sudden the entire area was bathed in harsh light. It was the searchlight beam from the Coast Guard cutter fifty yards off.

The President clambered up. "Shut that thing off."

Seconds later all went black, with retinal exploding spots. Blinded, I took a cautious step forward. There was a loud squish under my foot, then both legs were up in the air and I landed on my posterior, causing me to champ down on the tip of my tongue.

"Did you use your hands?" asked the President.

"I think I bit off part of my tongue," I said.

We walked—so to speak—some further distance along. Even in my pain I could see that it was a beautiful evening. All seemed at peace. The moonlight undulated on the water and seagulls flitted overhead—if seagulls flit; otherwise they were bats.

We came to a particularly nasty-looking piece of cliff that in some glacial age had split off the face and toppled over at a thirty-five-degree angle. The President had a name for it: Old Snaggle Tooth. "Come on up," he said gaily. "We can talk here."

I asked if I couldn't talk to him from the foot of it. "I can hear you quite well from here."

"Come *on*." It is difficult to say no to the commander-in-chief. He didn't do these kinds of things out of mischief. It was simply that there was a touch of the boy in Thomas Tucker.

I was a few feet up when I pitched forward and fell flat. The rock was coated with globs of the wretched rockweed. I slid back down, covering the entire front of my body with slime.

"You have to take a running start," said the President.

"I don't understand," I wheezed. "How are you supposed to get up there?"

"Momentum!"

"Right," I said, and started up at a great clip. I succeeded in getting almost all the way up before the seaweed arrested my progress. "Oh!" I said, feeling myself about to start sliding back. I didn't want to. It was a good fifteen feet down.

"Here," said the President. "Grab my hand."

As I reached for it, I began to slide. My fingernails dug into the rockweed and scraped, rather painfully, down several feet. Finally, I was able to brake myself by grabbing fistfuls of weed anchored to the rock. I had stopped myself from sliding any further; on the other hand, I couldn't move back up. Every time I tried to pull myself up, my fistfuls of rockweed ripped out. The only thing to do was to hold on in this awkward position.

"Aren't you coming up?"

"I'll just stay here," I said, spitting out a bit of marine algae I was sure was infecting the wound on my tongue.

"I love it here." He sighed and called up to the agent, "Ask them to move that vessel out of the moonlight, would you?" He chuckled, "I don't think any fish will try to kill me tonight."

If there was any dying to do tonight, no doubt I would be doing it.

The cutter gunned its engines and maneuvered a hundred yards to one side.

"*Much* better," said the President. My forearms were starting to cramp. "I guess I won't have to worry about Coast Guard cutters fucking up my moonlight much longer." He leaned back and laughed. "I've really fucked up, haven't I?"

I didn't think it was right for him to go into a campaign with that kind of attitude. "Just because you're trailing in the polls—" I was unable to finish my sentence because one of my handfuls of weed tore loose, causing me to swing to one side.

"Twenty-five points isn't trailing, Herb. It's drowning."

"But the advantages of the incumbency—"

"When they start throwing eggs at you—*on Pennsylvania Avenue.* What did Feeley call it? 'Like Caracas.' *Caracas!*" He laughed.

"A handful of radicals," I puffed, having regained my handhold. "The majority of the American people—"

"Hate my guts." He reached into the pocket of his windbreaker and took out a flask. "Well, at least I don't refer to myself in the third person. When they write their fucking memoirs, they won't be able to say that about me."

Let him get it out, I thought. *Then work on his self-confidence.*

"So," he said. "Have you got a publisher lined up for yours?"

I was surprised, and not a little hurt, at the question. "Of course not. I don't plan to write a memoir."

He laughed. "That's not what Feeley told me."

"What?"

He took another swig. "The day Jessie beat you up. That's why I hired you back. He said you'd already signed with a publisher and were going to spill everything about our marriage."

Feeley! So *that* was it. I clenched my fistfuls of rockweed tight, imagining they were his throat.

"I gotta admit, Herb, I really hated you there for a while. Then I figured, what the hell. *Everyone's* going to write a book."

I began to tell him it was an outrageous falsehood, that Feeley was only—in his *devious* way—trying to get me my job back.

He only shrugged. "Doesn't matter. Ah, I love it here."

I clung on, raging inside at Feeley. The President was gazing out to sea.

"You want some?" He offered me the flask; peered down at me. "You okay down there?"

"I'm all right," I said, still piqued.

"Say, Herb," he said, "something I always wanted to ask you."

"What?"

"You like being an accountant?"

I was not in the mood to discuss my work, frankly. I mumbled something about how I enjoyed working with numbers. You could trust numbers.

"I dunno," he said. "Sounds boring."

"I quite liked it," I said. My arms were knots of pain.

"The South is going to be a real problem. You saw what [Mississippi Governor G. V. "Sonny"] Montgomery called me last week?"

"Maybe if we had a few more unity breakfasts," I groaned.

The President grunted and pulled on his flask. "Unity breakfasts! You've gotta beat these people over the snout. Cut off their highway funds, close their military bases. It's all they understand."

"We tried that. It doesn't seem to have gotten us anywhere."

"*Us?* What is this, a hospital? 'How do we feel this morning?' "

"I was speaking," I said with mounting anger, "of *our* administration."

"Maybe it was the staff. Maybe that's where I went wrong. Sorry—we."

I sighed. This was old ground. "If you're not happy with the staff *we* selected, why didn't *we* do something about it?"

"Well, maybe *we* should have!"

"Fine," I grunted. "I could suggest a number of changes right off hand."

"So could I!"

We were now snarling at each other across an incline of moonlit seaweed.

"Well, if that's the way you feel about it, I resign!"

"Accepted! Effective immediately!"

"Good! Maybe I'll go work for George Bush—"

"Great! It'll give me an edge over him!"

"—*after* I write my memoir!"

"Go ahead! Put me down for a recommendation. They won't hire you to run a Tastee Freeze!"

"Ha!," I said. "I bet they won't even give you a presidential library! Who'd want your papers and your terrible speeches?"

"Harvard!"

"University of Caracas, you mean!"

In the midst of all this I let go of one handful of weed to shake my fist at him. I should not have. I slid to one side and the remaining fistful started tearing off the rock. I began to slide.

"Ahhh!" I cried. I managed to grab two fresh fistfuls and stopped sliding.

"Here," said the President, reaching down, "take my—"

I looked up and saw him starting to slide. "No!" I said, but it was too late.

His head slammed into the space between my shoulder and neck. The impact caused my fistfuls of weed to rip off the rock with a sickening, slimy, ripping sound. I endeavored to brake, but succeeded only in causing the most extreme and painful sensations under my fingernails. Thus locked together like two belligerent elks, we slid down the slope of Old Snaggle Tooth.

26
REST AND RESPITE

Arnold wants me on sedatives. Tempted as I am, must keep
wits about me. —JOURNAL (dictated), SEPT. 7, 1992

Feeley showed up at my bedside at Bethesda Naval Hospital shortly
after ten the next morning.

"Urrr," I said.

"I've just seen the boss," he beamed. "He looks *terrible*. Both eyes
are black and blue. His forehead has a lump on it the size of a golf
ball, and he's got a hairline fracture of his ulna."

"Why," I moaned, "does that please you?" The pain in my chest
was extreme, making it difficult to breathe. My toes felt hot and
itchy inside the cast.

"The switchboard's going bananas. We've logged twelve thousand
sympathy calls. And the fucking flowers. We're sending them over
to Arlington cemetery."

Pleased as I was to hear that the American people were pulling
for their President, I said I was surprised at the extent of the out-
pouring.

"Well, considering the circumstances," said Feeley.

"Circumstances?"

"Yeah. I mean, it was a great thing he did. I tell you, they're
shitting bricks over at Bush headquarters."

The remark cut through the pain like a horn through fog.

"Tell me," I said, "about this great thing he did."

"Saving your life."

Joan told me afterward that I attempted to lunge out of bed and
attack Feeley. In doing so, I apparently rebroke my collarbone and
passed out from the pain.

When I came to, a Navy doctor was leaning over me. Joan was sitting beside me looking worried.

"Feeley," I moaned. "Feeley."

"Of course you're not feeling well, Mr. Wadlough," said the doctor.

"No, Doctor," said Joan, "Mr. Feeley was the one he—"

"Ah," nodded the doctor. "You need rest, Mr. Wadlough."

Several hours later Joan fed me some homemade meatloaf. She was a great comfort to me.

"How are the children?" I asked. "Do they miss me?"

She told me Herb, Junior, had been put in the "B" section of ninth grade.

I sighed. "What other good news do you have for me?"

"We had a letter from Mr. Urrutia-Bleyleben's lawyer."

"*Joan*," I said. "I was being sarcastic."

We lived next to the Uruguayan military attaché. He was a singularly unpleasant man who owned nine basset hounds that bayed all evening long at the moon, whether it was out or not. After being pleasant about it for some months, I had finally threatened him with legal action. Then Herb, Junior, had taken his bow and arrow and wounded one of the beasts in the hindquarters. Neighborly relations had been very strained thenceforward. Whatever the new development was, it could wait.

After Joan left, I had a nurse dial the White House and ask for Feeley.

"Tell him I want to see him. Immediately."

She got him on the phone and told him. "He says he's very busy right now. Can he come tomorrow?"

"Tell him he has one hour. After that I start giving interviews."

She gave him the message.

Forty-five minutes later the door opened.

"Jesus, what a day." He had that altar-boy smile and was carrying a large and hideously ugly house plant.

"Where did you steal that? Arlington?"

"How you feeling?"

"Miserable. Miserable and betrayed."

"That's terrible." The worst thing about it was he was sincere.
"Can I get you anything?"
"You can. What sordid prevarications have you been spreading?"
"Would you like to read the press release?" He offered it to me.
"I can't use my arms."
"I'll hold it for you."
"Just put it there!"
I read.

THE WHITE HOUSE

August 31, 1992
12:00 AM EDT
Office of the Press Secretary
For Immediate Release

The President is in "very good" condition this morning following
an accident last night on Monhegan Island, Maine. He sustained
soft tissue injuries, ecchymosis under the right eye, and a hairline
fracture of the ulna. His personal physician, Major Todman F.
Arnold, expects him to be released from Bethesda Naval Medical
Command tomorrow, and to be able to fully participate in the
general election campaign.

"You split an infinitive," I said. Feeley shrugged. I read on.

Herbert A. Wadlough, deputy chief of staff and assistant to the
President, sustained slightly more serious injuries.

" 'Slightly'?"

His condition is being termed "good" by doctors at Bethesda. He
sustained a contusion of the forehead, a fractured clavicle and a
ruptured plantaris. Doctors expect him to be released within the
week. It is not known at this time if his injuries will preclude his
full participation in the election campaign.
    The incident occurred at 11:08 Eastern Daylight Time while

the President and Mr. Wadlough were walking along the rocks on the eastern shore of the island. Mr. Wadlough slipped on seaweed and began to fall down the side of a rock. The President, attempting to break his fall, jumped and interposed his body between Mr. Wadlough and the base of the drop. It is the opinion of Major Arnold that Mr. Wadlough would not have survived the fall if the President had not acted as he did. In so doing, the President sustained the above-mentioned injuries, which, though not life-threatening, were serious enough to require his immediate evacuation from Monhegan.

"You're responsible for this," I said.

"Herb, before you get all bent out of shape—"

"Bent out of shape? You perfidious— Look at me!"

"Oh, sorry. Didn't mean that. It's just, the thinking was—"

"Don't tell me what 'the thinking' was. Whenever I hear that, it means there wasn't any thinking at all, just conniving and deviousness. Usually both, in your case."

He grinned, which annoyed me considerably.

"You were probably exploiting my injuries for political purposes before I even got medical attention."

He tried to look hurt. He wasn't very good at it. "Do you really think I'd do that?"

"You'd blow up the Girl Scouts building."

"Do you really mean that?" he asked.

"Yes," I snapped. "And if I could think of something more sacred, I'd have said that."

"Do you want to hear what happened?"

"I *know* what happened. He fell and almost killed me."

"You were knocked unconscious—"

"I *know* I was knocked unconscious."

"It's a miracle it wasn't more serious, you know. Arnold—"

"I'm grateful—grateful I only sustained injuries to the head, neck, shoulder, and ankle."

"What about Tucker?" he said defensively. "He could have broken his neck. And you broke his fall." He paced. "Don't you see?"

he said excitedly. "You saved the life of the President of the United States. You ought to be proud, Herb. How many—"

"*Please.* What about this?" I gestured with my neck toward the press release.

"That?" he repeated.

"Yes. This tissue—this industrial broadloom carpet of lies. What about it?"

"I dunno," he said. "I thought it was pretty good for the middle of the night."

He grinned. He was genuinely, professionally proud of himself. That was what made Feeley innocent, no matter what outrages he perpetrated. I lay there pondering this, and my anger dissipated somewhat. Perhaps it was the medication. I could feel the fight going out of me. Being in politics requires an awful lot of resignation.

"He wants to see you," said Feeley. "I think he feels bad about what happened."

"Well, he ought to," I said. "He ought to feel extremely bad about what happened."

"Great. I've got it laid on for eleven tomorrow. We'll do pool coverage. You don't want a lot of cameras and reporters in here."

27
SAMARITAN

Am appalled by what is going on on the road.
—JOURNAL, SEPT. 28, 1992

The President profited greatly from my injury. As Feeley had predicted, the American Red Cross gave him its Great Samaritan award. Indeed, by the time the whole hubbub had died down, he had received twenty-two such humanitarian awards.

I was trotted out at these wretched award banquets like the March of Dimes child. At the appointed moment the spotlight would be turned on me and I would struggle to my feet, with my crutches and clavicle brace, and fawn gratefully in the direction of the President. Feeley called it "dynamite photo op." I called it unseemly.

One Friday afternoon we were about to fly out to Council Bluffs, Iowa, where the President was to be given another award for nearly killing me. I refused. I couldn't go through with another. There was a commotion, calls from Tucker/Reigeluth campaign headquarters saying it would cripple the Iowa effort.

"Codswallop!" I said.

Feeley soon got into the act, begging me to go. I threw my crutch at him. Finally the President called.

"Herb," he said, "I hate doing this as much as you do."

"I doubt that," I said. I had grown more independent of mind and outspoken since the Snaggle Tooth affair.

"Don't do it for me. Do it for us."

"You're appealing, I presume, to my patriotism?"

"I'm appealing to your sense of job security."

"Since you put it that way," I said huffily, "I will definitely *not* be attending tonight's banquet."

For one consequence of the whole deception was to *guarantee* my job security. It would hardly have helped the President's image to fire the "indispensable aide" whose life he had so gallantly saved.

"Herb, it's all laid on. Feeley says this sort of thing really goes over great out there. We're up three points."

So I relented, as I always did with the President, and went to Council Bluffs. It was an especially vulgar affair. To this day I break out in a rash when I hear the quotation "Greater love hath no man than this, that a man lay down his life for his friends."

The President sought to keep me happy during this period of public humiliation by giving me additional duties and responsibilities. One of those included "riding herd"—as he put it—over the staff. It proved to be an almost full-time job.

My first suggestion was that Lleland donate his yacht, the *Compassion*, to some charitable refugee organization. Needless to say, Lleland became enraged at the idea and told me to mind my own business. Feeley leaked word to the *Post* that Lleland was planning to give it to Ecuador for use as a hospital ship. He was forced to deny "an unofficial report" that he was giving his pleasure yacht to a humanitarian cause.

I kept close tabs on Charlie Manganelli those days. There had been the incident during the Democratic convention when he had threatened a reporter with bodily harm after the reporter had made disparaging remarks about the President's acceptance speech.

I had wrested speechwriting away from Withers—another payoff for attending those miserable award banquets—so I was able to keep a weather eye out.

Charlie's rhetoric had become fairly vehement. In one speech he referred to Mr. Bush as a "twit." I was all in favor of a vigorous campaign offensive, but this simply exceeded the bounds of good taste. I sent it back with the comment "Too strong by half. Change." He sent it back. He had changed "twit" to "twat."

I said, "See here, Charlie, we can't call a former Vice President either a twit or a twat. What's gotten into you anyway?"

"About half a pint of Jim Beam. Change it to fuckhead if you want. Come on over'n have a drink."

"No *thank* you," I said pointedly.

"It's after six."

"Don't you think you ought to lay off the sauce, Charlie? At least during the campaign."

"Nah," he said. "I write great, drunk. Listen to this. 'Let us join arms, not make arms.' "

"Very nice, Charlie." *Time* had called him "a young Ted Sorensen with a dash of Jimmy Breslin." Lately I feared Caliban was in danger of overwhelming Ariel.

"Fucking poetry is what it is. We'll use it in the Evangelicals speech Thursday."

"They're hawks, Charlie."

"Right. I'll throw in something about plowshares."

"Whatever," I said, "but no more name-calling."

"I'm just tired of hearing those douche bags blame everything on us," he said. "Every time some piss ant country gets invaded by Soviets, it's our fault."

I had to agree with him in principle. Bush had set the tone of the campaign with his blistering attack the day after Labor Day, calling the Great Deal a "Raw Deal" and the President's cabinet a "collection of spivs and drones." (This was especially insulting to the many highly qualified ethnic minorities in the cabinet.) He had criticized the President for refusing to send troops into Chiapas to help the Mexican government there put down the insurgency. He'd blamed us for the Soviet invasion of Pakistan, denounced the STOP Treaty as "non-verifiable"—whenever Republicans don't like something, they call it "non-verifiable." Pausing only to pronounce our tax policy "Marxist," he criticized the turnback of the U.S. naval base at Guantanamo Bay as "pandering retreatism" and the introduction of Coast Guard user fees as "undemocratic." He ended with his ominous reference to the Bermuda crisis: "I do not intend to stand by while another American vacation spot is turned into a Soviet satellite."

I suspected that Bush's dislike of the President was personally motivated. When he was Governor, Mr. Tucker had declined to attend the funeral of C. Fred Bush, the Bush family's cocker spaniel. (I had urged him to go, but he refused.)

Our chief advanceman, Leslie Dach, was showing his customary admirable zeal, but we could ill afford another episode such as the time he took it on himself to have the U.S. Fish and Wildlife dump 15,000 rainbow trout into the Allagash River a day before the President's annual fishing trip.

He was also insulting so many people in the line of duty that it was necessary to revamp our CAS (Computer Apology System).

To get some idea of what dealing with a White House advanceman is like, imagine someone bursting into your house at seven o'clock on a Sunday evening and telling you that you and your family will have to move into the basement for the next two days; that the dining-room walls will have to be knocked down for security reasons; that the dog will have to be kenneled, the walls repainted, the staircase widened, bathrooms added, the children farmed out to relatives; that part of the roof will have to be removed to accommodate the communications equipment; that you will be required to feed 450 people breakfast; and that the buzzing noise is the dogwood trees (the ones planted by your grandfather) being chain-sawed off at the stumps because they might block NBC's view of the pantry window. Advancemen are, by nature, not popular.

Our apology form now read:

Dear

The President has asked me to apologize profoundly for the unfortunate episode involving Mr. Dach's handling of (1).

He especially regrets the fact that (2).

He wants you to know that he has spoken to Mr. Dach, expressing his disappointment that such a (3) as yourself would have experienced such (4).

At the same time, he hopes you will understand the enormous pressures of Mr. Dach's job, knowing, however, that no matter what its demands, behavior such as his has no place in the Tucker administration.

With warm personal regards,

Herbert Wadlough
Assistant to the President
and Deputy Chief of Staff

One typical letter went out with the following insertions:

(1) the California Club luncheon
(2) your wife was spoken to in such a brusque manner
(3) outstanding California state legislator
(4) personal humiliation

I would choose the insertions and then have the letter written out in longhand. I think people appreciate that personal touch.

A campaign is a time of intense fraternization. You spend six, sometimes seven days a week putting in eighteen- and twenty-hour days with the same group of people. Invariably, romances form aboard the plane. I understand this. It is human nature. But eventually it became clear that things were getting out of hand.

Because of my injuries, I did not travel aboard Air Force One until late in the campaign. Joan moved back to Washington temporarily to help me during my recuperation. When I finally did "go out on the road," as they say, I was struck by the youth and attractiveness of the volunteers who manned the hotel staff offices.

How wonderful, I said to myself, *that so many young and attractive people should be getting involved in politics.* It seemed a bit odd that they were entirely female, but the Democratic party has always been in the forefront of the women's movement—unlike the Republicans—so I did not give it further thought.

One morning at six a.m. in Kansas City the real reason for this abundance of youthful pulchritude became clear. I was limping down the corridor of the Hyatt as one of the volunteers emerged from one of the rooms, wearing the shortest nightgown I have ever seen. I smiled at her and wished her a good morning. Even at the early hour I was taken with her freshness, her blond, tousled hair, her milk-warm voluptuous body.

Shame on you, Herbert Wadlough, I chuckled to myself. *If Joan were here, she'd pinch your ear.*

As I was shucking off these idle thoughts, I chanced to notice whose room it was that this sex kitten had emerged from. (The campaign always put name stickers on doors.) Bamford Lleland IV! Chief of staff to the President of the United States and "devoted" father of three.

Wouldn't Mrs. Lleland be interested to know? Of course I never told anyone.

I continued on my way to Feeley's room and knocked.

"What? Who?" came the voice from inside his room.

"It's me. Let me in." I was only fifteen minutes early.

"I'll meet you in the staff room."

"No. I need to talk to you."

"I'm in the shower."

I'd been in his room the night before, and I happened to know the bathroom was right by the door. His voice was coming from the bedroom. He was no more in the shower than I was in Cleveland.

"Is something wrong?" I demanded. "Why don't you let me in?"

"I'm getting dressed."

"For heaven's sakes, I've seen you without clothes before."

"Go away," he said. "I'll meet you in the staff room."

It is not in my nature to spy, but I positioned myself at the end of the hall where I could see the door to his room. As I was standing there, another volunteer emerged from another room, carrying her shoes, and tiptoed down the hallway. There was no need to tiptoe on the thick carpet—it was probably a conditioned reflex she had learned in front of her parents' bedroom door. After she'd rounded the corner, I hobbled down to see whose room she had just left. To my horror, it was that of a very senior White House official.

This was outrageous! Were we running a bordello or a campaign?

I renewed my hallway vigilance. After ten minutes Feeley's door opened. I recognized her immediately. She was the kind of person you remembered. I'd met her at a Young Democrats reception. She bore a resemblance to the actress Annette O'Toole. After she had disappeared into the elevator, I stormed down to Feeley's room and banged on the door loudly. This time he opened it.

"You ought to be ashamed of yourself!" I hissed.

He pretended not to understand, but I was having none of it.

"Good to have you back on the road, Herb," he said with pronounced weariness.

"Sorry! Sorry to cloud your sexual horizons! It's just that I thought we were trying to re-elect the President."

"I'm working my ass off. What do you want me to do? Sleep with Republicans?"

"Your extramarital affairs are no concern of mine."

"Then why, Herb, are we having this conversation?"

"Suppose she's a spy? Suppose she's working for the Bush people?"

"No, no, no. She worked for us in '88."

"When she was in the eighth grade?"

"Go away, Herb." He finished knotting his tie. "Remember the Golden Rule," he said. "Don't fuck anyone on your staff. But if you start"—he winked—"don't stop."

On the way home aboard Air Force One, I called Rob Dickinson, coordinator of volunteers at Tucker/Reigeluth. I told him that henceforward he was only to use women volunteers over forty years of age, or males. "No more of this teenage fluff," I said. I was in no mood to trifle.

The change was noted immediately, and my heavens, what a great gnashing of teeth and pulling of hair. You'd have thought I'd ordered everyone to wear chastity belts.

It did nothing for my popularity. People started calling me "Jonathan Edwards." Feeley said it was having a "disastrous" effect on morale. I told him it was having a far less disastrous effect on morale than a tabloid headline on the order of

COEDS VOLUNTEER
MORE THAN TIME
ON CAMPAIGN TRAIL

BOOK SIX
CRISIS

28

WE HAVE A SITUATION

Spending most days in Sit Room. Wonder if air there healthy.
Will look into.   —JOURNAL, OCT. 9, 1992

At 4:54 a.m. on Wednesday, October 7, my phone rang. It was the duty officer in the Situation Room at the White House to say that the U.S. Naval Air Station on Bermuda was "under attack" and that the President had called a meeting of the Emergency Situation Team (EST) for six a.m.

Groggily, I slipped on my clavicle brace. It's what they give you when you've broken your collarbone: a harness contraption that keeps your shoulders straight. It was soaking wet.

"Joan," I said, "why is my clavicle brace soaked?"

She told me that she'd washed it the night before.

"Well, why didn't you *dry* it?"

She said she hadn't put it in the dryer, thinking the elastic might melt.

There was nothing to do but put the wretched thing on. It was an exceedingly unpleasant sensation.

After searing the inside of my esophagus with a hurriedly gulped cup of scalding coffee—I was now drinking coffee—I had collected myself. The car arrived, and I sped off in the pre-dawn darkness.

On the way in, I reflected on the developments that had brought Bermuda to a boil.

I am not a colonialist, or a neo-colonialist, but I fervently wished Great Britain had not chosen to expel Bermuda from the Commonwealth. The status quo in Bermuda was pleasant enough: overemployment, full integration, bicameral legislature, a vigorous tourist economy. Her Majesty's government made a great to-do about how it desired her former colony to enjoy full self-determination, but the real reason was economic: Bermuda was costing the Exchequer too much in subsidies.

"Liberation," as it was exaggeratedly called, emboldened impetuous and extremist elements within Bermuda. With the benign specter of British authority removed, these elements quickly coalesced under the leadership of Mr. Makopo M'duku and all hell had been breaking loose ever since, beginning with the incident on the golf course several years earlier.

M'duku, whom a National Security Council officer had nicknamed "M-and-M," advocated expropriation of all white-held property, abrogation of the 1941 agreement between Britain and the U.S. whereby America had established her naval bases on the island, and abolition of the island's sweater retail industry, which M'duku, ardent cultural nationalist, was said to regard as demeaning.

At the White House the atmosphere was charged, electric. The corridor outside the Situation Room was crowded with admirals and Marine colonels. The smell of bacon, eggs, coffee, and fresh-baked buttermilk biscuits was in the air. I'd called the mess and told them to prepare emergency breakfast for 5:30.

Feeley greeted me with a smile entirely out of place at a quarter to six.

"You're looking exuberant," I said.

"This is fantastic."

I assumed he was talking about the breakfast. "Yes," I said, "Sanborn has outdone himself."

"Not the *food*, for Chrissake. Bermuda."

"What," I said, "is so 'fantastic' about an American base being attacked?"

"Everyone's been calling us pussies for four years. Treating this asshole M'duku like George Washington. Not saying anything when he was going to hang Wells."

One of Mr. M'duku's more intemperate statements had been his threat to hang our Consul General, Cecil Wells, from the flagpole outside the consulate. The President had written it off as "bluster," but Wells had been greatly alarmed and had asked to be recalled. The President told him it would be a "bad signal" to withdraw, and asked him to stay on and "show a little flag." Wells finally agreed, but with the most pronounced reluctance.

"Oh," said Feeley. "I called Manganelli and told him to get to work on a declaration of war."

"*What?*"

"Think I woke him out of a hangover."

I took strenuous exception to this. After all, presidential speech-writing was my bailiwick.

Feeley said, "Herb, this is no time for a turf battle."

"But *war?*" I said. "Don't you think that's a bit . . . premature?"

"We'll edit if we have to."

"God," I said. "A month before the election."

"Yeah. I just hope this thing doesn't peak too early."

It was time for the EST meeting. My clavicle brace was killing me.

"Why," yawned the President, "did they attack so early?"

Admiral Boyd, chairman of the Joint Chiefs, and Clay Clanahan of CIA, also yawning, suggested it was because the torches they were holding would look dramatic on the TV news. Feeley nodded.

The President asked about the base's integrity. General X. O. Gilhooley, commandant of the Marine Corps, said it was "watertight but not airtight." The President creased the left side of his face and asked what that meant. "It means we can hold for another few hours. Maybe three. They've breached at four points, but they were repelled."

"How?"

"Dogs, sir. They seem particularly averse to dogs."

"Good," said the President. "Let's get some more flown in. I want the place covered with dogs. Hundreds."

"Can I say something?" said Feeley.

"If it's constructive."

"You put a lot of German shepherds in there and it's going to look like Alabama in the early Sixties."

"What do you want, Feeley? Pekingese?"

"I'm saying if you want to be compared to Bull Connor, go ahead and unleash German shepherds all over the place."

"Feeley," said the President, "I'm not trying to keep Negroes from sitting at lunch counters, for Chrissake."

"Fine. Maybe you'll get off being compared to the Prime Minister of South Africa."

The President glared at him, then turned to Admiral Boyd. "Bud," he said, "is there a peaceful way of doing this? I mean, without anybody getting killed?"

Admiral Boyd and Gilhooley suggested rubber bullets and water cannon.

"Okay," said the President. "Let's go with the rubber bullets and water cannon. And don't tell me about Northern Ireland, Feeley." He turned to Edelstein. "Are we in touch with BUPI?"

Marvin said they weren't answering their phone at headquarters.

The President frowned. "Clay?"

"Most of the phones on the island are out," he said. "BUPI blew up the satellite dish two weeks ago. We've been using private channels. You want to get a message to him, we can do that."

"Tell him to give me a call," said the President. "Collect."

Feeley snorted. "Clay," he said, "if you can get a message to him, why can't you stick a grenade or something up his ass?"

Clanahan smiled. He had a gentle manner, despite all that he'd seen and done.

After issuing instructions to Edelstein, Clanahan, and Boyd, the President adjourned the meeting until noon.

The EST convened at noon. Admiral Boyd reported on an ominous development. Our P-3C aircraft were drawing small-arms fire. People were shooting at them as they came in to land.

The Orion P-3Cs are the old workhorses of America's anti-submarine warfare. They fly sorties out of Bermuda every fifteen minutes to drop sonar buoys that listen for Soviet submarines. Indeed, anti-submarine warfare was at the heart of the island's strategic value to this country.

The President sighed. "Are they doing any damage?"

"Mr. President," said the Admiral patiently, "American planes are being fired on."

"I appreciate that, Bud. But are they just plinking at them, or are they really trying to bring them down?"

From the Admiral's expression, it was obvious that the distinction was inconsequential to him. "Those are sensitive planes, sir. And if they blow out a wheel, hit a cable . . ."

The problem was that though the base was American soil—as per the 1941 agreement—the people shooting at the planes were on St. George's Island, across a stretch of water called Ferry Reach.

The President suggested landing a small assault force of Marines across the Reach to "neutralize" the snipers.

Lleland and Edelstein started shaking their heads. They said that would be tantamount to "an invasion."

"Invasion?" said the President. "We're the ones being fired on."

"Yes," said Edelstein. "But they are firing from Bermudian soil. It's one thing to defend the base, but if you start helicoptering in Marines, then you are, technically, escalating. And it could go beyond manageable dimensions."

Feeley lit a cigarette; smoke was now coming out his nose, mouth, and ears. He said, "Why are we dicking around with these people?"

"I beg your pardon?" said Edelstein, affronted.

"Not you," said Feeley, without conviction.

Edelstein suggested grounding the P-3Cs until the situation could be rectified through "dialogue." Admiral Boyd didn't like that idea at all. He said that anti-submarine warfare was a "continuum." If you stopped the flights, Soviet submarines would go undetected.

While he and Marvin disagreed, the President asked Clanahan if he'd established contact with M'duku.

Clanahan nodded. "He's not in a talkative frame of mind just now. Apparently he'll be making his position clear on the evening news tonight."

"Well, get this message through right away. Tell him this shooting has got to stop. If those men are still there by dawn tomorrow, they suffer the consequences."

"That might provoke him," said Edelstein.

"Marvin," said the President, "you're reminding me more and more of Cyrus Vance."

"Let me talk with him," said Edelstein.

Lleland spoke up in favor of the idea.

While they discussed it, Feeley leaned over and whispered, "They think it'll be good material for their books."

The third EST meeting that historic day began at nine p.m.—or, as I had begun thinking of it, at 2100 hours. Joan had brought me another clavicle brace; the other had shrunk, cutting off circulation in several major arteries and causing my arms to turn blue.

Clanahan had brought along someone whom he'd introduced simply as "Mr. Smith." Smith was short and nondescript and carried a gray briefcase that looked as if it might explode if you tried to open it.

M'duku had indeed made his demands on the evening news with all of America tuned in. Afterward he'd done a one-on-one with Barbara Walters, discussing some of his favorite movies and telling her that Gandhi had been a major influence on his political philosophy.

"Gandhi!" snorted the President, calling the meeting to order. "Well, he doesn't remind *me* of Gandhi."

"Maybe he's into enemas," said Feeley.

Clanahan reported that our Consul—the now hysterical Cecil Wells—and the entire consular staff had been moved to a safe house in Hamilton and would be evacuated by boat before dawn. The President remarked that he hated sneaking them out of there like that, but that he earnestly desired to avoid a consulate seizure. Clanahan warned him that M'duku would be sure to use the empty consulate to propaganda advantage, turning it into an "imperialist museum" or something similar. It was discussed whether to "blow" the consulate with explosives, but the idea was discarded as "too Libyan."

Marvin Edelstein reported on his plan—approved by the President—to fly down and attempt to hold talks with M'duku. Clanahan had cautioned against it on grounds that M'duku was too unpredictable. The President had considered sending Jesse Jackson. Edelstein had argued that it might introduce "too wild a card." I suspect what he really meant was he thought Jackson might steal his best

memoir chapter. I personally was disappointed that we weren't sending Jesse, though it was true he had a habit of "getting out in front,"
as they say, making the kind of concessions that had led to our
abandoning our former naval base in Guantanamo Bay, Cuba.

The Admiral reported that the sniping was continuing and that
the belly of one P-3C looked like a "tea strainer." Morale, he said,
was very low among the pilots; it was taking the edge off their sub-
hunting capabilities.

Clanahan gave us the worse news. Between 2,000 and 4,000 people were massing across the causeway separating the air base from
Hamilton parish and the main part of Bermuda.

"What are they doing?" asked the President.

"They're going to storm the base."

The room fell silent, except for the slight hissing noise caused by
the anti-bugging machine.

"When?" asked President Tucker.

"Sometime after sun-up. Apparently the BUPI leadership wasn't
satisfied with the TV coverage of the night raid, so they want this
one with proper lighting."

"Shit. Do they have weapons?" asked the President.

The CIA director handed him a sheet of paper.

The President read it. "Jesus. These are American weapons.
Where'd they get all this stuff?"

"The serial numbers trace them to Reagan administration arms
shipments to Pakistan. After the Soviet—"

"Right. Thank you." The President shook his head. The Admiral
suggested "taking out" the causeway. Edelstein objected. The Admiral counter-proposed moving the carrier *Weinberger* into Bermudian waters. Edelstein called it "gunboat diplomacy." Feeley fumed.
The President hit the desk with his pencil.

Clanahan spoke up. "Mr. Smith here has something that might
be of comfort." This was the first time I or most of the people in
the room had heard of GB-322.

The idea of putting large numbers of people to sleep struck me
at first as being eminently sensible. Feeley, however, became extremely agitated. He devotes three pages to his argument against
GB-322 in *The Outrage of Power*.

"Gas?" he said in a loud, demonstrative voice. "You want to *gas* them?"

But the President was intrigued. He pressed Mr. Smith, asking him if GB-322 was non-toxic.

The curious Mr. Smith explained, in his gray monotone, that the effects were temporary, and that the "target audience"—as he quaintly called them—would awake feeling mildly nauseated. "They won't be in the mood for politics when they come to," he said.

Feeley turned to the President and pleaded, "Boss, we're in the middle of an *election*. You want to gas people, gas them *after* November fourth. Hell, drop the big one on them. But not now— *please*."

Mr. Smith had brought slides. One showed a flock of sheep grazing. In the next one they were lying down with their legs up in the air.

"Will it work that way with people?" said the President. "I mean, are their arms and legs going to do that?"

Mr. Smith shook his head and said that was just the way sheep were.

The President asked for a vote. He went around the table. Only Feeley and Admiral Boyd objected.

"Look, let's just shoot the bastards and get it over with," said Feeley. "You know, the old-fashioned way. Why, I bet the Admiral here could—"

"I don't *want* to shoot anyone, Feeley."

"But *gas* . . ."

"People get gassed all the time. Tear gas, laughing gas, ether." He tapped his temple with his forefinger. "You know, this could be the start of a whole new ballgame. Non-lethal warfare."

Admiral Boyd shifted in his seat.

"If we solve this thing without killing anyone, Feeley, you're going to be out of a job. I won't even *need* a press secretary."

Four minutes before eleven o'clock—or at 2256 hours, as they say in the military—Operation Sandman was given the green light.

29
GB-322

Have become something of a celebrity due to appearance on *Today Show*. Joan uncomfortable with all the publicity.
—JOURNAL, OCT. 12, 1992

In the history of American military operations, there has never been one quite so successful as Sandman, nor so misunderstood.

The world greeted the news as if President Tucker had reintroduced mustard gas.

The fact that not a single person got hurt should have counted for something. President Tucker chose a course humane, yet firm. (My phrase, incidentally; Lleland stole it for the title of his Bermuda Crisis chapter, adding the question mark.)

"Barbaric," proclaimed the *London Times*. "*Méchant*," said *Le Figaro*. "*Brutto!*" cried *L'Osservatore Romano*, which carried the full text of the Pope's denunciation. *Pravda* ran the famous photograph of them all conked out across its entire front page, with a headline saying they were all dead. This from the same folks who had supplied BUPI with its weapons.

The domestic press wasn't much better. Only the *New York Post* approved, with its full-page READY, AIM, WHOOSH! The *Washington Post* editorial was titled "Jonestown Diplomacy."

The U.N. convened the Security Council. Greece introduced the resolution condemning us for "crimes against humanity." The vote was 14–1. We vetoed the resolution, but then our Ambassador to the U.N. was quoted in the *Times* as saying he had been "privately appalled" at the President's decision.

The President was truly dismayed by all this. "All I did was put them to sleep for two hours," he said.

West Wing morale was not good. Feeley looked like a man being
led to the guillotine. He wandered through the corridors of the West
Wing looking dazed.

"Feels," I said, catching up with him, "are you okay?"

He looked at me as though he didn't recognize me. I didn't like
the look in his eyes. "Yeah," he said in a faraway voice. "I'm on my
way to the press room."

"What's up?" I said cheerily.

"I have to release this. It's the chemical breakdown of GB-322."

"Are they giving you a hard time in there?"

He looked at me with his drugged look. "No. They're just asking
questions about chemical warfare. ABC wants to know if he's sent
an apology to Mrs. Outerbridge."

"Who?" I said.

"The lady who got accidentally dosed while she was making
waffles. The one who fell asleep on her waffle iron?"

"Oh, yes. Her. Dreadful."

"They're running pictures of her. Her face looks like a crossword
puzzle. Well," he sighed, "I have to go now."

I told him I'd draft something for Mrs. Outerbridge. Watching
him shuffle off to the press room, I felt sorry for poor Feels.

There were a lot of "unnamed senior White House officials" falling
all over each other in the press saying they'd tried to talk the President
out of this "rash" course of action, but I knew who they were. Lleland
adopted a superior air. Marvin rolled his eyes and spoke of dialogue.
It was a dark time for the Tucker administration. I relaxed my
prohibition on alcoholic beverages in the White House mess and
doubled the number of staff cars, knowing this would help morale.
There are times when you have to put aside your personal beliefs.

The President called for Truman biographies—he wanted to know
how Truman coped after dropping the atomic bomb. I ordered them
from the White House library, using a system whereby the library
wouldn't know who was ordering them. Some of the librarians were
holdovers from the Reagan administration. It would not have played
well if it had leaked that the President was seeking comfort in the
ashes of Hiroshima and Nagasaki.

. . .

"This is getting out of hand," the President said to me in the Oval late on the evening of October 9.

M-and-M had just given a press conference, attended by 800 reporters, denouncing the President as "a war criminal."

"At least I'm in Henry Kissinger's league," he said, looking out the window. We could hear the demonstrators chanting in the distance. "Maybe I should go talk to them," he said. "You know, like Nixon did." The idea was quickly dismissed.

To his credit, the President stood firm. The following exchange occurred during the press conference of October 10.

> Joel Ackerman, NBC: The world community has condemned your use of chemical-warfare agents in quelling the Bermuda uprising. In light of this, do you feel you owe the world an apology?
> The President: No.
> Ackerman: That's—would you care to expand on that?
> The President: Let me get this straight: the world wants me to apologize for saving American lives from a mob without killing anyone?
> Ackerman: But in using gas, haven't you lowered the chemical threshold so that this kind of warfare is more likely?
> The President: Frankly, Mr. Ackerman, I prefer this kind of warfare to the alternatives.

The President went on to make a very persuasive case for the use of GB-322 instead of bullets, rockets, napalm, and the like, but it was lost in the emotionalism that had enveloped the Sandman controversy. The headline in the *Washington Post* the next day announced:

TUCKER FAVORS CHEMICAL WARFARE

Petrossian's polls showed an alarming trend. The President was down six to eight points in his strongholds—the urban Northeast, the upper Midwest, the industrial mid-Atlantic states—but he was up an astonishing fifteen percent in the South.

Hump Scruggs, our Southern strategist, called in. "Gawdamnawmighty," he said, "the Klan is fixin' to endorse him!"

I didn't even pause to get details. I called Manganelli. "Drop whatever you're doing and get cranking on a vicious attack on the Ku Klux Klan," I said.

"The *Klan?* Everyone knows our position on—"

"They're fixin' to endorse him!"

There was a pause on the other end. "Herb," he said, "why are you talking with a Southern accent?"

I explained the situation, and told him to drop a one-page insert into the noon speech before the Asian-American society, a business group.

"It's a foreign-policy speech, Herb. It doesn't make any sense to attack the Klan in the middle of a discussion of our Pacific Rim."

"Charlie," I said, "I don't care if it doesn't flow. Use a lot of conjunctions. Now let's have one page of insert. And don't hold any punches."

I told Feeley about it. He slumped in a chair. "At this point," he said, "any endorsement would help."

The Asian businessmen were somewhat mystified to find themselves being treated to an unusually virulent denunciation of the Ku Klux Klan, but the Klan did not go ahead with its endorsement, and afterward the President thanked me for avoiding a potential disaster.

Three days after Sandman, BUPI announced the first "deaths."

The sealed coffins of the six "martyrs" were buried amidst full BUPI pomp on the fifteenth hole of what had formerly been the exclusive Mid-Ocean Club golf course. M-and-M gave the eulogy, denouncing the "American genocide" and calling the President "The Great Pestilence." Ironically, the Mid-Ocean Club was situated in a part of Bermuda known as Tucker's Town. It was now renamed Uhuruville.

We had been warned by Clanahan that they might try something like this.

As soon as BUPI announced that their people had been "poisoned" by GB-322, we asked the International Red Cross to investigate. The Red Cross agreed, but of course BUPI quickly refused, on the grounds that we had infiltrated the Red Cross with CIA agents. The Soviet Union, which steadfastly refuses to allow the Red Cross into any of the countries it invades, seized on this and echoed the denunciation. Indeed, the ties between the Soviet Union and Bermuda were improving daily. This was a valuable lesson. President Tucker confessed to me he was surprised by the developments and was "learning a lot" about the Soviet Union.

This nonsense over empty coffins should have been dismissed as propaganda, but the charismatic M-and-M had been so successful in portraying this as a David-versus-Goliath showdown that a lot of the world believed it.

George Bush was busy saying it was a time for "America to pull together behind the President," a shrewd tactic. The fact was he had broken a Senate tie back in 1983 and voted for the production of nerve gas. *He* wasn't about to start throwing canisters.

At the next EST meeting the discussion centered on neutralizing the "martyr maneuver." Secretary of State Holt—who seemed to regard the Bermuda crisis as a nuisance distracting him from the Middle East—said we had to discredit the tactic. No one disagreed. Clanahan and Edelstein concurred. There was consensus. The President then made the bold and extraordinary proposal that he be gassed on live television with GB-322.

For the first time since the morning of Sandman, Feeley displayed enthusiasm. He said it might "reverse everything." I opined that it would certainly be dramatic, if un-presidential.

There was passionate and heated discussion. Admiral Boyd opposed the idea in the strongest language I had ever heard him use. His Brooklyn accent became more and more pronounced. At one point he called it a "lunatic" idea, which in my view was improper, but the President did not take exception.

Boyd's arguments weighed on the President. But he was intrigued by his idea. Someone proposed gassing the Vice President instead. This idea had broad support, but after discussion the President vetoed it on the grounds that the press knew he didn't like the Vice President. "They wouldn't consider it a sacrifice," he said. "It has to be someone close to me."

Two days later I found myself in the NBC studios with Bryant Gumbel. Feeley had insisted on Gumbel, in part because he is black and Feels thought he would appeal to Bermudians, but also because he projects an affability that Feeley felt would offset the "chemical warfare" aspect of the show.

My gassing on the *Today Show* received a Nielsen rating of 13.2, with an audience share of 33, meaning that 27 million television sets were tuned in. In addition, Vision of America broadcast the event live around the world. When I woke up—feeling quite refreshed, I might add—Gumbel said, "Thank you, Herb, from all of us."

My celebrity was a mixed blessing. There were those who chose not to believe I had volunteered for the demonstration. In some cases I have to conclude the motivation was jealousy. Lleland said in his book that I "had to be dragged, whimpering, to the NBC studio . . . like a child being taken to the dentist." It is hardly necessary to dignify that vile canard by saying there is not a mote of truth to it.

The press scoffed. Patrick Buchanan of *The New York Times* said in his column, "If President Tucker wanted to rectify the catastrophe he has brought about in the North Atlantic, he should have used more potent vapors—on Mr. Wadlough and his other advisers." I thought it was mean-spirited of him to say such a thing.

The splenetic Michael Kramer of *New York* magazine attacked me personally, writing, "With this feat of derring-doze, Wadlough is striving to expand his portfolio. No longer content with the role of presidential baggage handler, he has now staked his claim to a more exalted post: administration guinea pig."

Despite this sort of carping, my *Today Show* appearance had a significant impact. GB-322 was seen for the harmless substance it was, the Uhuruville burials came under suspicion, and for the first time since the crisis began, M-and-M and BUPI were on the defensive.

Great Britain introduced a resolution in the U.N. calling for exhuming the Uhuruville coffins under internationally supervised auspices. When M-and-M announced that the former U.S. Consulate would be turned into the People's Museum of American War Atrocities, our foreign-policy people took it as a sign that his offensive had "gone theatrical." BUPI snipers continued to take occasional potshots at our P-3Cs, but the mob remained on the other side of the causeway, content with its bonfires and nocturnal chanting against the Great Pestilence.

Back home, the Republicans were doing their own chanting, accusing President Tucker of impotence and of not defending America's interests "the old-fashioned way."

Marvin, meanwhile, kept pressing the President to reactivate the plan to send him down to Bermuda to hold talks with M-and-M; Marvin's mission kept getting postponed at Clanahan's urging, due to the volatility of the situation.

On October 12, the sixth day of the crisis, the President finally instructed Marvin Edelstein to send a communiqué to M-and-M indicating our willingness to talk, but added, "No funny business, Marvin."

After our meeting Feeley followed the President back to the Oval and tried to talk him out of sending Marvin to Bermuda. "Anyone," he said, "send *anyone* except him." But the President said that Marvin was his NSC director and that it was decided.

Walking out, Feeley muttered, "No good will come of this."

Marvin devoted the last third of *Power, Principle, and Pitfall* to the Bermuda crisis. I found it as interesting as some other novels I have read.

At the next meeting Marvin reported that M-and-M was anxious for a meeting "He sounds like a reasonable man," he said. The Admiral, Gilhooley, Feeley, Clanahan, and I looked at each other.

"He'd better be," said the President.

Tucker wanted the meeting to be private and on board a ship. Marvin wanted it to be a media event. He maintained that the public pressure would be a "salubrious influence" on M-and-M. And he wanted to walk across the causeway separating the naval base from the BUPI encampment "as a symbol of U.S. willingness to reach out."

Admiral Boyd murmured that he'd like to reach out to M-and-M with a "wing of F-20s." An argument erupted between Marvin and Boyd which the President had to quell.

Lleland offered the use of the *Compassion* for the meeting. A shouting match erupted between Feeley and Lleland which the President had to quell.

These arguments probably played a fateful role. The President was so weary of the divisions among his staff and so anxious to solve the Bermuda affair, which had seriously affected his re-election campaign, that he approved Marvin's plan. In a calmer atmosphere he might have made a more judicious decision.

Watching the start of Marvin's "Long Walk"—as the networks dubbed it—across the causeway, even one as skeptical as I was filled with a sense of history and optimism.

Trailing him, sufficiently behind so as to be out of camera range, were his two deputies, Cromattie and Baum. (I later learned that Marvin had told them to walk thirty paces behind him; clearly, this was to be *his* walk.)

M-and-M and his cohort met him at the other end. Following the greeting ceremony, Marvin and M-and-M climbed into his Jeep and, with M-and-M at the wheel and half the world's press following, drove off. But not, as planned, to his headquarters at People's House. "The Long Walk" turned out to be a long gangplank.

30
*ESTI*MATIONS OF MORTALITY

Things sticky. —JOURNAL, OCT. 13, 1992

If you look closely at the TV footage of M-and-M roaring back
across the causeway in the direction of the naval base, you can tell
by Marvin's expression that he was stunned by what was happening.
(I never disputed that much.) There was also that tense, memorable
moment when it appeared that M-and-M was going to charge the
front gate: the Marines cocking their weapons, their confused looks
as they wondered whether they should also shoot the director of the
National Security Council. When M-and-M started giving Marvin
a tour of the site of the "massacre" instead of charging the base, the
soldiers were greatly relieved.

The only ones relieved.

As M-and-M, with a mute Marvin in tow, began pointing out
spots along Kindley Field Road where the "martyrs" had fallen
during Operation Sandman, my phone rang. It was the President.
His voice was a croak. "Better get everyone in here," he said.

I canceled the President's appointments for that afternoon. Together with Feeley and Lleland—Clanahan arrived shortly—we
watched the events of that stressful day unfold on television.

There was not much talking during the wreath-laying ceremony
at the Uhuruville cemetery. By this time Marvin clearly realized
that he'd been had. Unfortunately, that did not project on TV.
During the playing of the revolutionary anthems and the nineteen-
gun salute, the President leaned forward and shouted at the screen,
"Frown, god-dammit—frown!"

The next stop on the itinerary was the April 17 Re-education
Facility, formerly the Ocean View Golf and Country Club. I re-

member well the President's expression as M-and-M ushered Marvin
into that room where dozens of former sweater magnates now spent
their days sewing uniforms for the BUPI Revolutionary Guards. He
looked like a man on the verge of a stroke. The spectacle was a
distressing one, and sure to inflame Republican voters. The incident
involving Mr. Brown—one of the imprisoned magnates—spitting on
Marvin and being rifle-butted by the guards was especially unfortunate. Feeley made low groaning sounds.

The President said quietly, "Get him on the phone."

This turned out not to be immediately feasible. The White House
advance team had not installed phones at these places since they
were hardly on the itinerary, and the kind of talk the President
desired to have with his NSC director would have been imprudent
to conduct on a line supplied by BUPI.

Urgent messages were dispatched to the naval base. I found myself in unproductive—and extremely vexing—conversation with a
BUPI "communications officer." By the time the messenger from
the base arrived at the Re-education camp, the Jeepcade had departed
for the next stop. Clanahan and the President discussed the possibility of "complicating" the itinerary—CIA talk, I presume, for sab-
otaging this ridiculous dog-and-pony show. Though my views on
the use of force are a matter of record, at this point I would have
favored "complicating" M-and-M's little tour with a low-yield nuclear device.

The next stop, of course, was the former American consulate on
former Par-La-Ville Road. Here the *leitmotif* was Iranian, with
M-and-M leading a now-zombielike Marvin through the rooms of
the former "spy nest," pointing out various telex machines and des-
canting upon their counterrevolutionary functions. At one point he
held up a calculating machine and began denouncing *it* as a "spy
tool." Clanahan burst out laughing. The President did not join in.

By now his anger and frustration had spent themselves. He merely
rubbed the bridge of his nose as he watched the TV. He did show
some evidence of renewed interest when M-and-M announced that
the consulate would henceforward become the October 7 Political
Consciousness and Physical Fitness Center.

The President took a call from Sig Beller, our campaign manager.

I did not listen in, but the gist of it was clear enough from the number of times the President had to ask Sig not to resign.

The President finally reached Marvin as they were leaving the consulate. The Navy had dispatched a portable KYX-2 field-unit scrambler. M-and-M, on learning that Marvin was about to have a conversation with the President, insisted on being permitted to send the President his "warm personal regards." This was relayed to the President. The suggestion was quickly vetoed.

The first several minutes he was on the phone with Marvin, the President expressed himself freely. My notes of the conversation show that the word "idiot" occurred twice. When that phase of the discussion had ended, the President told Marvin to get back to Washington "on the double."

But Marvin was not eager to be recalled with his portfolio between his legs, so to speak. He went to work on the President, telling him that to retreat now would be to accept humiliating defeat. The President replied that defeat would be a "relief" compared to this.

At this point Marvin told him that he was "on the verge of a breakthrough."

The President expressed mirth of a sardonic variety.

Marvin said that M-and-M was putting on the show for domestic consumption, and that once they sat down at the bargaining table, "the concessions [would] flow like honey."

I wondered at the metaphor, since honey does not flow easily. As the President listened to this tommyrot, Feeley and I made frantic hand gestures. Clanahan, also listening in, tapped his foot. Lleland, on another phone, merely nodded as if listening to Pericles.

"Now's our chance," said Marvin in his best Alliance-for-Progress tone, "to prove we meant what we said in our inaugural."

Feeley grunted, " 'Our'?" Marvin was always doing this, trying to make the President feel he was breaking promises by not following his advice.

He told the President that M-and-M wasn't anti-American, that he was just trying to keep his constituency happy. "He knows whole chunks of the Bill of Rights by heart," he said. "He's been quoting them to me in the Jeep."

Feeley, working on an embolism the size of a golf ball, broke into

the conversation and started screaming at Marvin. The President
had to order him off the line. Marvin concluded his plea by telling
the President that M-and-M was a "vibrant personality."

The President scowled. "Then you better pray," he said, "he does
a lot of vibrating soon. And no more sightseeing, you got that?"

Marvin said there were no further stops on the schedule, and
with that the conversation ended. Feeley would later tell me this
was the moment he finally knew the Tucker Presidency was "cooked."

In his own memoir, *The Sorrow and the Power*, President Tucker
writes that once Marvin arrived in Bermuda, the die was cast, and
that to recall him, as his "closest" advisers urged him to do, would
only have "ratified a disaster." While I always admired the President's capacity for not giving up, perhaps a diplomatic "disaster"
would have been preferable to what ensued.

After he had hung up, the President sat without speaking for a
moment or two. He smiled wanly, buzzed for his steward, Aquinas,
and asked if anyone would like anything.

"Barbiturates," said Feeley.

The "concessions" Marvin had been so confident of did not mater-
ialize over the next three days. The international press, meanwhile,
spoke of the negotiations at People's House in Versailles Conference–
like language, building a supercharged atmosphere that had the world
thinking its future depended on what Marvin and M-and-M had for
lunch.

The President was denounced in the British Parliament for "con-
doning" the "inhumane" treatment of former British subjects. The
Soviet and East Bloc countries found the President's handling of the
matter "statesmanlike," causing great worry in the West Wing.

Tucker and Marvin spoke three, four times a day. The President
would press for something tangible, and Marvin would tell him that
the atmosphere was "encouraging" and so forth. The Joint Chiefs
looked gloomier every day. The afternoon of the second day, the
President called Marvin from Chicago after an especially disagreeable
demonstration outside the hotel. His patience was ebbing.

"Why," he said after listening to Marvin's report, "can't you get
some of the sweater people released or something?" Marvin replied

that M'duku considered them an "internal matter" and that he hesitated to inject it into the negotiations over the bases.

He then told the President that M-and-M was willing to renew the base's lease for one billion dollars.

The President winced.

"I think we should take it," said Marvin. "And he's willing to let us claim we bargained him down from four."

Grinding his molars, the President said, "Our lease on that land—which did not even *exist* before we dredged it up—expires fifty years from now."

"Not the way Commander M'duku sees it."

"I don't care if he sees purple hippos. I've bent over backwards for this clown, and every time I've had something unpleasant shoved up my ass. Now you tell him I'm in a nasty mood, Marvin, in a neo-colonial kind of mood, and that you don't know *what* the hell I'm capable of when I'm like this, but if he's smart he will cessate fucking with me."

He certainly was exercised. The veins on his neck were bulging above the top of his bulletproof Kevlar undershirt. We now wore this most everywhere, even to small receptions.

The President concluded that conversation by telling Marvin his "visa" was good for twenty-four hours. In his book Marvin claims this put "intolerable" pressure on the negotiations, precipitating subsequent developments.

They spoke five times the next day. Each time the President's blood pressure shot up and he would mutter the word "honey" with a sort of "Rosebud" inflection that frankly worried me.

The last call to Chicago came shortly after seven p.m. Central time.

"Five hundred million," said Marvin. "He'll do it for five hundred million. And we can *still* claim we screwed him down from four bil."

If M-and-M had been more "romantic"—to borrow Clay Clanahan's phrase—in his dealings with Thomas Tucker, the President might have agreed to the settlement. But this was not seduction, it was what law-enforcement people call "penetration."

"Get on the plane, Marvin," sighed the President.

Three hours later we were flying home on Air Force One. The President was holding a drink and staring out the window. "I should have made him Secretary of State," he mused, watching the strobe light on the end of the starboard wing. "He shows a remarkable talent for lobbying on behalf of countries that don't like us very much."

Somewhere over eastern Virginia he was handed a message saying that our naval air station on Bermuda was again under attack.

31
DESPERATE MOLAR

New and unpleasant ingredient has been added to this already
unsavory stew.   —JOURNAL, OCT. 15, 1992

"You know that scene in *The Longest Day*," said the President, "where the two Germans in the bunker look out and see the whole horizon covered with ships? I want it like that."

Admiral Boyd, sullen from four years of defense-budget cutting, replied, "I don't know if we have enough Navy left to cover the horizon."

"Then use tankers or whatever and paint them gray. I want him to look out his window in the morning and shit in his pants."

The Admiral pointed out that in order to be visible from M'duku's bedroom window, the Task Force would have to situate itself on top of a coral reef.

"Then put them so he can see them from his dining-room window."

Surveillance photographs were consulted, revealing that his dining-room windows looked out on his garden. The President declared that he wanted the garden defoliated.

We were in the Situation Room. It was past four in the morning and I was very tired, but there was a lot to do. Feeley had taken on martial airs—from having spent so much time with admirals and Marine generals—and had taken to walking around with his telescoping display-chart pointer in the manner of an English colonel. He kept repeating the phrase "Americans love a crisis." It was a sort of mantra he had devised for the occasion.

Throughout the night there had been discussion of sending in an "extraction team" from Fort Bragg to rescue Marvin and the hapless Cromattie and Baum. But there was no consensus on the point. M-and-M was disputing our charge that he was holding them hostage, saying that since it was impossible to get through to the airfield—which his troops were besieging—they would remain his "honored guests" at People's House for the duration of the "unpleasantries." Every so often the former Cedric Pudlington in Makopo M'duku bubbled to the surface.

The phones, of course, were down—cut by "elite Imperial American commandos," as BUPI claimed—so there was no communicating with Marvin, but Clanahan's "assets" were reporting that People's House resembled a fortress more than a governor's residence.

It was uncertain whether a rescue raid would aggravate or alleviate the situation.

There were some who wanted to leave Marvin where he was. General Gilhooley kept saying, "Well, if he's their *guest* . . ." Feeley began laughing. When the President asked him what was so funny, Feeley said it was the thought of Marvin having his toenails pulled out one by one. Everyone in the room denies having laughed at this, but the truth of the matter is that only Lleland did not. But then he never laughed.

It was then the President decided to approve the extraction mission, code-named Desperate Molar. It is possible that Feeley's joke was inadvertently responsible for that approval. I think that, despite everything, the President was disturbed by the thought of Marvin's toenails being pulled out.

Emissaries from Secretary of State Holt continued to arrive. The Secretary had determined that the Middle East might survive another week or so without his constant attention and had deigned to give the impending war in the North Atlantic some of his time. He, of course, was opposed to doing anything about it. "There are no instant solutions," he told the President. For a moment I thought there might be a scene, but then the President said in a quiet voice, "Thank you, Darius," and resumed questioning the Admiral about how many Rangers could be parachuted into the town of Hamilton.

Toward five a.m. all the elements of the "land-sea interface"—as the Admiral referred to it—were finalized. Boyd told the President the operation would involve over 30,000 men. "About all we have left," he mumbled.

"Thank you, Admiral," said the President. "I'll try to return them to you in good condition."

The Pentagon had code-named the operation Certain Fury, but the President preferred Extreme Displeasure—he thought it more understated, yet just as emphatic. He had also dropped his insistence on defoliating M'duku's garden. "I don't want to appear vindictive," he said. "You have to think about history."

With that, the session adjourned. I looked at the clock over the door. It read 5:45 a.m. I was filled with a sense of history, but I also had a slight headache.

After a few hours' sleep on my couch I dragged myself to my desk and spent most of the morning going over Charlie's draft of the President's address to the nation that evening. It needed toning down. Charlie had worked himself into a lather. There was one too many quotes from Henry V's "Once more unto the breach" speech; and anyway the President's tongue did not curl easily around Shakespeare. I also asked Charlie to beef up the supportive references to Marvin. His first draft had not even mentioned him by name, referring only to "U.S. personnel."

Charlie did not take well to my speech suggestions. The problem was that I knew more than he did about the TOP SECRET/TYPHOON-classified Extreme Displeasure than he, but was not at liberty to discuss it. After we had barked at each other for fifteen minutes or half an hour, I solved the problem by informing him I was no longer "suggesting" the changes.

He called me a "wimp."

I was not in the mood to be spoken to this way by a speechwriter.

I reminded him of what John Ehrlichman had told one of Nixon's speechwriters: "You writer types are a dime a dozen."

"So were Nixon's speeches," he snarled. "At least Ehrlichman had balls."

"Now, Charlie—"

"Go on, give it to Peterson. He'll give it that nice, simpering touch you like."

I made a note to look into Charlie's medication. I didn't think they were giving him enough of the pills that calmed him down.

At 3:10 p.m. I got a call from Clay Clanahan. "Something's just come up," he said. "I don't want to be the one to tell him."

I knew it must be bad.

"Guess who's in Bermuda," he said.

I hadn't a clue.

"First Brother."

I wasn't sure I wanted to tell the President either. Dan Tucker had arrived on the vexed island—by boat.

Clanahan's people had him under surveillance. Apparently he had gone straight to the Chancery building on Front Street that was serving as the Political Office of BUPI. Clay didn't know what he was doing in there, but he had a few ideas.

The President was briefing Speaker of the House Ferraro and the congressional leadership on Extreme Displeasure when I slipped into the Oval to give him the news.

From the look on Ms. Ferraro's face, the briefing was not going well. I managed to catch the President's eye and convey to him that I had something important for him.

"Well?" he said after they'd left.

I told him. He walked over to his desk and didn't say anything for a few moments.

"Remind me, Herb, is he still a Muslim?"

"No, sir. He's been living in Michigan with the Bhagwan."

"Oh, yes," he sighed. "That's right. He sent me some of their cheese for Christmas. It wasn't bad, actually. Little lumpy. Card said they make it from beans."

I felt badly for him.

32
URGENT LAUNDRY

Must speak with Herb Junior about his grades, stealing, etc.
—JOURNAL, OCT. 16, 1992

I slept on the couch in my office the night of the President's historic address. I was awoken shortly before six by a banging sensation on my forehead. It was Firecracker. He was in his pajamas and was carrying about four pounds of comic books. He got in under the blanket and handed me the comic books. Thus I began one of the most decisive days in American history by reading aloud from *Newbold the Wonder Slug* and *Titanium Kid*.

The spectacle of a U.S. Naval Task Force steaming at full speed toward Bermuda had certainly caught the world's attention. The morning papers were full of reaction to the President's speech. I winced at the *Post* headline, AMERICA GOES TO WAR. I hadn't recalled anything in the President's speech about war. Though he had made it clear he was no longer in a mood to be trifled with, the true mission of Extreme Displeasure remained a secret. The purpose of the speech was to persuade M-and-M that if this nonsense continued he might end up on the business end of the battleship *New Jersey*'s sixteen-inch guns.

The Soviet Ambassador, Vassily Kritkin, relatively new to Washington, arrived at nine. He was a stout fellow with watery eyes and strong cologne. He suffered from some skin condition and was constantly scratching. (I had advised him on some ointments.)

He had come to warn the President that the Soviet Union would be "forced to respond" in the event of a U.S. attack on Bermuda. The President nodded and steered the conversation toward the Ambassador's eczema or whatever it was, which seemed to throw the

Ambassador off guard. The interview concluded with the President giving him a good whack on the back and admonishing him, "Don't be a stranger." I saw to it that he left with several boxes of White House matches. Those always sent the Ambassador off with a smile.

Shortly after ten I received a call from the Uniformed Secret Service division saying I was needed "urgently" in room 103 of the Executive Office Building. There had been "an incident."

When I arrived I found two officers restraining Charlie and attempting to soothe him. He had each of them by their ties and was saying belligerent things to them. One of the White House medical staff had a blood-pressure sleeve around Charlie's arm. Charlie had a wild look in his eyes. His hair was mussed and he was breathing heavily.

Another officer told me that he thought Robin Peterson would be "all right" but that he had been taken to George Washington University Hospital just "to have some X-rays taken."

He said they had been called by Peterson's secretary, who told them "Mr. Manganelli is in with Mr. Peterson and there are strange banging sounds going on."

I was not able to get much from Charlie—he was in quite a state. But clearly the problem was the speech. I'd asked Peterson to rework Charlie's draft. He'd done a perfectly workmanlike job, and had added the line "We must never shrink from force, just as we must never force others to shrink from us," with its Kennedyesque echoes. Charlie, however, took strong exception to it. Writers are a sensitive lot—too sensitive, in my opinion.

After bundling Charlie off to Bethesda, I called Dr. Saladino at George Washington. There was no serious damage to Peterson, nothing broken, just a swollen lower lip and a bruise below the left eye. I told him of the need for discretion, and he assured me the matter would remain "private." Very agreeable man.

At one o'clock Clanahan called me. "More good news," he said. "Cain is making a speech this afternoon on TV." Cain was our private code word for Dan Tucker.

I really did not feel like being the one to tell the President this. We argued for five minutes about whose job it was. It was a truly inverse Washington phenomenon: two top-level government officers, each trying to convince the other one that he was closer to the President. Of course, I *was* closer; it was just not a distinction I felt at the moment like enjoying. In the end we tossed a coin. I did the tossing and it came out heads. Clanahan had said tails. He didn't believe me. So we set up a conference call with Marshall Brement, a mutual and trusted friend and Assistant Secretary of State for Political Affairs. Without telling Marshall what was at stake, we had him toss. I lost.

"More good news," I said, walking into the Oval Office, trying to sound as perky as popcorn. The President did not take the news well.

Feeley spent an hour on the phone trying to convince the U.S. networks not to carry the speech live. Hah!

Even now, years later, I sometimes dream about that speech. Joan tells me she knows I've been having the dream when I begin hurling pillows at the dresser.

I watched Dan's speech with the President and Feeley in the Oval. It was just the three of us. He didn't want anyone else.

I don't know what made Dan tick, but his clock was not working properly. I don't know if he ever would have made good his promise to immolate himself in public the moment the first U.S. landing craft or paratrooper hit Bermudian soil. The point was that M-and-M might not have given him the option of changing his mind. The President convened another session of the EST.

My heart went out to the man. Here he was doing everything in his power to keep the North Atlantic from becoming a war zone, and now his baby brother was threatening to douse himself with gasoline and light a match to himself.

The President apologized to the EST members for the "awkwardness" of the situation. I thought I caught a faint trace of a smirk on Lleland's face. Admiral Boyd and Gilhooley seemed to have a hard time looking the President in the eye. I think they pitied the man too.

The situation did not require much discussion. Admiral Boyd was directed to assemble another extraction team and to coordinate with Clanahan. The operation was code-named Urgent Laundry, and was to be given priority over Desperate Molar—a fact which obviously grated on Marvin, to judge from his book.

M-and-M's forces, emboldened by Dan's promise of self-immolation, pressed the attack on the base throughout the day. The President was kept in direct contact with the Pentagon. The fighting was fiercest at the main gate and along Kindley Field Road. Gilhooley wanted to "blow" the causeway, cutting off the base from the western end of the island, but the President refused, saying he did not want to escalate the conflict. This was admirable restraint, I thought. Gilhooley did not see it that way.

"Then can we at least give them a dose of 322?"

But the President did not want to use GB-322 again. His appetite for chemicals had been ruined; besides, there was the other danger. "General," he said, "if they so much as get a whiff of that stuff, you know what they might do to Mr. Edelstein?"

From his silence it was clear General Gilhooley was indifferent to the fate of Marvin's toes.

"We just need to hold twelve hours longer, Gilhooley."

"Sir, we may not have twelve hours."

"Have you tried the hoses?"

Gilhooley sighed. "The water pistols. Yes, Mr. President. We have. And those people appear to be enjoying themselves."

"Good, good," said the President. "I'm glad there's something redeeming about all this."

All day the giant C-7A Universe cargo jets roared in and out of the base continuously on their secret missions, setting the stage for Operation Extreme Displeasure. I'm told by those who were there that it was a sight to rival the Berlin airlift.

Toward seven p.m., with the fleet only five hours from rendezvous point Sierra off St. George's, the fence along runway ten was breached. This was the scene of the heroic repulse by Master Sergeant Stephen Wagner.

Wagner directed his men to charge the attackers with the firefighting trucks. Outnumbered nearly ten to one, he and his unit foamed the invaders to a standstill until reinforcements arrived to complete the repulse with rubber bullets and tear gas.

One of the President's happiest duties as commander-in-chief was pinning on Wagner's Bronze Star with V device in the Rose Garden.

In the midst of all this my wife, Joan, called. "Herb," she said, "I'm worried about Herb, Junior."

"Joan," I said, "this is not a good time."

"He bought a crossbow at Sears."

"Joan, *where* did he get the money to buy a crossbow at Sears from?"

"That's just it. I think he's stealing from my purse."

"Joan, you're going to have to cope with this. I can't—"

"You remember what he did with that slingshot."

"All right, tell him to put it away. I'll speak with him when I get home."

"When will *that* be? You haven't been home—"

"*Goodbye,* Joan."

Shortly after midnight we boarded the motorcade for the Pentagon. The President wanted what he called a "no-frills" motorcade, so we went in just ten vehicles, not counting motorcycles. We reached the Pentagon seven minutes later, and a few minutes after that we were ushered into the National Military Command Center. It sometimes goes by the name "the War Room."

"Welcome to Ground Zero," said a general to me with a Disneyland smile. I suppose it was just his way of trying to make me comfortable, but I found it unsettling.

Behind a glass plate there were men working at computer terminals. In the center of them stood a gray metal box latched shut with seven padlocks, each one a different color. I didn't even ask what was in it, but I had a pretty good idea. I noticed that each time the door to the NMCC opened, a sign lit up saying: THIS ROOM NOT SUITABLE FOR SENSITIVE CONVERSATION.

If truth be told, the place gave me the heebie-jeebies. I said to myself, *Steady now, Wadlough, your country needs a cool head,* but that only made me more nervous. I was beginning to think I might not be cut out for government service.

After a half-hour the motorcade was sent back to the White House with an advanceman sitting in the President's car. Soviet intelligence monitors motorcade movements, and we did not want them to know we were staying at the Pentagon until Operations Desperate Molar and Urgent Laundry were complete.

At exactly 0207 hours Eastern Standard Time the President gave the go-ahead order. I felt a little chill as he said to Admiral Boyd, "Let's do it."

The Admiral had offered the President CVM, or Continuous Visual Monitoring of the operations. Small TV cameras with infrared capability embedded in the headgear of selected commandos could instantly relay the picture up onto the six screens in the NMCC. The President had declined, however; "This isn't the Superbowl," he'd said. He did agree, however, to CAM, Continuous Audio Monitoring. Through headphones we would be able to hear the sounds of Desperate Molar and Urgent Laundry.

The President was too nervous to listen to his brother's rescue mission, so we both would be tuned in to Desperate Molar.

It started with a *whop-whop-whop* noise, followed by a *zzzzzzt* as the Alpha Group commandos rappelled out of the helicopters to the sound of heavy breathing. Then there was some thumping, followed by a most awful gurgling noise, which I took to be some wretch having his source of oxygen curtailed. I winced.

Steady, Wadlough, I said to myself.

More thumping followed. Then there was a series of noises that sounded like someone with a lisp trying to say "Stop." A military aide explained that those were silenced machine-pistol shots. Each *thupp* was followed by an "Unh!" or, in some cases, an "Ah!"

There were quite a few more *thupp* noises. Then some muffled explosions followed by coughing. Then a voice.

"Who are *you?*"

I have never been so pleased to hear Marvin's voice.

"Come on!"

"Wait a minute—"

"Hurry! Hurry! Keep down!"

"I can't leave like this."

Then there were loud explosions. An alarm. Barking. A siren.

"I'm in the middle of nego—"

That was the last we heard of Marvin. There was an abrupt
"Unnnh!" followed by the sound of something being dragged. I
deduced that something was Marvin. The major leading the operation had apparently elected not to stand about and discuss it with
him.

Thereafter the soundtrack was chaos. Shooting and shouting and
barking and screaming and a series of "Move it, move it!" After the
most excruciating length of time the *whop-whop-whop* returned. Distant at first, it grew louder until it overwhelmed the explosions and
shouting.

"His legs!" I heard through the *whop*ping. Then, "Go! Go! Go!"
as the helicopter blades grew louder, almost deafening.

Suddenly there were two shots, close together. A groan. Someone
shouted, "Major!"

There was a crunch that jolted me. The sound of breath going
out. The *whop-whop* of the helicopters faded and soon there were
only voices, a distant barking, and the croaking of tree frogs.

"Sir? Mr. Wadlough? Mr. Wadlough."

I opened my eyes. A colonel had his hand on my shoulder. He
gently lifted the phones off my head.

"They're safe," he said. "They're on their way back to the carrier."

I looked over at the President. He had never before sent men to
their death, nor had I ever seen him weep before.

I whispered at one of the generals to find out if the President's
brother was safe yet.

He shook his head and asked me if I cared to listen in. I wasn't
especially anxious to, but if something went wrong, I felt it would
be better if the President heard it from me.

The First Brother was in another house, the former Cabinet building on Front Street. It was even more heavily guarded than People's
House. Of the two missions, it was the dicier.

I put on the earphones and right away heard a lot of *thup*ping.
Doors were being kicked in to the accompaniment of shouting. They
hadn't found him yet.

Wincing at every "Unh!" that indicated a deceasing BUPI guard,
I listened as the Alpha Group team swarmed through the rooms. It

was almost as harrowing as being there. Little droplets of perspiration beaded over my upper lip.

Presently I heard what sounded like several zippers being rapidly fastened at the same time, followed by a spate of "ooh"s and clumping sounds. Then two loud *phoomps*—concussion grenades, so the General said—went off.

Burst of *thupp* noises.

"We're American! It's all right!"

I could not make out the next words, but they sounded like chanting of a religious sort. Then I realized: it was Dan. He was safe!

"Put that down, Mr. Tucker!"

"Oh light, oh truth, oh, Baba. . . ."

Baba?

"Don't do that, Mr. Tucker!"

"Baba—AHHHHH!!" There was a *whoomp*. The sounds of scuffling. A great *phoosh*ing; then nothing but heavy breathing and running footsteps. Two minutes later the audio was drowned out by helicopter blades.

The General explained that the Alpha Group team had anticipated that Dan might try to set fire to himself on the spot, so they had equipped themselves with fire-extinguishers. I was able to inform the President that his brother was singed but safe. As we left the War Room, I made a note to ask the Attorney General to look into this Bhagwan fellow. I have always been a stout upholder of freedom of religion, but I take a dim view of pukka sahibs of any stripe whose followers go about setting themselves on fire.

33
AMERICA GOES TO WAR

M-and-M apparently in a rage. Am delighted.
—JOURNAL, OCT. 17, 1992

The President and I left the Pentagon a little after four a.m. He
asked the Secret Service not to use their sirens so we wouldn't wake
anyone up. The Potomac looked beautiful and calm in the moonlight.
The President didn't say anything until we pulled up in front of the
South Portico.

"You want a drink?" he said.

He poured two large bourbons. I started to decline, but he seemed
to want company, so I accepted my first drink of hard liquor. I
confess it wasn't all bad. We sat in the Yellow Oval Room with the
lights out.

"It's pretty from here," he said finally, looking down at the fountain. "I'll miss this."

I made a noise to the effect that it wasn't over till it was over.

"No," he said. "My lease is up."

We continued staring out on the Ellipse. "Until a few hours ago
I could claim something few Presidents could."

I said, "You were trying to save lives."

"I wonder how the others felt. Kennedy, Johnson, Nixon."

"Worse, I suppose."

"The death of millions, a statistic. Show me the death of one
man—now, *there's* a tragedy."

I thought about this for a moment. "That's not bad, you know,"
I said. "We might use that sometime."

He smiled. "No, I don't think so."

"Why not?"

"It's one thing to be progressive. And I think I *have* been progressive. But I don't think we ought to be quoting Lenin."

"Oh," I said. "No, I guess not."

He winked at me. "At least not before November 4."

I slept on the couch again. Mrs. Metz arrived at 6:30 a.m. with a clean change of clothes. Alcohol leaves peculiar aftereffects. The inside of my mouth tasted like a used Dr. Scholl insole pad.

By about 7:15 my phone was ringing constantly. Mostly it was White House staffers who considered themselves more senior than they actually were, demanding to know why they hadn't been let in on the extraction missions. Some of them had already had calls from the media and were obviously having a hard time pretending they knew anything about it. I told them I'd give them a briefing at the regular 8:00 a.m. staff meeting in the Roosevelt Room.

Ambassador Kritkin called, full of *de rigueur* outrage over the "acts of war," etc., etc. I listened blearily. Finally there was a lull in the monologue, during which I stuck in an "Oh, go stick it in your samovar, you old fraud." I just didn't care anymore.

I expected him to resume bellowing at me in Russian, but instead he started to laugh. Great, aspirated, phlegmy, loud sounds. Not a pleasant sound, especially.

"That was a clever maneuver with the limousine, Herbert," he said, wheezing.

"I thought you'd like it, Vassily. Actually, the President forgot the nuclear codes for bombing your country. We had to send the driver back for them. By the time he got back to the Pentagon it was too late and he was tired. But we're going to do it tonight. Would you like to come? We're having a few people over."

He found this amusing. "You make jokes!" he chortled. "Like Reagan!"

He said he must talk with the President. I told him he could have ten minutes around eleven.

At nine I had a call from Marvin, aboard the *Eisenhower*. He was furious, saying he'd been trying to get through to the President all morning. He wanted to be flown back immediately. Moreover, he thought it would be "appropriate" if he were helicoptered from

Andrews Air Force Base to the South Lawn and greeted by the President. I took the greatest pleasure in telling him I'd have to get back to him on that.

"Whose idea was it anyway?" he demanded angrily.

"You won't find too many people taking credit for it, Marvin," I yawned. "There wasn't much of a consensus about rescuing you, frankly."

"But I didn't *need* rescuing!"

"No," I said. "I'm sure you had everything under control."

"I had a dialogue going!"

"Yes, I'm sure you did. Frank, candid, constructive—"

"I need to speak to the President."

"Well, he's awfully busy, Marvin, mopping up after your diplomatic triumph down there. He thought he might tie up a few loose ends for you. He doesn't want anything to get in the way of your Nobel."

"Now, Herb," he said, "I've got to debrief him."

"Absolutely. But you've been through an ordeal, Marvin. The Navy doctors want to keep you under observation for a while."

"But I'm fine!"

"What can I do? Doctors' orders. Anyway, the salt air will do you good."

"Salt air? You're not leaving me out here!"

"Goodbye, Marvin."

"You don't understand. I'm not good on boats. I get sick. I threw up once in a rowboat on Central Park Lake."

"Goodbye, Marvin."

"*Herb!*"

The day was improving. Sometimes public service can be enormously rewarding.

As for the First Brother, the Navy people informed me he was in deep meditation with his legs pretzeled under him in a meditative posture. Just the same, he was being kept under the watchful eye of a stout chief petty officer named Collins.

I decided it would also be best for Dan to enjoy the salt air for a while. Feeley and I worked on a statement saying that both he and Marvin were experiencing "trauma" associated with the rescue mission.

Vassily came in to talk to the President just after eleven. On the way in, he gave me a chuck in the ribs—in one of my bad ribs.

The President greeted him with a grin and, after we sat down, told him, "Let's cut through the usual horseshit today, shall we, Vassily? Now what can I do for you?"

Vassily, a man of high-protocolarian nature, was momentarily taken off balance. Then he announced that the Soviet Union would "view seriously" any further military operations on Bermuda.

The President digested this and said, "Vassily, I view *movies* seriously. Do you mean you're going to send aid to this asshole?"

Unaccustomed to such parlance, Vassily could only nod at the abrupt short-circuiting.

Tucker smiled. "I'm going to make an announcement this afternoon. You're not going to like it. But I hope you'll still come by. I enjoy our little visits."

Shortly after noon the President took a call from Admiral Boyd saying that the last of the C-7As had flown out of the base. Everything was in place—or rather, out of place.

At 12:35 that afternoon the President went on television and made the announcement that even today causes stimulating discussion.

I was in the Oval, standing to one side as he made his historic speech.

"Under the terms of the lease signed by President Roosevelt and Prime Minister Winston Churchill," he said, "the 694.33 acres on St. David's Island will remain the property of the United States government until the year 2039.

"This arrangement, which the new Bermudian leadership seems not to comprehend, is as binding upon them as it has been on the successive American administrations.

"However, recognizing that the presence of a U.S. military establishment has given the present leadership a pretext for aggressions such as those which the events of this morning were necessary to remedy, I have taken the following measures.

"After due consultation with the Joint Chiefs and the congressional leadership, I have determined that our satellite submarine-detection capabilities are sufficiently viable to warrant the dismantling of those present facilities.

"The military is, however, in need of other kinds of facilities. Given the present climate in Bermuda, the land now under dispute highly recommends itself for a new purpose.

"Accordingly, as of noon tomorrow, the U.S. Naval Air Station Bermuda will officially cease to exist. At that time it will become, officially, the U.S. Naval Air and Sea Practice Target Range Bermuda.

"All Bermudians, and I address this especially to those currently attacking that facility, are advised to remove themselves from the immediate vicinity. Failure to do so may result in sharing the defunct status of the present air station.

"I realize this decision will have the effect of depriving Bermuda of an airport. The U.S. has always permitted commercial aircraft to land on the base, and to service Bermuda's once vigorous tourist industry. That tourist industry is, however, now non-existent, in accordance with the country's new policies. Bermuda will therefore find itself less in need of an airport than before.

"Perhaps their Soviet allies will build them a new airport on some other part of the island. While they are at it, they might also build them some new concentration camps. The Soviet Union is expert at this form of architecture, having built so many of its own. Mr. M'duku seems fond of concentration camps, to judge from the ones the world had a chance to view last week before my adviser, Marvin Edelstein, was taken hostage. He will probably be building more. This is customarily the case with dictatorships that forge close ties with the Soviet Union."

A change came over the President after making that speech. He seemed more relaxed than he had been since assuming the Presidency. Perhaps it was the relief of having made a decision. But I think it must have been something else too. None of the ensuing criticism—and there was, Lord knows, no small amount of it—reached him. He seemed *content*.

George Bush, whose sense of patriotism—we never denied he was *patriotic*—now permitted him to go on the attack, called it the "moral equivalent of filling in the Panama Canal," and promised to reverse the decision if elected. At this point, unfortunately, there was little doubt that he would be, since we were now seriously behind in the polls.

There was something in the crowds too that had changed, especially among the young. They liked the line in his speech about beating swords not just into plowshares but into fields, which, indeed, the former naval air station had begun to resemble following the rather vigorous target-practice sessions. I think these young people saw in Thomas Nelson Tucker a leader who went beyond all the idle talk about disarmament. Here was a man who turned the weapons on themselves.

The night of November 4 was not a suspenseful one as election nights go. We were buoyed by the decisive vote in the Virgin Islands, toward whose statehood the President had devoted so much energy, as well as by the news that we would only lose Massachusetts by a margin of 400,000 votes. (Respectable: Gerald Ford had lost the state by the same margin to Jimmy Carter.) And of course we were immensely pleased when we squeaked over the top in Idaho. It is always gratifying to carry your home state.

The atmosphere at Tucker headquarters in the Boise Sheraton has been described in the press as "funereal," but I think this was an exaggeration. Certainly people were tired—who wouldn't have been after such a grueling campaign?—and obviously no one was gladdened by the fairly dismal returns. But as I looked about the ballroom, I felt there was still a sense of purpose and idealism in the air. I kept saying, "It's not over until it's over," to the reporters. The press said I was "oblivious to reality," but I was only trying to keep up morale.

Petrossian, Feeley, and Sig Beller were in a corner of the suite going over the concession statement.

"No," said Sig. "No, no, no. It makes him sound like Walter Cronkite leaving the air. Let's just end it with 'God bless you.' "

"He *hates* 'God bless you,' " said Feeley. "We'll end it here with the bit about how the dream doesn't die but goes on flapping in the wind."

"Flapping?" said Petrossian. "Where does it say flapping?"

"Waving. Whatever. This isn't a fund-raiser, we can afford to leave God out of it."

I interjected that it was cavalier to discuss God this way.

"Shut up, Herb," said Feeley.

Beller said, "I want this out. Where it says, 'The good that men do is often voted out of office with them.' It stinks and I don't get it."

"I don't get it either."

"It's gone."

Petrossian said the President had put it in himself.

"It's still gone."

I added: "Maybe he should say something about the Virgin Islands."

"We can't mention everyone who voted for him."

"Why not?" said Sig. "It would only take a paragraph."

"Can we finish this, please? Can we just finish?"

"ABC wants to know why we haven't gone down yet. They say the Bush people are calling us ungracious for not conceding."

"Tell them we're in the bathroom passing a kidney stone."

Just before eight o'clock we were about to go down. There was a kafuffle at the door. It opened and in walked the First Lady.

I personally was delighted. But there were others on the staff, notably Bamford Lleland IV, who were resentful of her for having accepted Mr. Weinberg's offer.

The President's marital situation during the campaign—rather, the lack of one—has been dragged through the mud of at least a half-dozen White House memoirs, and I do not propose to do the same here. But there she was, stunning in red fox and black leather pants. She had flown in from location to be with him in his hour of defeat. I have always said that Jessica Tucker was a woman of character.

If anyone of the senior staff had any doubts as to whether or not the President and she still loved each other, they were dispelled moments after she walked through the door when they embraced.

Frankly, I was worried that they might fall to the floor, they were so demonstrative. I immediately shooed people out of the suite so they could have a moment of privacy before going down to face the cameras.

After ten minutes had gone by, they still had not emerged from the presidential suite. By now Sig and the others were frantic, saying that we *had* to concede or it would look really terrible. So I knocked. And knocked. And knocked. Finally I was prevailed upon to open the door, which I did, only to find it chained.

It was a good forty-five minutes before the President and First Lady appeared. I must say that he looked more refreshed than he had in months, and the First Lady, but for a hair or two out of place, looked radiant.

EPILOGUE

We promised George Bush the best transition in the history of transitions, and I believe we made good on that promise. The President put me in charge of it. He also took the extremely unusual step of publicly firing Bamford Lleland IV shortly after the election. I would be dishonest if I said I regretted his departure. To judge from the vindictive tone of his memoir, he seems to have found the experience quite humiliating. I cannot say that I blame him.

As I look back on that postscript to my four years at the White House, the thing I most often remember was a little ceremony that to this day has remained a secret.

Two days after that last Christmas in the White House, Theodore died. The First Hamster succumbed to something called "wet tail," a disorder, I believe, of the lower GI. Firecracker had stayed up with Theodore all through the night. In the morning the First Lady came in and found them. Firecracker was standing at attention, saluting. On the ground, covered with a small American flag, was Theodore.

Firecracker was incensed when later in the morning his mother suggested it was time to flush Theodore down the toilet. He asked me to take charge of the funeral arrangements.

So, early on a cold, crisp morning in December, the seven-man Army Honor Guard arrived from Fort Meyer. In honor of his special contribution to the Tucker Presidency, Theodore was laid to his final rest to the accompaniment of a nineteen-gun salute. The President himself gave the eulogy. It was one of his better efforts, in fact; an oration, as Charlie would say, not a speech. I am told that the little marker is still there, beneath the American Elm planted by John Quincy Adams.

As for me, I had always expected to return to Boise, but such was not to be.

Old man Skruem passed away in December; Skruem *fils* came in. He was one of the new breed of CPAs, and a bit too flashy for my money. So when it became apparent that my old job at the firm was no longer open, Joan and I had a heart-to-heart talk. The children had made friends at school—though not the best kind, perhaps—and Joan had made close friends within her church social group. We decided to stay on in Washington.

Quite a few firms in town tried to "headhunt" me, dangling large salaries and perks in front of me. But after you've worked at the White House, you become a bit blasé, as the French say. After taking my time looking around, I accepted a high-level position with the National Association of Part-Time Railroad Employees. With the extra money I took Joan on a two-week cruise of the Caribbean, which she greatly enjoyed, despite a slight case of sun poisoning. (She has always been sensitive to sun.)

It was for her, in the end, that I wrote this book. After all poor Joan had been through, I couldn't ask her just to turn a blind eye as all these mendacious tomes climbed the best-seller lists and tongues wagged at the checkout line. As for those who have yet to publish their memoirs of the Tucker years, let them write what they will about Herbert Wadlough. Only the Good Lord and your tailor know your true measure, as Father used to say.

ACKNOWLEDGMENTS

I am indebted to a number of people. My wife, Joan, typed and retyped the manuscript, kept me supplied with endless cups of hot water, and urged me to go on when I would have faltered. My personal physician, Dr. Robert Ascheim, was also a great consolation.

I would also like to thank Martha Brown, Andrea Nash, Catherine Smythe, and Julia Woody of the TNT Library in Boise. I should also thank Christopher Buckley, who rendered editorial assistance in the preparation of the manuscript.

Finally, I would like to thank former President Thomas Nelson Tucker and Jessica Heath Tucker for giving me a unique opportunity of serving them during a difficult period in this nation's history.

A NOTE ON THE TYPE

The text of this book was set in a digitized version of Janson, a typeface thought to have been made by the Dutchman Anton Janson, who was a practicing type founder in Leipzig during the years 1668–1687. However, it has been conclusively demonstrated that these types are actually the work of Nicholas Kis (1650-1702), a Hungarian, who most probably learned his trade from the master Dutch type founder Dirk Voskens. The type is an example of the influential and sturdy Dutch types that prevailed in England up to the time William Caslon developed his own designs from them.

Composed by Maryland Linotype Composition Co., Baltimore, Maryland.
Printed and bound by Fairfield Graphics, Inc., Fairfield, Pennsylvania.
Designed by Iris Weinstein.